Dan Watters

ROAD TO RUMOUR

As I was goin' over
The Cork and Kerry Mountains
I met with Captain Farrell
And his money, he was countin'

I first produced me pistol
And then produced me rapier
said, "Stand and deliver for I am the bold deceiver"

Mush a ring um a do um a dah
Whack fol the daddy-o!
Whack fol the daddy-o!
There's whiskey in the jar

I counted all his money
It made a pretty penny
I put it in me pocket
and I took it home to Jenny

She sighed and she swore,
That she never would betray me
But the devil take the women,
For they never can be easy

Mush a ring um a do um a dah
Whack fol the daddy-o!
Whack fol the daddy-o!
There's whiskey in the jar

*Only a few years ago,
Jack Harrigan…an experienced bushman
climbed Black Mountain during the
search for a missing woman.
"The boulders at the top," he said
"are the wobbliest of the lot.
Touch them, and they tip over."*

*Jack's description of the gaps
between the rocks was graphic…
"Fall down one of those, and
you'd drop from here to about that house
across the road. And," he added explicitly,
"that's where you'd stay."*

'The Mysteries of Black Mountain',
1987, by Maureen Kozicka.

ROAD TO RUMOUR

CHAPTER 1

Standing over her sleeping husband in the half-light of the morning, Constance Harvey-Fairchild tried to remember what it felt like before love greyed-off. She couldn't. The memory was lost, or perhaps she didn't want to remember.

"John," her voice was deep with sleep. "Get up."

John was on his back, mouth open, snoring. She'd listened to it all night, the fleshy rattle grating on her nerves. She shoved his shoulder, shaking his soft body making little difference. He was such a heavy sleeper that she could take a pillow, place it over his face, and he'd never wake up.

But she couldn't let him sleep. Not today. There were things to do and somethings could only be done without John at home.

She shook his body, harder and turned on the bedside

lamp.

"I'll go later. Turn it off." John groaned.

"No. You did this last week. I had to do your shift. Get up." Connie tugged on the sheets.

John's hand shot out, grabbing her by the waist and pulling her rough into his soft body. She cringed at the feel of his clammy skin and reeled at the smell of stale beer and grease.

"You stink. You didn't shower before bed did you?" she complained, fighting her way free of her husband's arms. "Get up. You have to go." Connie straightened her top with a tug.

John threw off the sheets exposing his pale, naked body, glowing in the dark.

"Happy anniversary," he said his voice flat.

She looked at him deadpan and crossed her arms.

"It was yesterday. Get in the shower."

The floorboards down the length of the hall creaked. In the kitchen, an old light shade lit the original cabinets re-coated recently in a fresh coat of duck egg blue. Inside one of the cabinets, Connie found her favourite mug in a matching duck egg blue colour, a mother's day gift from her step-daughter last year. The cutlery drawer was devoid of teaspoons, and Connie measured out a scoop of coffee with a soup spoon.

Somewhere down the hall, a door opened, and the sound of bare feet padded towards the kitchen, floorboards creaking. A teenage girl appeared. She had long, straight, dark hair and squinted into the light.

Connie smiled.

"You're up early."

Karla didn't smile back.

"Where's Dad?" she croaked.

"In bed. Although he better be up. Can you bring the

teaspoons out of your bedroom, please?"

Karla gave a flat 'yes' and shuffled zombie-like to the long island bench taking a seat.

"You look miserable."

"I am." The girl wrapped her arms around her stomach.

"What's wrong?" asked Connie.

"I don't know."

"Is it your period?"

Karla shrugged.

"I don't know."

Connie set the kettle boiling and circled around the island bench, reaching out and rubbing Karla's back.

"Do you want to go to the doctors? Your Dad's going into town."

Karla hummed a monotone.

"Use your words." They'd talked about communicating like an adult. Connie refused to play guessing games with a teenager. "Can you take me?"

She couldn't, not today.

The floorboards in the hall groaned. Karla's face lit up with desperation, and she whispered, "Please?"

Connie shook her head.

"I'm sorry. I can't."

"You can swap with Dad. You've done it before," said Karla.

Connie made a pained face. She'd lost her chance last week when John had slept in. She couldn't miss it again.

"Why can't your Dad take you?"

John was in the doorway, wearing a pair of boxes and a tight singlet.

"Take you where? Into town?" he said, entering the kitchen, his tall frame shrinking the room.

"To the doctors," said Connie.

Karla's expression flattened. She shot a look of hate into the corner of the room. John crossed to the fridge, opening the door and scanned the contents.

"Sure, I can take you."

"Don't worry about it." Karla jerked her body out of her seat and stormed out of the kitchen.

John shrugged and closed the refrigerator. Down the hall, a door slammed. Connie felt bad for Karla. She made a mental note to check in when John wasn't around.

John pulled open the drawer of cutlery, rattling around.

"Our anniversary isn't today?"

"No. It was yesterday."

"Why didn't you say something?"

"I don't-"

"Where are all the fucking teaspoons?" John slammed the drawer. "It doesn't matter. I'll get a coffee in town," he said.

"Eat before you go, please," said Connie.

John flinched like he'd been stung and his jaw clenched. They'd talked about dieting. It was more of an argument. They both knew if he didn't eat before he left, he'd end up with his face in a box of fried chicken and chips from the China Diner.

John growled something, taking off into the hall.

Connie pursed her lips to stop her from biting back. It would only start an argument, and that would waste time. She poured hot water over her coffee and listened to the sounds of her husband down the hall, throwing his weight around the bedroom and shook her head inward at herself wondering how John had become so volatile. Some of it was her fault. She'd made one mistake. One drunken walk to another man's house and the locals made it out to be worse than it really was. It wouldn't have happened if John had paid her closer attention.

The water pipes in the wall thumped and rattled, whistling.

John was in the shower.

Connie put down her coffee, took up a set of keys from a hook on the wall and headed out the front door into mottled darkness.

A soft glow from the eastern horizon gave her enough light to see the steps down from the porch and across the open ground of a gravel car park. Her footsteps crunched loud, disturbing the silence of the early morning as she made her way towards a large rambling building of rusty tin sheets and a low, corrugated roof. As she closed in on the back door to the building, she held her breath. The smell coming from the bins and the stack of cardboard boxes could turn an empty stomach.

Inside with the door closed, her first breath drew in the sting of bleach. A cluster of fluorescent tubes hummed overhead, lighting up several flat stainless steel bench-tops, a tall dishwasher, a commercial-sized double sink, an old heavy oven and cast iron cooktop and a collection of mixers and deep fryers. She took a takeaway container from under one of the benches and went to the sink, reaching to a shelf above, drawing out a single key. Connie crossed to a large white door where a padlock was clasped around a chunky steel handle. The padlock clicked open, the handle rattled, and the door swung open. Cold air swirled around her body as she stepped inside where she was flanked by shelves loaded with trays of raw meat, bouquets of fresh herbs and buckets of broccoli, cauliflower and carrots. There was enough food here for a week of trade. She removed the lid from a sealed bucket and filled the takeaway container with a fruit salad mix. With the takeaway container in hand, Connie closed the coolroom door, returning through the kitchen, out the back door, across the gravel car park and up the steps of the porch into her home.

The water pipes were hissing.

She took a set of car keys and placed them with the takeaway container on the kitchen bench with a single fork. Across the hall was an office. She took an A4 sheet of paper from the printer and, returning to the kitchen, made a note.

'Breakfast.'

She looked at the note. The single word on its own was abrupt. Not unlike John. There was a time when her letters to John were long and loving.

Connie bent over the note again.

'Made with love,' she wrote and drew a love heart.

The love heart would probably come across as overkill. But, maybe overkill was what they needed to…

Bullshit.

She had to stop thinking like that. These were the lies she'd been telling herself for years. All the love hearts and notes hadn't worked then, and they weren't going to work for them now.

The water pipes in the walls changed pitch, rattled and squealed and went silent.

John was done.

Connie didn't want to get caught with John and have to explain the note. She hurried out of the kitchen, pausing in the hall at the entry to Karla's bedroom, pushing back a lock of blonde hair, her mouth close to the door.

"Karla? Your Dad is leaving. Are you going with him?"

"No." Her voice was petulant—nothing unusual there.

Connie remained at the door, her stomach knotted, head bowed knowing Karla was going through hell and there was nothing that she could do.

"I'll come back and check on you later, OK?"
Silence.
John was in the bedroom.
She would come back when she could.

Back in the small commercial kitchen, with an armload of single-serve cereal boxes, Connie pushed through a swinging door into a large dining room of uncommon construction and unusual decor. Knobbly timber posts sprouted from the floor holding up wonky, hand-hewn rafters supporting a corrugated tin roof. The tacky timber floors pulled at the soles of her shoes as she wound through a maze of old timber tops, bench seats and rickety chairs. She passed beneath the white skull of a horned bull, a dried leather bridle, several sweat-stained bras, scratched hard hats and dirty high vis shirts hanging from the rafters, collecting dust. The fibre cement walls were decorated with a display of car number plates from different states and countries, dinner plates signed by travelling bands, a collection of neoprene stubbie coolers, a cluster of branded cardboard coasters and a colourful swarm of glittering bottle tops. Above the cash register, a long line of foreign banknotes were pinned to the bulkhead of the bar. A corkboard by the front door displayed homemade notices and photographs of locals holding prized Barramundi and Coral Trout. Where there were gaps, the wall exposed, customers had taken to crafting handwritten messages in red, black, blue and green.

'NYE, 1987, Gary, Mark, Matty, Scott, John'.
'Gary's 5th Beer 12 of Sep' 69' Friends of Gary'.
'Mark is Satan'.
'Lyn has big Norries'.
'Tim, Greeny and Jacko arrived in a blaze of glory'.
'Lee + Eric XMAS 92'.

Where words wouldn't suffice, there were drawings. At the far end of the restaurant, a large amount of blue ink-stained the walls, in the shape of a hideous man-beast. By the bar, two small stick figures were posed in a crude position. And, perched high above the window, beyond the reach of drunk men with sharpies were two beautiful parakeets in bright red and green.

Connie laid out the cereal boxes on a table at the back of the room by the upright piano. Above the tables were a series of framed, black and white photographs, old photographs of people in period clothing. Of hills, denuded. Of men smeared in dirt crouching at the dark, open mouth of a small mine-the Lion's Den Tin mine.

And this was the Lion's Den Hotel. Her hotel.

Outside, the horizon had taken on a pink hue. Birds began to sing. In the morning light, the landscape around the hotel took shape. Mountains of blue-green ringed the valley where the hotel stood. The floor of the valley was open grassland crossed with fences and cut through by a single dirt road. Shiptons Flat road. In one direction, the road lead across the bridge over Mungumby creek, onto the Bruce Highway and into town. That was the only safe way out of Rossville. In the other direction was the Bloomfield Track, slow and tricky in the dry and deadly in the wet.

Connie watched the road waiting for John.

From the side of the hotel, she heard the sound of feet and voices drew closer. Five boys, barely men fresh out of high school, came up from the campgrounds at the back of the hotel to the front door, speaking a mix of foreign, European accents. They greeted her, paid cash and loaded up with food from the table at the back of the room, eating more than their money bought. Connie turned a blind eye and stood at the entry to the hotel, watching the road, her frustration growing. John was taking his time.

She could hear the foreign chatter inside, and it became distracting. Among the jumble of unfamiliar, accented words, the boys repeated two words she knew. Connie turned to the boys.

"You shouldn't go there," she said. They looked at her with blank stares. "Black Mountain."

The oldest of the boys sat up and raised a spoon.

"We want to explore there," he said.

Their peach fuzz faces were so innocent. They had no idea of the dangers in Black Mountain.

"People go missing on the mountain. Read the signs. They're there for a reason."

"We have big mountains, much bigger, at home. Your mountain is not so big," said the oldest boy, chest out.

Connie had never been overseas, but she was sure there was nothing in the world like Black Mountain. On days when the mornings were cold, and the sun rose hot, the boulders, some as big as a double-decker bus, would explode. She could hear it from the hotel. The explosion would leave a mark; a white spot against the massive pile of black boulders. The mountain was hollow, like a giant bowl of rice bubbles. From time to time, the rocks moved, tumbling, settling, falling and grinding. Inside was a maze with no fixed path. That maze was home to deadly snakes, giant pythons, spiders, lizards and bats. At places, the rock opened, forming dark bottomless wells. From those wells, toxic gasses would rise up stinging the eyes and lungs. Anyone climbing the mountain suffered from headaches reported hearing voices and acted paranoid.

"Just, don't do it," she said to the boys. The rumble of an engine drew Connie back to the entry, and a brown

Mitsubishi Pajero turned out of the car park onto Shiptons Flat road, the wheels kicking up a trail of sulphur-yellow dust.

Connie considered leaving things as they were.

She needed answers.

Hurrying through the swinging door through the kitchen and out into the car park, Connie entered the house. Karla was in her bedroom, the door closed. The place was quiet.

John's office was a small room off the hall, the desk covered in receipts and letters addressed to the director, addressed to John. Connie rifled through the papers.

'Why don't I get letters, for me?', she'd asked, John. He'd explained it away-an explanation that had left her unsatisfied.

She needed evidence. She needed to see her name on something besides a receipt from the fishmonger.

Searching the desk, the drawers, lifting and looking under the tray of stationery, Connie pulled on the handle to the filing cabinet. It was locked. The keys were in with the stationery. She took them out, and the drawers rattled open revealing rows of hanging files. She pulled out the first file and laid it on the desk flipping through forms from the tax department. Every letter was addressed to the director, singular, or addressed to John. The papers in the second and third files were insurances, all addressed to John.

Connie worried about leaving the hotel unattended. If a local didn't get service, John would hear about it, and he'd ask why she wasn't there. And yet, she couldn't leave the office without answers. Those answers had to be here in these papers. She was desperate.

Removing file after file, and flicking through I, K, L Connie noticed at the bottom of the drawer, a manila folder lying flat under the files. She took it out. Dust flew into the air, and she laid it on the desk. Inside were several leaves of paper, the first with a coat of arms and the heading 'Notice of Change of Directors to a registered body'. It had been five years since she last saw the document, but she recognised it immediately. When she'd signed it, John had opened champagne, and they'd celebrated. The document was wordy and official with boxes, crossed, and answers completed in John's handwriting. He'd nominated Constance Harvey-Fairchild as a director of his company. The ink on the document had faded, and the last page, while signed and dated showed no stamps, no approvals. The form had never been sent.

Her stomach dropped. John had lied.

"Bastard." She slammed a fist on the desk, swatting the air with the papers, shaking, angry, screaming. "Bastard." She kicked the metal cabinet, making a dent and swore, kicking out again at the office chair sending it clattering out into the hall.

"Liar."

Ten years she'd given up for John and the business, thinking she was an owner and he'd lied. She'd given up her time and her body, raised his daughter, giving everything she had. He'd given her nothing in return. She was stupid.

Pressure filled her body. She reached over the desk with clawed fingers flinging the files into the opposite wall and stood with hunched shoulders drawing breath and exhaling.

"Are you OK?"

The voice from the hall startled her. Karla was standing beside the overturned office chair, peering into the room at the mess, alarmed.

Connie's hand went to her forehead as if her palm

could hold back her tears.

"I didn't mean to scare you," said Connie, shaking.

"What's wrong?" Karla's voice was small.

Connie held back a rolling ball of rage.

"It's nothing. Go back to your room."

Karla held her ground, concern etched in her face.

"Is it Dad?"

She was going to kill him.

CHAPTER 2

In a dry, yellow paddock, at the edge of bushland, a cow lay tangled in the wire of a broken fence, kicking and writhing, stained in blood, eyes wide, bellowing desperately.

From the far end of the paddock, a white, rust-stained Landcruiser approached, bouncing over the uneven ground, the burble from the engine growing louder. As it came close to the cow, the brakes screeched, and it stopped. Two cattle dogs jumped from the back tray and ran to the cow, barking. The cow kicked, and the wires strained, clattering like swords, cutting deeper into the skin of the animal.

The drivers' door opened with a crack, and a man stepped out, his hair white, his face creased by time. He threw on a cattleman's hat and drew a rifle from the vehicle, ambling, stiff-legged to the fence line.

"Back," his voice crackled like fire, growling and kicking at the two dogs.

The cow bellowed, mournful.

"Whoa, girl. Whoa." The old farmer took slow, deliberate steps around the large beast, through the wires, circling in close and bent down. A deep cut had opened the cows flank, and a cluster of flies festered around the wound. The creature bucked and moaned, and the farmer stepped back, talking to the animal, in a calm voice. He continued to circle at a distance and stopped at the sight of a limp hoof, bent at an odd angle—a broken leg.

The farmer dropped his head. A moment of silence. A deep breath. He moved in, slow, taking up a position behind the large bovine head, planting his feet in a broad stance, pressing the butt of the rifle into his shoulder and looking down the barrel of the gun, taking aim.

The gun cracked, blood sprayed across the grass, and the sound echoed off the hills and back into the valley. The two dogs startled and cowered.

"Awful business, girls."

Beside the old man, the bush erupted with sound crashing and smashing and feet thumping. Through the trees, he caught a flash of short hair, powerful legs, pointed ears, long bodies and a snout.

"Pigs."

The dogs leapt forward their eyes wild and ran barking at the bush, jumping over the dead cow when a piercing whistle filled the air, and the dogs stopped. The old man took two fingers from his mouth to growl, "Get in the truck."

The dogs turned circles, whimpering. The thumping of trotters grew distant. The farmer growled again, drawing the dogs back from the tree line, telling them to get into the truck. The dogs obeyed, and he patted them, told them to stay and went to work. Pulling a length of cable from a winch, the old farmer hooking the cable on a mechanical arm above the driver's cabin and swung the arm out to the side of the vehicle. Pulling the cable through the arm he made his way to to the fence line, dropping the heavy metal hook on the ground. With a pair of pliers from the glove box, he clipped the wires away then pulled the cable under the cow, looping it back onto itself in a metal lasso before returning to the Landcruiser and starting the engine. At the base of the mechanical arm was a switch and he turned it on. The winch turned, retracting the cable and dragging the limp body of the cow through the dirt, up the slope and alongside the Landcruiser. The vehicle tipped to the side as the winch took up the weight of the cow, the wire taut, bones cracking, lifting the creature into the air. He pushed at the cow swinging the mechanical arm over the tray back of the truck and dropped the animal onto the vehicle, the dogs dancing around the dead body. After tying down the cow and packing away the winch, the old man's weathered hands were covered in blood and grease. He lowered himself to the ground, kneeling in a patch of dry grass and wiped his hands on the grass.

From the tray back of the Landcruiser, the dogs began to whimper, their bodies stiff, their muzzles pointing east.

Standing and wiping his hand on his chest, the old farmer produced a pair of spectacles from his breast pocket and shielding his eyes from the rising sun, he looked over the slow-running creek, above the treetops of the bush onto a dark mound of boulders, piled high. Among the black rocks, he saw movement. Five figures were jumping, pulling and pushing each other up the giant rocks towards the summit.

"Hey! What the hell are you doing!" he shouted, "Get down!" The boys didn't respond. The distance between them was too great for his worn voice to carry. The dogs began to bark. The old man cupped his hands to his mouth and took a deep breath.

"Get down!"

The five boys didn't respond to the shouting or barking and continued to climb. He watched them, his face creased. Their climb brought them to a large, smooth oblong-shaped boulder, too steep to climb. It was a dead end. They had to come down. But they weren't coming down. They were just standing there. Talking.

"Come down," said the old man, his face twitching.

The larger of the five boys pointed into the rocks.

"Don't do that."

The same boy knelt and crawled between the rocks, into a dark void and disappeared.

The old man took off his hat and waved it in the air.

"No. Stay outta there."

The other boys closed in on the gaping void and one after the other, followed their friend, crawling between the boulders until only one remained, standing on Black Mountain. The farmer rushed to the Landcruiser and pressed the horn, holding it down and waving his hat.

The remaining boy paused, looked up and scanned the landscape for the source of the sound, looking in the direction of the old man. The boy lifted an arm and waved back before dropping to his knees, crawling forward and disappearing.

"You fucking idiot."

On the tray back of the Landcruiser, one of the dogs howled setting off the other, their voices seesawing. The old man turned a pale shade and climbing into the driver's seat, kicked over the engine, turning the Landcruiser around, gathered speed, bouncing across the straw-dry paddock, the shadow of Black Mountain looming in the passenger window. Ahead, over the curve of the land, a large, tin shed appeared alongside a white weatherboard home. The old man, scowled through the windshield, gripping the wheel and steered towards the house.

CHAPTER 3

In a small room cramped by two, clean and organised desks, a broad-shouldered man in a blue, short-sleeved shirt, epaulette on each shoulder and a nameplate on his chest, hunched over a keyboard, jabbing two fingers at the keys. The computer screen blinked, and a smattering of white and blue pixels advanced down a map of brown and blue divided by a sawtooth coastline. The tight cluster of pixels grew in size moving towards a pin on the map labelled Cooktown. The Sergeant lent into the screen. A tall, lean man in uniform entered the room, helping an elderly woman into a chair at the opposite desk. The phone rang.

"Hey, Sticks. Have we had a weather warning from the bureau today?" The Sergeant asked.

"No, boss. Nothing."

The Sergeant frowned at the screen. The phone rang. The image on the screen reloaded and the dark cluster of pixels ballooned, larger. The phone rang.

"Can someone get that?" The Sergeant shouted into the next room. The screen blinked and reloaded. A second cluster of pixels stuttered into view.

"What is that…?" said the Sergeant under his breath.

The phone rang.

The Sergeant reached out, snatching up the handset.

"Cooktown Police. Sergeant Cross speaking."

"It took you long enough." The voice was rough and horse, breathing heavy down the line.

"What do you want, Wes?" said Andy, his eyes fixed on the computer screen.

Ken Wesselman, the old farmer, stood in his kitchen, the handset of an avocado green, bakelite phone to his ear.

"Five boys just went into Black Mountain," he said, taking off his cattleman's hat.

"What do you want me to do about it?" asked the Sergeant, frowning at the screen.

"Get them out."

"I'll make a note of it, Wes."

"A note won't do them any good."

"They'll be fine. Tourists climb Black Mountain all the time," said the Sergeant.

The computer flashed and reloaded. The two colourful masses of pixels jumped down the screen closing in on the same point on the map. Cooktown.

"They're not climbing over the rocks," Wes' voice crackled down the line. "They went inside."

"Wes, we're police officers not park rangers. Unless they're committing a crime, there's nothing I can do."

Wes growled.

"It'll be your problem when their parents come knocking on your door," said Wes.

The Sergeant sighed loudly, sat up, pinning the phone to his shoulder and took out a note pad and pen.

"How many were there?"

The Sergeant took notes as Wes described a group of five boys. He'd seen them before. They were staying at the campgrounds at the Lion's Den Hotel.

The computer screen reloaded. The Sergeant looked up from his notepad. The two masses of pixels continued to expand and advance.

"Wes, I'm sorry. I've got to go."

"What about these kids?"

The phone still pressed to his ear, the Sergeant rose, shouldering a bright yellow, high vis jacket.

"Call me tomorrow if they don't turn up." Andy hung up. "Sticks. Get your binoculars. I need a second opinion." He apologised to Mary Bosco and asked the old lady to wait. The Sergeant lead Sticks out the double doors striding down a narrow footpath towards a hard, dirt road.

"I just had the Weasel on the phone. He says a bunch of kids went inside Black Mountain," said the Sergeant.

"I hope you don't expect me to go in there after them," joked the tall, lanky man.

They crossed a dirt road into a thin strip of parkland walking briskly toward a large body of clear, turquoise water.

"Every time he sees someone up there on the rocks he calls. He wants us to search the mountain. I think he knows they're in there," said the Sergeant.

"His family? Have you heard back from the District Inspector?" said Sticks.

"They turned me down. I need more evidence before they'll reopen the case."

"After forty years?" Sticks scoffed. "Unlikely. Have you tried your old man?"

They passed by a brass statue of a strident English sailor.

"Not yet. I need something to take to him," said the Sergeant. "Reopening the case would have done it."

"You interviewing your Dad. Awkward."

The two officers reached the edge of the park. A huge snaking river wove through the emerald green mountains down into a calm body of blue water, opening into the turbulent ocean. On a nearby pier, a sailboat tethered, bobbing in high tide. Two men were on board arguing, their voices raised. A bearded man with long, straggling hair shook a fist full of cash at a tanned and tattooed man with windswept hair. The tanned man refused to take the money and wanted more.

"Everything alright?" said the Sergeant.

The wild man saw the officers, his hairy face twitching. He pulled out an extra fist of cash and shoved it at the tanned man telling him to leave, then turning into the cabin shouting instructions at a woman inside to pull the mooring. The negotiations over, the tattooed man put on a shirt and shoes and stepped ashore, counting his thick fold of notes.

"What's that for?" asked the Sergeant.

"Services rendered," said the man continuing to count. The officers came closer. The man looked up from his counting. "I repaired his sail." The tanned and windswept man looked satisfied and headed for the shore passing the two policemen.

"Jakes. Wait." The Sergeant stopped him. "Corrections called. They're letting Reggie out."

Jakes' face dropped, his eyes shading over with fury.

"When?"

"Today. This morning."

"Where is he?" asked Jakes.

"I don't know."

"You should know."

"That's not our job."

"Why couldn't you keep him in gaol for another month?"

"Again, not our job, sorry," said the Sergeant, holding up his hands and glancing out to sea. "I'm just asking you to avoid him. If you see him, don't talk to him and don't start a fight. If he gets hurt, it won't play out well in court next month."

"We're going to court? I didn't think the state had enough to get a conviction?"

"The attorney is going with what we've given them."

Jakes had his head down, thinking.

"What if he gets off?"

"That's in the hands of the lawyers."

Jakes' eyes narrowed.

"He's not getting away with this," he said, taking off, reaching the end of the pier and turning north along a narrow strip of parkland towards a cluster of buildings in the distance.

"Do you think he'll do anything?" asked Sticks.

The Sergeant shook his head.

"No. He knows it'll put the court case in jeopardy."

The Sergeant turned to the ocean, fixing his eyes on the horizon. Without the binoculars, he could pick out in the distance a bank of dirty cotton clouds billowing on the horizon. Further out to sea, the second cluster of grey clouds cast a shadow over the ocean.

"It's not a cyclone," said Sticks, the binoculars pressed to his face.

"I'd say it's monsoonal," said the Sergeant.

The dark shadow over the ocean lit up, shooting out a finger of lightning.

"It's a bit early for the monsoon," said the Sergeant putting out his hand for the binoculars and pressing them to his face. Through the tunnel lense, he saw rain. Lots of rain.

"Call the port," he said. "Raise the alarm."

CHAPTER 4

Connie stood in the kitchen of the hotel, one hand on her hip, the phone pressed to her ear, tapping her fingernails on the stainless bench. The phone rang out, and she slammed the receiver into the cradle.

"Where are you?"

"Is that John?" At the back door to the kitchen, a short, stocky man in chequered pants kicked off his sneakers and slipped into a pair of black, shoes. "What's he done now?"

Connie was about to say something but stopped herself. She hadn't told Karla, and before it got out and spread like wildfire around town, she had to talk to John first.

"What is he doing in town that's taking him so long?

He did this last week."

Sherbet Ray, buttoned up a white, Chef's jacket and wrapped himself in a black apron.

"With any luck, he won't come back," he said.

"Careful. He still pays your wages."

Sherbet Ray, scoffed.

"Everyone knows you run this place."

That may be true, but she didn't own it. The thought of it triggered fury.

The Cook lit the gas on the cast iron stove.

"What are the bookings like for tonight?"

It was Friday.

"Half the restaurant is booked out."

"How many are out there now?"

"None." The lunch guests had cleared out an hour ago.

"There's a car out the front."

Connie looked up at the clock, realising she'd been trying to reach John for the past thirty minutes. She darted through the swinging door into the restaurant, but the restaurant was empty. In the car park at the front of the hotel, she could see a silver sedan and Connie peered around a corner into the bar. There a thin man with wispy blond hair was looking around the room at the bric-a-brac on the walls. Connie recognised him.

"Quicks?"

The man jumped, and the two of them made eye contact. Quicks flashed a thin-lipped smile.

"Here she is," he said, loud as if he'd gone deaf.

"Sorry. Were you waiting long?" said Connie.

"Oh, no. Not long." Quicks glanced sideways at the front door, the smile dropping from his face. At the doorway into the hotel, she saw a shadow. A man appeared. He had windswept hair, a bronze, clean-shaven face and a fresh shirt, open at the chest, showing the dark lines of half-hidden tattoos.

"I've been waiting."

Connie felt a jolt of electricity.

The last time she saw Jakes Jenkins, she'd gotten herself into trouble. Panic rose in her chest, stealing her breath. Jakes couldn't be here.

"What are you doing here?"

Quicks drifted out the front door leaving her alone with Jakes.

"You look good," Jakes said, his cheeks creasing back in a smile.

The compliment made her float. She pulled herself back to the floorboards.

"Jakes." His name was thick, like peanut butter. She swallowed. "This is serious. You can't be here."

"Well, I am."

"What do you want?"

"Dinner and a drink?" He was smiling and crossed the floor coming close enough for her to pick up the smell of the ocean. It reminded her of the taste of salt on his lips.

"You have to go. John-"

"John's in town."

Her eyes narrowed as her suspicion grew.

"You know he's not here."

"It doesn't make a difference to me if he's here or not."

"It does to me."

"I can talk to him if you want?" Jakes raised a brow.

"John's not the talking type," she said.

"Do you want to talk?"

Connie would love to talk, to tell someone about John's lie, to pour out her feelings to someone she could trust. But, she couldn't trust Jakes. Someone had told somebody about their kiss. Connie settled into her hips, squaring up to Jakes, dropping her voice.

"Why are you here?"

"I've got a booking."

"No, you don't. Stop playing games."

"I do," he laughed.

"Then, I'm cancelling it. You can't be here, Jakes."

"I miss this place." Jakes stepped up to the bar and pulled out a stool to sit, and Connie rushed forward, blocking him.

"No."

They were close. She could feel the warmth of his body. The electricity sparked in her chest, spreading to her legs and arms.

"Please, don't sit." The edge had gone from her voice, and she couldn't seem to find the strength to fight back. She was tired of fighting.

"He's been talking about you," said Jakes.

"Who?"

"John. He's been talking to Fred Abe. Abe thinks your marriage is over. He's been telling everyone in town."

"Is that why you're here? You think my marriage is over?"

Jakes threw her a wry smile.

"I wish. It's Josie's birthday. She made a booking."

Connie remembered taking the call between her repeated attempts to reach John.

"And where's Josie?" said Connie, sceptical. Josie was a lot younger than Jakes.

"She's getting ready."

"And she's spending her birthday with you? Shouldn't she be out with friends? People closer to her age?"

"I am a friend. Closer actually. She moved in with me."

Connie felt sick.

"Josie? She's half your age."

Quicks swung his head inside the front door.

"He's coming," he said.

Outside, a cloud of yellow dust billowed up from behind a brown Mitsubishi Pajero. A chill spread through Connie's veins.

"Jakes. Please. Get out of here."

Jakes followed the vehicle with a grim stare as the Pajero pulled into the front car park beside the silver sedan. The driver's door opened, and John got out.

"Too late," said Jakes offering an apologetic smile. He planted his feet on the old timber boards and faced the front door. He knew what was coming.

Connie knew too and backed away, distancing herself from Jakes.

CHAPTER 5

John entered the hotel carrying a polystyrene box filled with milk and ice, his face sweaty and red. He saw Connie and began to give her an excuse for returning late when he Saw Jakes.

"Hello, John." Jakes, lean and light stood his ground.

John's face flushed with anger. The polystyrene box dropped hitting the floor, ice scattering, and in a second, John was across the room throwing his body at Jakes. The two men hit the floor, the impact shaking tables and rattling glasses. John had Jakes beneath him and started swinging his arms with balled fists at Jakes' face.

Connie screamed.

"John. Stop."

Quicks entered the bar throwing himself into the fight trying to pull John off Jakes. John gave Quicks a shove.

Quicks stumbled back falling on his backside. John continued throwing punches, some hitting their mark, splitting skin and blurring Jakes face with blood and spit.

A loud crack split the air and Connie jumped, the fight stopped, the gunshot coming from the open doorway. A tall, old man in spectacles and a wide-brimmed hat, a cigarette in the corner of his mouth, stepped into the hotel, smoke trailing from the end of a long-barrelled rifle. He pulled back the bolt on the gun - snick, clack, click - shunting another bullet into the chamber then took aim at John, his finger on the trigger.

"What's going on here?" said Wes.

Jakes squirmed. John held him down.

"Wes, get that gun out of my hotel," said John, fierce, staring down the barrel.

The swinging door to the kitchen opened, and the Cook appeared, a knife in hand, making eye contact with Connie. She shook her head at him, and the Cook retreated into the kitchen.

Ken Wesselman stood his ground, the rifle on John.

"Let him go."

John looked at Connie for support. She wasn't going to give it. His face turned ugly and gave Jakes a shove before standing and facing his wife.

"Why is he here? Why'd you let him in?" John took a step towards her. The rifle followed.

Connie didn't want to have this conversation in front of these people.

"Go home," she said, her voice shaking with fear.

John turned to Jakes, eyeing him off and Wes stepped forward, placing himself between the two men. John gave the old farmer a cold stare.

"You really want to take his side?" John said, short of breath, his clothes twisted, spotted with blood, his knuckles raw.

"I don't take sides," said Wes.

"Go home, John."

John looked at Wes and the rifle, at Jakes beaten and lying on the floor. He held up his bloody knuckles and seemed satisfied.

"When I get back, you better be gone," he said to Jakes before turning towards the swinging door to the kitchen. Connie wanted to throw a salt shaker at the back of John's head.

When John was gone, Wes lowered his rifle.

"You should have shot him," she said.

*****

Jakes held a wad of paper towel to his face, apologetic.

"That went as well as it could."

Wes was outside in the car park depositing the rifle into the cabin of his Landcruiser.

Connie was still shaking. She started cleaning up the ice and milk that had been dropped. When she was done with the mess, she poured herself a short drink. Jakes had moved with Quicks to a table the back of the hotel where he was cradling his injuries. At the back of the bar, a storage room lead through to the kitchen. Sherbet Ray came through, wringing his hands on a tea-towel.

"Everything alright," he said. "I thought you were being murdered."

She was fine. John had gone back to the house. Sherbet Ray promised to keep an eye out for her husband and returned to his work.

Wes came back into the hotel, unarmed and Connie served him a beer.

"It's on the house."

They shared a drink in silence. Wes was like that. If you wanted to talk, he would listen, and if you didn't want to talk, that was OK too.

She waved a finger at Jakes.

"Keep an eye on him for me." Connie finished her drink. "I have to talk to John."

Connie walked through the storage room into the kitchen where Sherbet Ray was sliding trays of meat into the oven.

"I've got to talk to John."

The back door to the kitchen opened, and Karla appeared, dressed in black, her hair tied up in a ponytail, an apron in her hand.

"Dad's in a mood," said Karla, her face a picture of teenage disgust.

Connie looked at the clock. The other waitresses would be here soon.

"Can you look after the hotel?" she asked Karla. "I've got to talk to your Dad.

The back door opened again, and a young man with brown hair and olive skin entered the kitchen. His name was Stephan, and he greeted everyone with a smile and a Spanish accent. Stephan was a backpacker and the kitchen hand. The job was often filled with young, foreign travellers, although Stephan had stuck around longer than most.

Karla and Stephan made eye contact, and Karla's cheeks coloured before she spun on her heels and left the room. Connie bristled with curiosity. She eyeballed Stephan. Stephan moved to the sink and began shuffling pots and pans. He was older than Karla, foreign and exotic. She could imagine Karla being attracted to him. She thought about quizzing Stephan to see if anything was going on and decided against it. That was Karla's business.

Besides, Connie had enough on her plate for now.

Outside, the air was sticky. The humidity had kicked up a notch. On the horizon, the sun had fallen into a sky of orange hues. Up the stairs to the porch and into the house, she could hear the water pipes in the wall hissing. John was in the shower, and Connie followed the sound of running water into the bedroom. John had tossed his dirty clothes on the bed, feet from the laundry hamper. It angered her. He was useless. She bundled up his damp, sweaty clothes to put them in the hamper and something fell out, hitting the floor. It was his cell phone. Connie picked it up. The screen lit up, showing a litany of missed calls and messages.

Connie deposited the clothes in the hamper. The shower was still running, and she unlocked the phone.

Altogether there were six missed calls and two voice mail messages, all from her. At the bottom of the list was an outgoing call. It had been logged to a local land-line at ten AM that morning, and the conversation had lasted twenty-eight seconds.

There was a lot you could say in twenty-eight seconds.

After that call had been made, John had ignored her calls for five hours.

There was a lot you could do in five hours.

She thought about calling the number, but the mobile had no reception. She'd have to phone from the kitchen. But what would she say? Whoever it was, they would probably know her by her voice. Everyone in town knew Connie.

She needed some way of knowing where John had been. Connie searched the pockets of John's pants. They were empty, although she picked up a waxy smell on his shirt. Wax and lavender. Her mind conjured up images of a bedroom and candles, blinds drawn and a faceless woman.

If John was using the trips into town to cheat on her, this probably wasn't the first time.

Connie took the business papers from the bedside table and weighed them in her hand. She didn't own the business. If he threw her out, it wouldn't make a difference. She had nothing to lose. So, with the papers in hand, Connie pushed through the door into the ensuite.

The hot mist in the bathroom swirled, and there was John, standing behind the wet shower screen, naked, his hand around his penis, masturbating.

Connie's mouth fell open. John looked up, his eyes widened in shock, and he covered himself.

"What are you doing here?" He said. "You should be at the hotel."

Her cheeks seared with embarrassment. She almost backed out of the bathroom. Then John looked down at the papers in her hand. There was no going back. Connie palmed the official form to the glass screen of the shower.

"Explain."

John's eyes scanned the paperwork, and his face turned pale.

"I know. I forgot. I didn't send it," said John.

"You forgot? For five years, you forgot! I found it in the bottom of your filing cabinet." She shook the papers through the glass screen. "You didn't forget. You were lying."

"I forgot, and then it was too late. It expired," said John.

"You're an arsehole. You told me I owned the business. You bought a bottle of champagne. We celebrated. I put off having a child for this. For you, and you lied." She slapped the papers on the glass, rattling the shower screen.

"I didn't know how to tell you." John shut off the

shower and got out, wrapping himself in a towel.

"Bullshit. You know how important this was to me. I've worked my ass off."

"I can get it fixed." He said.

"You better. And what were you doing in town all day?" The mobile phone was in her other hand. She held it up.

John's face tightened and filled with anger.

"Give me that," he said, taking a step forward snatching at the phone. Connie stepped back into the bedroom.

"Who did you call? Who are you seeing?"

He levelled a dead stare at her and ground his teeth. Silence.

"You can tell me, or I can call the number," she said.

John threw himself at Connie, colliding with her, body on body, his weight bumping her back onto the bed. He fell too, his weight coming down onto her pelvis and chest, his body hot and damp. He grabbed her wrist, pried the Nokia from her fingers and looked at the screen.

"Get off me." She tried pushing at him, tried wriggling out, but she couldn't move.

John was looking down at her struggling.

She stopped.

"John, get off." He was staring at her, his breath heavy, his pupils enlarged. She felt uncomfortable.

John tossed the phone on the bed.

"John, get off me," she repeated, her voice rising.

His eyes drifted from her neck, down her chest to the gap between the buttons of her dress. He lifted a hand to grab her breast, and she tried to push it away, but John forced his hand onto her.

"No. Get off." She pushed at his weight, to no effect.

His hips lowered onto her, pressing into her pelvis,

pushing her into the mattress. She felt his hand slide down her hip onto her thigh and his fingers clawing at her dress, pulling the hem up one leg.

"John. No."

He wouldn't stop.

Connie screamed.

CHAPTER 6

It was the scream that did it. John had lifted his body, the darkness in his eyes shrunk, and he told her to leave. Connie crawled off the bed and ran from the house shaken. Inside the back door of the kitchen, she felt safe. Sherbet Ray stood under the roaring sound of the extraction fan, Stephan, elbow-deep in a sink full of dishes. Neither of them had seen her enter, out of breath, her dress twisted and her hair a mess. No one had heard her scream. She straightened her dress and hair and took deep breaths to compose herself.

She'd never seen John like that before. He was getting worse.

Out the front of the hotel, the bar was quiet. Jakes was still seated at the back of the restaurant with Quicks, talking. Wes was at the table by the window with a half-empty beer.

"How'd it go?" asked Wes.

"Not good," she said.

A car pulled up at the front of the hotel, and two couples got out. They were locals: Maggie Dwight, Veronica Westcott and their husbands.

"Where's Karla?"

Wes nodded towards the bathrooms at the back of the hotel.

"She's been in there for a while. You might want to check on her."

Connie greeted the two couples with a smile and sat them at a table out of the direct line of sight to Jakes.

"Why are you still here?" she said on her way to the toilets. "You should leave before you start any more rumours."

"I didn't tell anyone about us."

"Then who did?"

"Not me."

"And why are we whispering? It's not like we're hiding anything. Nothing happened."

Jakes raised an eyebrow as if to challenge her. She didn't want to go into it and turned her back on him, pulling open the door into the women's toilet.

The air smelled acrid. Karla was standing at the sink, straightening her hair in the mirror.

"Are you O.K.?"

Karla's face looked pale.

"I'm coming."

"Have you been sick?"

Karla nodded, placing two hands across her stomach.

"It was the smell in the kitchen."

"If you've got a bug, you should go home."

"No, I'm fine, sort of. I feel better, I think." Karla

looked at Connie with searching eyes and didn't seem to be O.K. Something was off. This morning, Karla had wanted to go to the doctors. Then there was that look between her and Stephan just now.

"Are you sleeping with Stephan?" said Connie.

Fear flashed on Karla's face, and she burst into tears.

"Oh, God. You're pregnant."

Karla wailed.

Anger, like a sheet of hot iron, shot Connie upright. This couldn't happen to Karla. She was too young. And why hadn't she seen this coming? She had no idea Karla was seeing Stephan.

Karla was sobbing, snot glistening at the end of her nose. Connie reached into a cubicle and pulled off a wad of toilet paper handing it to Karla.

"We talked about boys. We talked about protection."

"I know," Karla sobbed.

"What happened?" It was a stupid question. Luckily Karla didn't offer an answer and Connie didn't need one. She knew what had happened. They'd got carried away. Despite her feeling about this, she could be wrong. Maybe Karla wasn't pregnant.

"When was the last time you had your period?"

"A month," sobbed Karla. "Maybe more."

Nope, she was pregnant. Fuck. She'd have to get tested to know for sure, but the results would come back positive for sure.

"You're getting a termination." The words just came out. Cold. Harsh.

Karla's mouth opened and closed like a goldfish.

Connie wouldn't give her the option. She was going to get an abortion.

"You're not having this baby. You're sixteen. A baby at your age will ruin your life." Karla wasn't putting up a fight and looked frightened.

Voices drifted in from the hotel. Connie had to get back to the bar. She thought about sending Karla home, but John was there and if John found out his daughter was pregnant...

"Can you still work?"

Jakes caught her eye as she came back into the restaurant.

"Everything alright?" he asked, wincing. The cut on his lip was somehow attractive. Over his shoulder, Connie could see to the bar. Customers were milling about, looking for someone to serve them a drink.

"What are you still doing here?" she said.

"Waiting for Josie," said Jakes.

She looked at Quicks.

"Why is he here?"

"It's Josie's birthday." Quicks shrugged.

"And you chose to bring her here?"

"She wanted to come here."

That was bullshit. Jakes knew turning up at the Lion's Den would start a fight and no one, not even Josie would want that on her birthday.

"Just dinner and we'll leave," Jakes winced, touching his lip.

His charm and their bullshit story made her curious.

"Fine. What's your favourite flower?"

Jakes looked confused.

"Frangipani?"

"I'll bring a bunch to your funeral," she said, walking away.

Wes was talking to her customers, keeping them

entertained, and Connie apologised for making them wait, getting them seated and headed for the bar with their drinks order. Karla was on her mind. Disappointment swirled inside her. She'd have to make an appointment to see the doctor and get a referral to a family planning clinic. She'd have to do it without John knowing. At the same time, she'd have to stay on John to get him to sign the business papers and make her an owner. He couldn't make her leave. The business wouldn't run without her.

"I'm so stupid."

Wes was at the bar with an empty glass, looking confused.

"You're the smartest woman I know."

"You don't know many women."

"You're not stupid, Connie."

"John lied to me. I don't own the business," she said in a whisper. "I found out today.

"I thought he made you an owner years ago?"

"Nope. He never sent in the papers. It's been years, and I didn't know. I feel like an idiot."

Wes shook a finger at her.

"No. Your husbands' just an arsehole." Wes waved a hand at Jakes at the back of the restaurant. "You should have bunked off with him when you had the chance." Everyone knew about the rumoured affair with Jakes, only Wes knew the truth.

"Yeah, but, how do you know when it's time to give up?"

Wes looked down at his hand, tapping his empty glass with a scratched and battered ring.

"Sure. I know what you mean." Wes' had kept wearing his wedding band long after his wife had disappeared. "But, I never had anyone chasing after me."

"He's not chasing after me."

Wes put on a pair of spectacles and squinted across the room at Jakes.

"Then why is he here. He's gotta be brave or stupid."

"Maybe neither."

"Is he here for you?"

Connie made a noise somewhere between a snort and a laugh.

"No. He's got a girlfriend. They've moved in together."

"Then, he is stupid," Wes said. "And you have to get John to make you an owner."

Connie couldn't disagree, although it was hard to hear the truth.

"Are you still taking shooting lessons?" asked Wes.

There was a rifle range out near the airstrip on the other side of Mungumby Creek. Connie had been taking women-only lessons. They spent more time shooting the breeze than hitting targets.

"I'm not to shoot John and go to gaol."

Wes smiled.

"No. There's some wild boar in the area. I was thinking of going hunting tomorrow. I could use a hand. You should come with me."

"I couldn't kill an animal," she said, pouring Wes a beer.

Wes shrugged.

"Also, I saw those boys from your campground this morning. They were climbing Black Mountain. Have you seen them come back?"

Connie hadn't seen them since their conversation at breakfast.

"I told them not to go up there."

"Did you tell them about the rocks?" said Wes.

"What about them?"

"They're poisonous."

"Isn't that an old wives tale?" said Connie.

"No, It's not," said a short fat man entering the hotel. He came to the bar with a wheeze and a waddle. "Not entirely. It's a psychotropic algae." His name was Scratch, and he was a local resident. One of the few that lived this side of the Mungumby creek.

Wes gave Scratch a dirty look and without a word, picked up his beer and crossed to the table by the window taking a seat. Wes and Scratch were neighbours. There were a few kilometres between them, but they were neighbours, and in all her years of managing the hotel, she'd never seen the two men have a civil conversation. Whatever had happened between them wasn't bad enough for them to stop frequenting the bar. Scratch climbed a stool at the bar.

"Hello, Scratch. What are you having?"

Scratch ordered a beer and dug one hand into his pocket, mining gold and silver and set a fist full of coins on the counter.

"So, this algae on the rocks won't kill you?" Connie asked, making conversation.

"The more you're in contact with it, the worse it gets. It won't kill you, but it'll make things a little weird."

Connie picked out enough of the coins to cover Scratch's drink.

"Have you tried it?"

"Sure. I didn't like it."

Connie laughed, serving Scratch his beer.

"I never thought you'd be the type to do drugs."

"Not on the mountain," said Scratch, serious. "It's dangerous enough up there without hallucinogenics in your blood."

"Why doesn't anyone know about it?"

"What are the council going to do? They can't remove the algae. It's been there for thousands of years. That's what makes the rocks black. And, if they put up signs about it, every hippie will be up here scraping it off the rocks and getting high."

A gaggle of female voices drew Connie's attention to the entrance where four women, from their early twenties to late forties entered, dressed in black, carrying aprons. One of the women, closer to Connie's age, gave her an apologetic look.

"Sorry we're late. We got stuck at Emma's. We couldn't get Ada and Bev away from her baby girl."

"Bev and I had to get in a few cuddles before we left," said Ada.

"You had a cuddle too, Tina", said Bev, turning to Connie. "You'd love Chelsea. She's so cute."

"I miss her already," said Emma.

"Welcome back, Emma. You'll be home before you know it," said Connie. She would be a mother by now if John hadn't played it off against the business and made her an owner, then lied about that too. Her own step-daughter would be a Mum before Connie if she refused to get the pregnancy terminated.

"Is that Jakes Jenkins?" Tina was facing the back of the hotel, looking puzzled.

Connie's face hardened.

"Yes. Just treat him like any other customer."

"Does John..."

"John knows." Connie cut her off. "He's already served Jakes." - A knuckle sandwich.

The four waitresses looked doubtful and Connie put them to work before they could ask any more questions.

Over the next hour, half a dozen dusty four-wheel drives and cars pulled up at the front of the hotel. An hour after that, the tables and chairs around the bar and the restaurant were near capacity. One of the customers, Evelyn Ashby, a retired nurse, ordered a shandy and reminisced about how, as a little girl, her father would bring her to the Hotel. Since then, very little about the old tin pub had changed. A big, barrel-chested man by the name of Fred Abe ordered a round of beers for his four friends who were already drunk. Connie considered refusing him service. Fred Abe, Jakes had said, was spreading rumours that her marriage was over. So, Connie put up four beers and a glass of water.

"The water's for you."

"Why would I want water?" said Fred Abe pushing back the single glass, his voice booming.

"You must be too drunk to figure it out," she said, hands on hips.

Fred Abe looked at her puzzled. He wasn't the smartest man.

"Apparently my marriage is over?" she said.

Fred Abe's face turned red.

"Well, … isn't it?" he said.

"No."

Not yet it wasn't, but it might be after tonight.

"Sorry," was all Fred said.

Connie glared at him, put up another beer and took his money. He took his beers to his small group of friends, men with names like Shakey, Gunner Jones, Slippery Pete and Kipper, the only names by which these men were known.

As drinks flowed, voices lifted drowning out the background music. The smell of hot chips and roasted meat wafted out of the kitchen. The waitresses were busy running plates and bowls, glasses and cutlery to tables. Connie stood at the bar controlling it all and money filled the till. This was her hotel. She ran it like she owned it and she'd be damned if she was going to give it up without a fight.

A wolf whistle cut through the noise from the crowd and the men in the bar parted. A young, full-breasted woman with straight brown hair threaded her way through the men on long legs dressed in short khaki shorts and a loose-fitting top. Josie Easten had grown up. She was in her early twenties, slim and attractive, even without makeup.

Connie felt a sense of resentment towards the younger woman and tried to put it aside. Jakes had made his choice, and it wasn't Connie.

Josie brushed off a man offering to buy her a drink, scanning the crowd. She spotted the towering figure of Fred Abe with his friends, and Josie's pretty face turned mean. She made a beeline for the group of men and came within arms-length of Kipper when Jakes Jenkins cut her off. His lip, split formed a crisp circle as he mouthed a. 'No.'

Josie clenched her fists. She was looking for a fight.

"Josie, what are you drinking?" Connie called out to the young woman, drawing her attention. She turned and came towards the bar, pouting.

"A beer. Thanks" Josie's voice was deep. Her face still burning with hate.

"I hear it's your birthday. Happy Birthday," said Connie.

Josie sneered.

"Yeah."

This wasn't your typical carefree, twenty-something-year-old woman out to celebrate. She was looking over her shoulder, anxious and angry. Connie handed her a beer.

"Are you planning on attacking any more of my customers? Because that wouldn't work for me," said Connie.

Josie gave a forced smile and held out a banknote.

"No."

"Jakes tells me that you moved in with him."

"It's nice that you two are talking." Another forced smile. Josie was hard to read.

Connie handed over the change.

"Stay out of trouble," she said.

Josie took her drink, found Jakes in the crowd and followed him to their table. Connie had the impression that Jakes, Josie and Quicks weren't here to celebrate. Worse still, everyone had seen Jakes and the conversation shifted to her rumoured affair with the local sailmaker. But they wouldn't be here long.

Connie called Tina to the bar and pointed out Jakes, Josie and Quicks.

"Can you take their order? Make sure Sherbet Ray knows it's urgent." With a little effort, Connie was confident she could get Jakes out of the hotel before John made an appearance and realised Jakes was still here.

Then someone tapped her on the shoulder and pointed across the room. Wes was out of his seat, pointing out the window. Outside it was getting dark. The old man called out over the noise in the bar.

"Those kids are back. They look hurt. One's missing."

Four boys hobbled into the hotel, leaning on each other. Their clothes were torn and covered in dirt, and they were bleeding from the hands and knees. One of the boys was crying, another cried out, desperate for water, and a third shouted into the crowd, telling everyone to get back. He was skittish, twitching, spooked, eyes bloodshot, pinpricks for pupils.

"Where's your friend?" said Wes.

"I didn't push him. He fell." said one of the boys.

"Is he still in the Mountain?"

"No, he's gone to the tent," said another, slipping a rucksack off his shoulder and unzipping the top.

"We found this," he said, reaching inside and lifting out a dirty, white object with teeth - a skull.

Connie felt a chill.

The room took a collective breath. Wes' eyes widened, his face turning hard.

The boy handed the skull to a friend and plunged his hand into the rucksack again, coming out with a second skull, smaller by half with a row of small teeth - a child.

Wes reached out to take the small skull, and the boy pulled back.

"What are you doing?"

Wes pointed at a dark spot on the back of the child's skull.

"What's that?"

The boy turned it over. At the base of the skull was a small, round hole that appeared to be the type of impact made by a bullet into bone.

Connie grabbed Bev Shay by the apron, pulling her close.

"Call the police. Tell them there's been a murder."

CHAPTER 7

Sergeant Andy Cross lent forward, his wet high-vis jacket dripping water over his desk and hung up the phone. The windows of the police station rattled, and rain lashed the glass.

"It has to be them," he whispered into the static-like hash of the storm.

Two deaths. An adult and child. The child shot in the back of the head, their skulls found by the boys who'd made it out of Black Mountain alive. In living memory, there had been only one disappearance that involved a child.

"It's got to be them."

Getting up from his chair Andy crossed the room and passed through a doorway into a cold hallway stopping at a solid, metal door. He took out a set of keys and opened the door into a storage room lined with shelves of brown archive boxes and grey metal cabinets. Locking the door behind him, he inserted a key into one of the filing cabinets and opened the drawer. From between the rows of files, he took out a brown folder placing it on top of the filing cabinet. The cover contained a case file summary printed by typewriter in fading black ink.

'Missing Persons, Wesselman J and K, Investigating officer Sgt. Andrew Cross, Archived December 1965.'

Andy turned through the contents quickly, flicking past photos and photocopied images checking everything was there, securing the bindings holding in the papers. Satisfied, Andy unzipped his jacket, lifted his shirt, slipping the folder into the waistline of his pants, tightening his belt. He pulled down his shirt, zipping up his jacket and locked the filing cabinet. Giving the folds of his clothes one final check Andy stepped out of the storage room into the hall, closed and locked the door and walked through the station and out the front door, jogging through the heavy rain to a marked four-wheel drive and climbed behind the wheel. As he drove, rain lashed the windshield. He'd forgotten to tell Bev Shay about the storm.

A block from the police station, under the sodium-yellow street lights of Charlot Street, Andy pulled over removing the file from under the folds of his clothes and laid it out on the passenger seat. With the engine running, the wiper arms swinging wildly and the deafening sound of rain on the roof Sergeant Andy Cross opened the folder.

Forty years ago, a woman and child went missing. They were the Wesselmans, the wife and daughter of Kenneth Wesselman, a farmer from the tablelands. The police had interviewed two suspects, but without a body, they were unable to determine why or how the mother and child went missing. The case had been closed without a conviction, and the disappearance became folk law. Andy had grown up with the story of the missing woman and child. The most popular theory was they'd been killed and dumped in Black Mountain. With the discovery of the bones and the bullet hole in the child's skull, the local stories were beginning to prove true. The next step would be to secure the evidence, conduct interviews and search for their killer.

To his own credit, Andy was ahead of this case. He'd been looking into the unsolved mystery and applied to have the case reopened. The District Inspector had denied his submission due to a lack of new evidence. The discovery of the two skulls changed that, and the case would be reopened with a phone call. Unfortunately, Andy wouldn't be investigating. Homicides were sent to Cairns. In about a week, a group of detectives in suits and ties would turn up in Cooktown asking questions, and that would be the beginning of the end. The locals wouldn't talk to anyone they didn't know and the police, from out of town, would reach a dead end. The case would go back into the archives.

Andy had a week to solve this. He had to start the investigation now.

Blasting fog from the windshield, Andy put the police vehicle into gear, steering away from the centre of town into the back-roads, winding his way through the streets with cyclone proof houses on stilts. The vehicle slowed and pulled into the driveway of a light blue weatherboard home with a tropical garden, lashed with rain. Andy jogged from the car, up a flight of stairs to the front door and let himself inside. It was dark. Light and sound from a television in the next room told him someone was home.

"It's me," he shouted, flicking a switch and illuminating a cream coloured kitchen with patterned linoleum. He pulled the case file out from under his jacket and placed it, face-up on the worn laminate of the kitchen bench, in plain sight.

"Hey, are you there?" he shouted again.

"Who's that?" a voice crackled, from the next room.

"Do you want tea?" Andy called out, louder this time and filled a white plastic kettle with water.

The TV cut off. The floorboards creaked. An old man in shorts and a singlet appeared. His skin was pale, his hair white, and he walked with a long stride and a hunch.

"You're dripping on my floor," he said, pointing a crooked finger. A trail of water led to the kitchen bench. The old man saw the file. He opened it, read the cover, flipped through the contents and closed it.

"Have you had any update on the Reggie Morris case?"

The old man seemed disinterested in the file.

Andy held up the tea bag and got the approval of the old man, dropping the tea into a mug and setting the kettle to boil.

"The prosecutor delayed the court date - not enough evidence. And they're saying someone else could be involved. We've had reports come in from other women. Someone's been looking through windows while Reggie was in gaol."

"He's out?"

"Got out this morning. He's on parole for the B and E. Must have a good lawyer."

"Lawyers," said the old man with obvious disgust.

The kettle clicked like the hammer of a revolver. Andy poured out two mugs. In the corner of his eye, his father cast a furtive glance at the case file. Andy smiled then straightened his face and slid the hot mug across to his old man who cupped it with two hands, blowing.

"Any proof we have around the photos is circumstantial. His lawyer is arguing that this second person connected to the peeping Tom had the camera and took the photos, and all Reggie did was develop them. If he tells us who he's working with the state is going to make him an offer."

Andy gave his father space to interject and ask about the offer, but his father didn't seem to be listening and glanced again at the police file. It was getting to him.

Andy continued.

"It's typical for this sort of thing to escalate when there are two or more people involved. You know how it goes. Either way, the prosecutor is asking us for more evidence to sure up a conviction, and I've exhausted most options."

"Where's Reggie?"

"In town. Probably at Top Pub."

"He came back into town? Like nothing happened?" said his old man.

"The only charges are breaking and entering. Nobody knows about the pending charges, except for Jakes and Josie and they're keeping it quiet."

There was a pause in the conversation. The line of conversation was running out of road. But Andy didn't want to be the first to deviate.

"He'll try it again. People like that don't just stop," said the old man.

"We know."

There was another pause.

"You should give the barman at Top Pub a tip about Reggie. Let him spread some stories. The locals will take care of him."

"It doesn't work that way," said Andy.

"It did in my day," said his old man.

"Not under my command."

"Justice isn't always served in the courts, Andrew."

The use of his full name was intended to be condescending.

Andy stared at the file on the kitchen counter, the coffee to his lips.

The silence became heavy.

"Get on with it," blurted his father, waving at the file. "What's this here for?"

"I just got a call from the Lion's Den. A bunch of kids were climbing Black Mountain and found human remains."

"It may not be the Wesselmans? Plenty of people have disappeared up there. You're jumping to conclusions."

"They found two skulls. One of them is a child." Andy paused, waiting for a response. His father's temperament seemed to cool, crossing his arms and his eyes wavered, but he remained silent.

Andy put down his mug and took a step closer to his dad.

"Your case just became a homicide," he said.

The old man spat out a breath.

"It's not my case."

"Your name is still on the file."

"I was fifty-two years in the force. My name is on a lot of files." The old man turned his back and crossed the room to sit at the table by the door. "And what makes you think this was a homicide?" said the old man.

"There's a gunshot wound to one of the skulls," said Andy.

"Have you got the skulls?"

"They're at the Lion's Den."

"Then how do you know it's a fucking gunshot wound? You haven't even seen these skulls. You can't go around saying they were murdered if you don't know."

"Don't get angry. This is just a conversation. We're talking like we normally do."

"Talk can be dangerous. Especially in this town. When you've got the skulls, you come back here, and we'll talk." The old man got up to walk out.

His father was on the defence.

Andy felt terrible. He'd been putting off this conversation for this reason, and he could let it go, right now. But the conversation had to be had. And it had to be now while the evidence was fresh. This wasn't a conversation between father and son. Nor was it a conversation between Sergeant and Officer. Andy was here in his uniform to investigate a forty-year-old murder. He had to put aside his feelings and do his job. If he didn't someone else would do it for him.

"Dad, wait. What can you tell me about the case?"

His Dad stopped in the doorway.

"Have you even read it? Everything is in there. You don't need me."

Andy held up his hands in surrender.

"OK. Sure, just take a seat. Finish your tea." His old man came back into the kitchen. Andy smiled.

"You know who dropped into the station today? Mary Bozzo. Sticks brought her in. Do you remember, she got bitten by that dog. Do you remember that?" said Andy, looking up at the ceiling with a smile and another soft laugh. "Who's dog was that?"

"Dusty Millen," said his father, taking a seat at the table and sipping his tea.

"I hated that dog," said Andy. "It scared the shit out of me every time I walked past. It was on Furneaus Street. I remember that. I'd walk around the block just so I didn't have to go past the Millen's house."

"Furneaus Street. Right. The damn dog was crazy. Wild. It kept getting out. Attacking the wildlife."

"Is it true it ate a whole kangaroo?"

"It was a wallaby," said his Dad, smiling.

Andy pushed off the kitchen bench and moved to the table, sitting close to his father, leaning in.

"I remember that whole thing as a kid. It ate the wallaby then a few days later it attacked Mary Bozzo. I remember you telling Mum about it. The next day there was a story about it in the local paper. You had to get the dog put down, and Dusty refused to let you do it. That was the first time I really understood what you did for a job and how hard it was for you. But I understood that you did that to keep people safe. So I could walk down Furneaus Street without being bitten. I wanted to do that. To keep people safe. I wanted to be a police officer."

"I didn't put the dog down. The vet did that," said his Dad.

"No. I know. Do you know I use that case as an example to new recruits? It was good solid police work. We have copies of the file as a point of reference. You matched the dog bite, got witness statements. The works."

Andy stood up and crossed the kitchen to the file on the counter.

"You did more work to get Dusty Millen's dog put down than you did trying to find out what happened to this woman and child," said Andy, his voice full of heat and fury.

"Fuck you." Quick as a clam, his old man closed up.

"We're talking about the life of two human beings. It's disgraceful what happened to her." Andy jabbed a finger at the file. "The lack of information. The lack of care. You treated them like dogs. Worse than dogs. What happened? Did you give up?"

His father's face was red.

"Don't lecture me about how I did my job. I had nothing to go on. There were no bodies. No evidence of a murder. For all I knew, she ran away with the kid."

Andy took the anger lodged in his chest and moved it out of his body. He put his hands up in a sign of surrender.

"OK. But there must be something you know that isn't in the file. Tell me about the Wesselmans." His voice was calm and commanding.

His father rose to his feet.

"You're not listening. Everything I got I put in that file," shouted his old man. It looked like his father wasn't going to give Andy anything more than he already had. Andy picked up the file and his car keys.

"It doesn't matter, anyway. You won't be talking to me. This'll go to homicide," said Andy.

His father's brow dropped.

"Bullshit. If you farm this out the whole things a lame duck. The locals won't talk. You need to stay on this," said his father.

"It's not my decision. It'll go to regional. This time next week I won't have anything to do with it."

Father and son stared at each other across the room. His Dad knew this is how things worked, and there was nothing Andy could do about it.

"I can investigate," said Andy. "But I won't have a lot of time. "On Monday I'll make the call. It's a cold case, so no one is going to rush this. That gives me maybe a week or two if we're lucky. Then it all gets transferred, and the guys in homicide are going to see what I'm seeing in this file, and they're going to start where I'm starting; with you. They're going to come here and ask the same questions I'm asking. But they're not going to be able to do what I can do.

"What are you talking about?" said his Dad.

"You've got to tell me, what's missing from the investigation." Andy shook the manila folder.

His Dad shook his head and dropped his chin to his chest, silent, thinking.

"It's not a lot of time, Dad. I can take care of this. You need to talk to me."

Silence.

"Dad!"

His father looked up.

"I can't help you," he said, "This is your case now." His old man turned away and disappeared into the living room.

CHAPTER 8

A group had gathered around the skulls with the boys jealously guarding their gruesome find. Wes stood among the boys, a weathered hand outstretched.

"Let me see it."

"No. It's ours. We found it," said the boy, clutching the small skull in two hands.

"Just let me have a look, and you can have it back," said Wes.

"What for?"

"Don't let him take it," snapped the oldest of the boys.

"I'm not going to take it, I just want to take a look," said Wes, extending his arm.

"Why?"

"I think you may be holding my daughter. And that is my wife." He said, pointing at the skulls. "I'd like to look at them."

One boy looked to the others for guidance. The oldest boy gave a cautious nod, and the skull was offered to Wes, the old man taking it to the bar and holding under the brightest light, looking into the empty eyes, examining the cheekbones and the row of tiny teeth. The crowd watched on with macabre fascination.

"Is it them?" said Connie.

The old man's eyes were glistening, and he didn't speak. One of the boys came forward.

"That's enough. Hand it back." He held out a hand.

Wes faced the boy, eyes burning.

"You shouldn't handle these. Put it in your bag." Wes nodded at the rucksack in the hands of another boy. He came forward with the bag.

"Both of them," said Wes waving at the boy with the other skull. The boy came forward and placed the skull inside the rucksack. The rucksack was thrust at Wes, and he put the skull in the bag.

"Zip it up." He told the boy.

The boy worked at the zipper.

At the edge of the crowd, Scratch was on the balls of his feet, eyes on the bag of remains.

The boy with the rucksack was struggling with the zipper. Wes lent in and grabbed the bag, yanking it from the hands of the boy. The boy looked at Wes, stunned. Wes pulled back a fist and punched the boy in the face knocking him to the floor. The crowd took a collective breath, in shock. Some of the men cheered. With the bag of bones in hand, Wes turned and ran for the door. The boys lunged forward, chasing Wes to the exit and caught him on the threshold, grabbing the bag and pulling him back into the hotel. It was tug-o-war with the skulls in the middle. But the boys weren't playing. Led by the oldest, the three boys leapt on Wes and began hitting and kicking. One of them made a fist, took aim and smacked Wes in the head. The old man's eyes rolled back, his face slackened, and his knees gave way. The rucksack slipped from his limp hand, and his body hit the floor- out cold.

The boys had the rucksack. They turned toward the exit and found it blocked by a dozen angry men. The peach fuzz faces of the four boys dropped as they realised they were in trouble. A roar went up from the group of men, and they pounced on the boys, swarming around them, grabbing, pulling, punching and kicking. It was an all-in brawl. Bodies stumbled and fell, crawled and dodged. Yelps from the four boys were punctuated by the thud and smack of fist on flesh. The fight rolled around the bar and into the hotel knocking over tables and chairs, flipping plates, spilling food and drinks. Customers scattered.

Connie's screams to stop were a whisper in a storm.

Among the stumbling feet, Connie saw the rucksack. It lay on the floor getting kicked about in the melee. Dodging and weaving through the brawling men, Connie snatched up the bag. But, as she turned head for the bar, she felt a tug. Holding onto the other end of the rucksack, gripping the straps were the short fat fingers of Scratch.

Connie tugged at the bag.

"Scratch, Let go."

Scratch tugged back.

"Let me have em," he said, his eyes darting in and out of the crowd.

"No. This needs to go to the police," said Connie.

Scratch opened his mouth to speak when Wes emerged from the brawl and threw himself at Scratch. The two men tumbled and rolled across the timber floor. Connie had the bag.

"No one is getting it," she said, stepping behind the

bar and dropping beneath the counter finding a resting place for the remains in lost property.

"What the fuck is going on?" The male voice yelled over the sound of the men fighting. Connie rose up from behind the bar and saw a red-faced, angry looking, John glaring at the group of men and boys. Without hesitation, John dove into the fight, but he was on the wrong side, shoving and pushing at the men, trying to defend the boys. Connie yelled at John to stop. She ran around the bar and grabbed at his arm.

"John, stop."

In the pulling and shoving and pushing, a stray elbow from her husband collided with the bridge of Connie's nose.

Pain exploded in a burst of colour and her vision blurred.

The noise from the fight stopped for a split second before an angry roar ripped through the room, and through a blurred vision, Connie saw the group of men turn on John. Men rushed in, grabbing and throwing punches. Roughing him up. John covered himself with his arms, and the group of men pushed John towards the exit, throwing him out of his own hotel.

Connie recovered her vision, her nose stinging and went out onto the veranda. John was shoved to the ground.

"That's enough," she said.

The men backed off. John was ranting and got to his feet with a stagger. He'd taken a hit to the face, and his nose had exploded like a tomato.

"Go home, John." Connie guarded the entrance.

John swayed on his feet, scanned the doors and windows of the hotel. All eyes were on him. His posture faltered, and he shot Connie a mean stare. Without another word, John turned, storming off into the night.

*****

The bar was a mess of broken glass and overturned tables. Older couples and parents grabbed their children and left. Connie was left shaking. Her nose stung. She asked Tina to take over the hotel for the night and, with a glass of wine, disappeared into the kitchen.

"Are you alright? What was going on?" Sherbet Ray wasn't aware there'd been a brawl in the bar.

"There was a fight. John hit me. It was an accident, but he got thrown out of the hotel. I think he was drunk," she said. Connie wanted to cry. She was exhausted. If she could, she'd go home, lay down and sleep for a week until all of this went away.

The phone rang.

Connie thought it might be the police calling back.

"Hello?"

"Is Kipper there?" It was an older male voice.

"Just a minute," she said, putting down the phone. Connie looked through the swinging door at the thinning crowd. Half the restaurant was empty. The only people staying on seemed to be the locals, eager to witness the undoing of Connie and John.

She turned to Sherbet Ray.

"I can't go out there. Can you get Kipper?" she held up the phone.

The Cook put down his tea-towel and went into the restaurant.

Connie slumped against the stainless kitchen bench hugging the glass of wine. John was a mess. She wanted him to sign her on as an owner of the business, but that would tie her to him and right now, she wasn't sure she wanted to stay.

The swinging door opened and Kipper entered the kitchen, his eyes bouncing nervously off the shiny metal surfaces. Connie pointed the thin, pale man towards the telephone. Kipper put the receiver to his ear.

Sherbet Ray came through the swinging door, stepping around Kipper.

"It's a mess out there," he said, diving back into his work, picking up a tea towel and removing a large, heavy pot from the boil. "It must have been a helluva fight," he said, taking the pot to the sink, tipping the contents out and balancing it on a mountain of dirty dishes. "Did John do all that?"

"No, it was mostly the locals and a group of boys, fighting." She told the Cook about the fight between Wes, Scratch and the boys and that the boys had found two skulls in Black Mountain.

"I miss out on all the good stuff," said Sherbet Ray.

The swinging door kicked open, and Tina entered with an armload of dirty plates circling around Kipper heading for the sink.

"Half of the people have left," said Tina, trying to make space on a bench for more dirty dishes. The kitchen was a mess.

"Where's Stephan?" said Connie, realising the Spanish kitchen hand was missing.

The Cook looked up at the clock.

"He's been on a break. Can you get him back in here?"

Connie pushed off the bench, put down her wine and headed for the back door.

Night had settled in around the hotel. A cold wind blew in from the east. There was a tapping sound on the tin roof and a wet smacking on the gravel in the car park. The dusty smell of rain hung in the air. From the horizon, a flash of lightning lit up a dark bank of cloud over Black Mountain and beneath the menacing cloud was a thick sheet of rain.

The boom of thunder hit her in the chest. Her heart hammered. Another flash of lightning lit up the campground. The sheet of rain hit the tents, flaps of canvas danced in the wind, and people were running for cover.

Connie looked around for Stephan. A row of plastic seats at the back door were all empty. She called out his name into the oncoming roar of the storm, her hair whipping her face. In the darkness, a beam of light caught her eye. Shining against the wet ground, the light came from a crack under the door of a small storage shed. A shadow fell across the threshold. Someone was inside.

Connie stepped out from under the eaves, cold bullets of rain showering her face. She reached the storage shed and pulled on the door. Inside, sprawled out on a pallet of flour was the half-naked body of Karla. A man stood over her, hands gripping her waist, pants around his feet, thrusting his bare hips into hers. Karla's head snapped up. She saw Connie and her face filled with horror.

"Shit."

Connie flushed hot, stepped back and closed the door.

CHAPTER 9

It would be impossible to get the image out of her head. Connie stood at the door to the shed in a deluge of rain, mortified, the vision of Karla, skin on skin with Stephan clear and fresh in her mind.

And they were on the clock. She was paying them to have sex. Fury filled her body and Connie raised a hand, bashing on the tin door, rattling the walls.

"Get out here, now," she yelled, through the howl of wind and rain.

Her hair was getting soaked, and it was cold. It only fuelled her anger.

The door to the shed opened, and the two lovers emerged from the light. She lined them up against the tin wall of the shed.

"Stephan. You're fired. Get your stuff, you're leaving tonight."

"No." Karla squeaked, grabbing Stephan by the arm. "You can't make him leave."

Connie turned on Karla.

"Be quiet. I'll deal with you later."

"If you fire him you have to fire me too," Karla said, defiant.

"You'll get worse than that," said Connie turning to the young man. "Stephan, when John finds out about this, you won't want to be here. Understand?"

Stephan nodded.

"I'll arrange for someone to take you into town," she said.

"No." Karla dug her fingers into Stephan's arm, unwilling to let him go.

"It's O.K. I'll go," said Stephan prying back Karla's nails.

"No," Karla screamed, tears coming to her eyes.

"Keep it down. Do you want your Dad out here?" said Connie.

"I don't care," she spat.

"O.K. Let's go tell him now." Connie was ready to march the two lovers into the house to cop John's wrath.

"No," said Karla, turning meek. "Don't tell him. It's none of his business. It's none of your business. Just leave us alone."

"You made it my business when you decided to have sex at work. I'm paying you both. What were you thinking?"

Karla didn't have an answer, and Stephan was fearful and silent. Connie pointed at Karla's hands.

"Let go of your boyfriend. He has to go."

"It's O.K. I'm going," said Stephan.

Karla broke into a loud cry, and Connie could sense the teenage heart, breaking.

"Where are you going to stay?"

There was another flash of lightning and a clap of thunder. It was dangerous outside.

"Leave that up to me. Stephan, pack up your stuff."

"I'm going with him."

Connie's clothes were soaked, and she was out of patience.

"The only place you're going is your room. Now, say good-bye," she said, her voice threatening.

Karla threw her hands to her face and cried. Stephan looked at Connie awkward, unsure of what to do.

Connie waved a hand at Karla.

"Say good-bye." They hugged and shared a kiss that was awkward for everyone. Connie pointed at Stephan.

"Get your stuff. Wait out the front of the hotel. Go." Stephan ran for the campground his figure obliterated by a thick swirling band of rain.

"I hate you," said Karla, her voice breaking, tears flowing.

Connie could deal with that later.

"Go to your room. And don't let your Dad see you."

*****

"Pity, he was a good kitchen hand," said Sherbet Ray.

Connie hung up the phone.

"Dawn Kirby is going to take him," she said, wicking herself dry with a hand full of fresh tea towels. "I just need to get him into town."

Connie couldn't leave the hotel, and she couldn't ask just anyone to take Stephan. Whoever took him would ask questions. Stephan might even say something himself and

Connie didn't want rumours going around about Karla. There was only one person she could count on to get Stephan away from the hotel without saying a word.

Wes stood outside under the veranda, the cold wind pulling at his hat, the rain splashing his feet.

"Awful weather," he said, flicking the stub of a spent cigarette out into the rain and lit up again. The red flame behind his cupped hand flickered in his eyes, casting a long shadow over the deep lines of his face.

"I need a favour," said Connie. "Can you take Stephan into town?"

Wes looked up into the dark clouds, the air thick with rain then turned to look inside through the window waving his cigarette at the bar.

"Give me those remains, and I'll do it."

"Why do you want them?"

Wes bowed his head and blew smoke out of the corner of his mouth. When he looked up, his eyes were hard.

"That's my family."

In all the years she'd known Wes, he'd only mentioned his wife and daughter a few times and never in any detail. Everything Connie knew about them, she'd heard from locals.

About forty years ago, they'd disappeared. The police had investigated at the time, but they were never found. The rumour was Wes had killed them. Connie had never believed it.

"I want to take them home." Wes' voice shook with emotion.

Connie put a hand on the arm of the old man.

"Wouldn't it be better if the police took them?" she said.

Wes growled and pulled away.

"They're not going to be able to find the person that

did this. They couldn't do anything back then, and they're not going to be able to do anything now."

"What are you going to do with them?"

Wes glared at her through cigarette smoke, noticing her damp hair and dress. He ashed his cigarette.

"How bad do you want this kid gone?" he said.

"I'm asking you for a favour."

"And I'm asking you for a favour. Give me the bag behind the bar."

"If you take Stephan into town we'll talk about the about the skulls when you get back."

"It's not just the skulls," said a voice from the dark. From the end of the veranda, a young man came into the light dragging with him a large backpack. He was dirty and wet, marked with blood and hobbling. He was the last of the five boys who'd found the skulls in Black Mountain. "There are bones too. I can show you," he said.

"Do you have them?" Wes asked the boy.

"Yes, but you can't tell the others. I need to get out of here before they find out," said the boy. "Can I come with you to town?"

CHAPTER 10

Scratch sat on his stool at the end of the bar cradling a cold beer. "What was Wes saying out there?"

Connie gave Scratch a wary look. She wasn't sure how much she should tell Scratch.

"You know that's his wife and daughter?" said Scratch, pointing to the shelves behind the bar.

"That's what I keep hearing."

"I was around when they disappeared. He killed them."

"Wes, wouldn't kill his own family," said Connie. "Maybe they're not his wife and child."

Scratch leaned over the bar trying to look into lost property.

"Show them to me."

"Why, so you can steal them? Why did you want the

skulls?"

"To keep them from Wes."

"Maybe they're someone else, and this has got nothing to do with Wes."

Scratch frowned, tapping his beer.

"Plenty of people have disappeared in and around Black Mountain, but they've all been adults. Wes' daughter is the only kid who's gone missing around here and to find an adult and child together? It's got to be them. It can't be anyone else."

Connie thought of the grim contents of the rucksack under the bar. Outside on the veranda of the hotel, Wes had the foreign boy locked in conversation. She was sure Wes didn't kill them, but someone had.

"Why do you think it was Wes?" she asked Scratch.

"I saw him with the bodies. I was near Black Mountain the day they disappeared, and I saw him carrying the bodies. I knew they were in there all this time."

"Did you tell the police?"

"Of course. The police spent weeks searching Black Mountain."

"Did they find anything?"

"Nothing."

"But you saw Wes? You're a witness. If that's true, why didn't it go to court?"

Scratch shifted in his stool.

"Well…I didn't see his face."

"So you don't know for sure that it was Wes?"

"I knew it was Wes. It was a tall man in a hat. But they didn't believe me and put me in for questioning. I was scared out of my mind. Then they raided my house, took my stuff and searched through my parents' property. My parents didn't know what to think. The police were talking like I'd killed them, so I shut my mouth. Anything you say can be used against you, you know. Then months go by, and nothing got done. There was no court case, and we just went about our lives.

"Where did you see this man with the bodies?" said Connie.

"Near Wes' house, down by the creek. It was in the dry, and he walked straight across the creek bed into Black Mountain."

"What were you doing there?"

Scratch sipped his beer.

"I'd go for walks," said Scratch, shifting in his seat. "And the day before they went missing I heard her and Wes arguing."

"You were around their house the day before his wife and child disappeared, and the day they went missing. No wonder the police questioned you."

"I didn't do anything." Scratch looked frustrated. He pointed down the bar. "You've got a customer."

Connie turned to find Jakes Jenkins flashing a half-smile, the other side of his face swollen.

"You're wet," he said.

Connie became acutely conscious of the dress clinging to her skin.

"Does it bother you?" she said, hand on hip, chest out.

Jakes raised a brow.

"A little. Can I get an ice pack?" Jakes touched his tenderised face.

Connie produced a fresh tea towel from under the bar and filled it with ice.

"Why are you still here?" she said, bringing the four corners of the tea towel together and handing over the makeshift ice pack. Their hands touched.

"I can't seem to leave," he said. "Any chance of a drink?"

Connie turned to the refrigerator to take out a bottle and found Stephan blocking her path. He was dripping wet, eyes down, shameful.

She scowled at him.

"I forgot my jacket," he said, waving at the bar.

Sherbet Ray appeared from the storage room behind the bar, looking alarmed. He was about to say something when he saw Stephan and faltered.

"Um…You better come into the kitchen," he said to Connie.

"What is it, now?" Connie had had enough surprises for one night.

"It's Karla," he said.

Stephan stiffened.

Connie put up a hand.

"She isn't your concern, Stephan. You need to leave," she said, pointing at the front door.

Stephan bowed his head.

"I'm sorry," he said.

"We're all sorry," said Connie stepping into the storeroom at the back of the bar. She passed by a stake of beer cartons and shelves of wine and spirits and out into the kitchen. Karla was slumped on the floor by the sink, looking angry.

"What's going on? Why aren't you at the house?"

"It's Dad. He's gone totally nuts," she said.

"Does he know about Stephan?"

"No. He's just really angry. I'm not staying at the house," said Karla.

Connie asked Sherbet Ray to lock the back door.

"Well, you're not going to sit on the floor all night. Get up." Connie waved Karla to her feet. "We're short a kitchen hand, and Sherbet Ray needs help. You can wash the dishes." Connie handed Karla a tea towel.

"I know why he's angry," said Karla, flipping the tea towel over her shoulder and picking up a dirty pot.

"Do you want to tell me why you think he's angry?" said Connie.

"Because, that guy's here," she said, bitter. She was angry at Connie for sending her boyfriend away when her own boyfriend was in the restaurant.

"Jakes isn't the problem, Karla."

John was the problem, although she couldn't say that. Not to Karla.

The swinging door burst open, and Tina entered the kitchen.

"Those boys are back. They're angry. They want their bag back. The bag with the skulls."

Connie was fed up.

"They can take the damn things back for all I care."

"No, they can't," said Tina. "I already checked under the bar. They're not there. The bag is missing."

Connie rushed back to the bar. The boys were at the door, being held back by the group of men who'd thrown them out. They were shouting about their friend who'd stolen something from them. Connie dropped behind the counter, searching shelves for the rucksack. She pushed aside caps and clothing, a kids book, toys and a disposable camera.

"They're gone," she said, panic filling her veins like ice. She'd lost the remains.

Scratch stood on the footpegs of his stool, looking over the countertop.

"What's going on?"

"I put them right there," said Connie, placing her hands in the space among the lost property.

"You've lost the skulls?" Scratch said.

She didn't lose them. Someone had stolen them.

CHAPTER 11

Connie cast a suspicious eye around the hotel. Despite the commotion out the front, most people were trying to get on with their meals and drinks, and were engaged in conversation. Out on the veranda, the four boys were waiting, guarded by the same group of men who'd thrown them out an hour ago. In the darkness beyond the boys were the outline of vehicles in the car park and a space where one vehicle was missing—a white four-wheel drive. Wes was gone and he'd taken Stephan with him.

"Stephan." He was the last person Connie had seen in the bar rifling through the shelves for his jacket.

"Stephan?"

"The Spanish kid. The kitchen hand. He must have taken the skulls."

"I didn't see him with the bag," said Scratch.

Maybe it wasn't Stephan who took the skulls. Connie considered all the people who'd been to the bar in the last few hours. It couldn't have been Stephan.

"He didn't know about the bag. He was…" He was with Karla, but she didn't want to say it. "He was in the kitchen the whole time. There was no way he could've known about the bag or the skulls. Not unless someone told him about them." Wes was the only person who knew about the bones and had contact with Stephan. If Stephan had stolen the bones, Wes must have convinced him to do it.

"How could you not see someone take them? You were sitting right there," said Connie, waving at Scratch. Scratch had also wanted to take the bones and Connie focused in on the old man.

"Did you take them?"

"No. I couldn't reach them from here," he said as if he'd considered snatching them.

Outside the boys were shouting over the din of the storm, demanding their rucksack back.

"You must have seen something," she said.

"If I saw someone taking them, I would have stopped them, believe me."

Connie got out of the bar and went to the front veranda, pushing past the group of men guarding the door.

"I've called the police," she said. You can't have the skulls, and you can't have your bag. They're evidence," she lied.

"You don't have them do you?"

"That old man took them with him. We saw him leave with Dean. Dean has them," said the oldest boy.

Either way, the boys weren't getting back the bag or the skulls. She told them she still had the bag with the skulls. The rain intensified. She told the boys to go back to their tents and come back in the morning for breakfast. The boys didn't seem convinced, nevertheless they left.

Inside the rain hammered the tin roof with a deafening percussion, so loud that it became impossible to hold a conversation. Outside, water cascaded from the tin roof in glassy sheets.

Worried looks passed between couples and across tables, and car keys came out. This much rain was a problem. Rivers and creeks flooded cutting off the road into town. The floods were so severe, so quick that people got caught and drowned or trapped for days. It happened every other year to tourists who didn't know better and to locals who should know better. This much rain was more than Connie had ever seen and more than anyone had ever seen in a long time. Car keys stayed on the table. It was too late to make a dash for home. Safer to stay and wait for the storm to pass.

Wes was out in the storm, and Connie had sent him out there. She worried about the old man driving through the rain. He'd probably still be in town. She could warn him.

Connie picked up the phone to call her friend, Dawn Kirby. There was no dial tone. The phone was dead.

If Wes didn't stay in Cooktown, he'd have a hell of a time getting back to Rossville. It would take a few hours before the Annan river flooded. It was the smaller waterways like Mungumby Creek that could be a problem. These creeks filled, fast, with a high volume of churning water that stripped the banks of rocks, branches and whole trees, building into a wave of mud and debris.

Connie tried not to think about it. She kept herself busy, running the hotel, directing the waitresses and serving drinks from the bar. An hour passed, the rain kept a heavy flow. Then, out of the watery darkness came two yellow headlights. They pulled into the car park at the front of the hotel and a tall figure in a cattleman's hat, stepped into the open doorway of the Lion's Den, dripping, saturated.

"The bridge is out," Wes shouted above the rain. "The creek is flooded."

CHAPTER 12

A wave of shock and despair rippled through the small crowd and Wes approached the bar, water running from his fingers drawing lines across the timber floor. In addition to the water, Wes was covered in sand from his hands to his feet.

"We need to talk," he said spitting water.

Connie handed him a wad of tea towels and waved him behind the bar into the small storeroom where stacks of beer cartons, bottles of liqueur and wine were stored. She could see into the kitchen where Sherbert Ray was still at work handling pans.

"What's with all the sand?" she asked. Somewhere between here and town Wes must have gotten out of his car.

"The first thing you need to know is John is at my

place," Wes said.

"What's he doing at your place?" The last she knew John was at home.

"He was on the bridge. I was coming back from town and saw him standing there knee-deep in water holding onto the handrail. I think he got caught on the crossing."

"What was he doing on the bridge?"

"Why does anyone cross a bridge?" said Wes pausing. "I wouldn't have crossed the creek if he wasn't there. I tried to get him into the car, but he wouldn't let go of the rail, and I had to leave him out there. I made it across. Then the bridge collapsed."

"With John on it?"

Wes nodded.

"I took a torch downstream and found him washed out at the first bend. He was unconscious. I had to give him mouth to mouth."

"Is he O.K.?"

"He'll live."

"Why didn't you bring him home?" she said.

"He's not saying much, but he did say he didn't want to come back here."

John had left angry after being thrown out of his own hotel. Then there was the fight she'd had with him at the house, the rough treatment he'd given her and the fight he'd had with the men in the crowd. He'd been thrown out of his own hotel. And Karla had said he'd lost his temper at house.

Wes patted his face and neck with the tea towels.

"You've got to ask, what was he doing out there? I risked my life to help him." Wes shook his head. "I had my hand out, looking him right in the eye." Wes paused and shook his head. "He didn't want my help."

"You think he wanted to die?"

Wes shrugged.

"I think so."

She couldn't believe it. John wasn't suicidal. Selfish, yes, but not suicidal.

"He can say at my place for now. I don't mind. I'll keep an eye on him," said Wes.

"Are you O.K.?"

"I'll be better when I get out of these," said Wes, pulling at his wet, sandy clothes. "And we need to work out sleeping arrangements. There are a lot of people out there who need beds."

"I have to tell you about the skul-"

"Later," Wes cut her off. "Let's get these people into beds, and I can go home for a hot shower." Wes squelched as he made his way back into the hotel.

Before going into town, Wes had been desperate to get his hands on the two skulls. Now his priorities had shifted to a hot shower. It didn't make sense. The only reason Wes wouldn't want to talk about the skulls was if Wes already had the skulls.

Connie put aside her judgements and joined the old man in the hotel. She stood in the space between the bar and the restaurant and called everyone to attention. As she began to explain that about the flood, the bridge collapsing and that she'd find beds for everyone Connie noticed out the corner of her eye, through the window, the waddling figure of Scratch hustling through the rain. He got into his yellow station wagon, the wet ground lit red with the tail-lights, and a beam of yellow light cut through the dark and driving rain. Scratch took off home on his own. Besides the Lion's Den Hotel there were two houses in Rossville and Scratch had one of them. Leaving without taking someone with him was unforgivable.

By the time Connie turned off the lights in the hotel and ran home through the rain, everyone had a place to lay their head for the night. A large group of people followed Wes back to his farm, some of whom would be sleeping on the living room floor. Connie crammed families and couples into double rooms and huts dotted around the property at the back of the hotel, and the remaining men like Kipper, Slippery Pete, Shakey and Fred Abe were given sheets, cushions, pillows and blankets to make a bed on the hard timber floor of the hotel.

Connie got to the front porch of her house, soaking wet and jumped with fright at a figure waiting by the door.

"Jakes." Connie put a hand on her chest to calm her heart.

Jakes pushed himself off the wall.

"Sorry, I didn't mean to scare you."

"What are you doing here?" She looked back into the darkness towards the hotel for someone watching. If John knew Jakes was talking to her on her doorstep of their home, he'd go mental.

"I can't stay at the hotel with Shakey and the others. There'd be another fight," Jakes said.

"Why, did you sleep with his wife too?"

Jakes' eyes fell, and he held out his palm.

"Well…they were on a break when she…when we…" He squirmed. Uncomfortable.

"Jesus Jakes, is there anyone in this town you haven't slept with?" she said.

"I haven't slept with you," he flashed a half-smile.

"And you still fucked up my marriage."

Connie opened the front door. Inside she heard gasps and the hushed voice of Sherbet Ray and saw a group standing in the hall staring into the kitchen, waitresses with hands over their mouths. Among the group were Josie, Quicks and Karla.

"What's going on?"

"I told you, Dad went nuts," said Karla, waving a hand at the kitchen.

Connie stepped forward, the crowd parted. In the kitchen, the cabinet doors had been ripped from their hinges, drawers pulled out and tossed across the room, the walls punctured with holes, and the floor covered in broken plates, shattered glass and scattered cutlery.

"Your Dad did this?" Connie looked at Karla. The girl nodded.

John's journey, the path that had taken him to the bridge started to make some sense. He'd been into town doing God-knows-what and came home to find her with Jakes Jenkins, started a fight, she'd accused him of an affair, he'd almost assaulted her, and there was the second fight with Jakes, he'd been drinking, he hit her, accidentally, and was thrown out of his own hotel, he'd come home in a rage, tore apart the kitchen and left the house, headed towards town on the only road out of Rossville and got caught in the flood, drowned, resuscitated and didn't want to come home. He'd totally lost control.

Connie entered the kitchen, broken bits crunched underfoot. She picked up the cutlery drawer and tried to fit it back into the cabinet, but the frame was twisted out of shape. John had destroyed everything.

The waitresses offered to help clean; however, Connie told them to stay out.

"You'll only spread the mess," she told them when all she really wanted was to be left alone. Karla was the only one she didn't send away or didn't go. The two of them stood in the kitchen, surveying the mess.

"Are you O.K.?" said Karla.

Connie took a second to answer, sorting out the thoughts in her head.

"I'm O.K., but I'm worried about your Dad."

Karla burst into tears. Connie put an arm around the girl.

"I'm sorry about...what happened...with Stephan," said Karla, sobbing. "What's wrong...with Dad?"

Connie looked around the room. She wasn't sure where the problem started. It went back further than she could remember. Perhaps as far back as John lying to her about signing her onto the business.

"What do you think is wrong with him?" asked Connie.

Karla's forehead scrunched up, and she sniffed.

"I think, maybe he's unhappy," she said.

"Why do you think he's unhappy?"

Karla took a breath and held her breath. Words stuck in her throat as emotion blazed from her eyes, and in those eyes, Connie saw blame and hatred. She encouraged Karla to talk. It had to come out.

"What's he doing here?" she hissed, pointing a finger into the hall.

"You mean, Jakes? You can say his name," said Connie.

"He's the problem."

Jakes could have been another man at another time in a different place, and Connie could have made the same mistake. Jakes wasn't to blame. That was her fault.

"The problems your Dad and I are having go back before Jakes," said Connie, thinking of the lies John had told, the weight he'd gained, the arguments they'd had, all spot fires left to burn.

"Well, he better not be here when Dad gets home," said Karla.

"Your Dad is staying with Wes," said Connie.

Karla shifted her feet, looking dissatisfied.

"What's wrong?" Connie asked. She waited for Karla to speak.

"He shouldn't be in the house," said Karla, hatred on her breath and in her eyes.

Karla was right. Jakes had walked in with her. To anyone else it could have looked like he'd been invited to stay.

"I'll find him somewhere else to go," said Connie, not sure where that would be.

"Why isn't he at the hotel?"

"There's some men there that don't like him. And your dad is at Wes' farm so he can't stay with Wes."

Connie was tired, and they still had John's mess to clean up.

"It's late. If you're O.K. with it, we'll let Jakes stay tonight, and I'll make sure he leaves first thing in the morning."

CHAPTER 13

Connie woke up to darkness and screaming. She threw off the sheets and followed the screams to Karla's bedroom, throwing open the door and hitting the light. Karla stood pressed against a chest of draws in a corner, looking terrified. She pointed at the window. The blinds were open.

"Someone's out there."

Rain lashed the window in silver streaks against a black ink swirl of shadows. She rushed to the window and saw her own reflection. Sherbet Ray, Quicks and Jakes appeared in the doorway followed closely by Josie and the waitresses.

"Turn off the light," she said.

The room went dark, and Connie looked through the glass into the night. If someone was out there, she couldn't see them.

"He was trying to get in," said Karla.

She pulled the blinds closed, and the light came back on.

Connie went to Karla and put her arm around the girl.

Josie pushed her way into the room and knelt next to them.

"Did you see who it was?" she asked.

Karla shook her head and buried her face in Connie's arms, crying.

"I'm going out there," said Jakes, running for the front door. Quicks and Sherbet Ray went with him.

A sour smell drew Connie's nose to the bed. The covers were folded back and the sheets stained with white, dry rings—body fluid. A heat climbed her neck and into her cheeks. Connie crossed to the bed, pulling the covers over the mattress and noticed the stains were the type left by a male. The window was a few steps from Karla's bed. Stephan had been in her room.

Connie felt angry and wanted to say something. Now wasn't the time.

"Were the blinds closed when you went to bed?" asked Connie.

Karla nodded.

"And you heard a sound at the window?"

Karla nodded again. When Karla opened the blinds, she was looking for Stephan and met with the dark outline of an unfamiliar face.

Jakes and the others came back from their search dripping wet. They'd found no-one.

Karla asked if she could sleep in Connie's room, and Connie agreed. Before going to bed, she did a circuit of the house, locking the doors and windows and closing the curtains.

Safe in bed beside Karla, Connie lay listening to her step-daughter breathing, listening to the rain, feeling unsettled, wondering who had been at the window. Her thoughts drifted to other problems. John and his erratic behaviour made thoughts about her future unclear. The signs indicated that John was leaving her. He certainly wasn't happy in the marriage, and he could be having an affair. Or, he might want to commit suicide. At least then, she'd keep the house and the hotel. One thing was sure, Connie didn't know what to expect next from John. She had to be prepared for anything.

Sitting up and folding back the covers, Connie swung her feet onto the ground and crept through the dark into the walk-in wardrobe, closed the door and switched on the light. Reaching between two stacks of clothes, she grasped a cold metal tin, the size of small gift box flecked with red paint. Inside was a thick fold of banknotes. She counted the notes, checking they were all there and put the tin to the back of the shelf, switched off the light and crept back to bed.

Lying down, her eyes closed, Connie tried to think of a way to handle John. Tomorrow she would go to him, to talk. Perhaps his near-death experience would change him. She needed to try. If John didn't meet her half-way, if he didn't want things to get better, then there was no point in going on. She would take the tin of cash, pack the two suitcases under the bed and start again. The thought filled her with sadness and fear.

CHAPTER 14

In the darkness, a voice came to him, soft, feminine, penetrating his sleep.

'Wake up.'

The words repeated and he forced open his eyes. Someone was sat on the end of his bed, and he raised his chest to look. It was a woman. She was facing the window looking east out into the darkness. She had long, dark hair, a familiar shape, a familiar smell.

'Get up. You have to leave.' Her voice was clear. It was a voice he recognised.

"Jane?" His tongue stuck in his mouth.

The woman turned to face him. She was young and beautiful, and she smiled at him. His heart lifted, and he felt joy. She'd come back.

"You have to go," she said. The cry of a child came from somewhere deep inside the house, and the woman stood up. 'I have to go.'

He reached for her wrist and pulled her to the side of the bed, bringing her close. She sat next to him. He lent in, and they kissed.

'I miss you," he said. 'Please don't go.'

The baby was crying.

Jane pulled away, her smile was gone. A black spot bubbled up on her lip where they kissed.

'Get up.' Her voice was clear and commanding.

The black spot spread to the corner of her mouth. There was a desperate look in her eyes. 'Get up.' He tried to get out of bed but couldn't move. The spot spread like burning toast, growing like a rash, moving from her mouth to her chin and down her neck. It charred her clothes, burnt her shoulders, arms, body and legs until she was a nothing more than a shadow. A crack appeared where a mouth had been, and out came a scream.

Wes woke up, the scream ringing in his ears, his heart pounding, covered in sweat. The blinds were open and an early, predawn light filtered into the bedroom. The room was empty.

He pushed back the bedsheets, dressed, put on his hat and shoes. From behind the house, he heard barking. The dogs weren't used to being tied up, but he couldn't trust them with the people staying in the house. They'd never been around children.

Walking through the living room, Wes stepped over the scattered sheets and sleeping bodies to get to the kitchen. With his keys and spectacles in hand, Wes pushed through the back door of the house into the fresh morning air, a fuzz of light rain touching his face. Down a cracked concrete path to a large tin shed the dogs were pulling at their chains and barking. But they weren't barking at him. The door to the shed was open, the light on. Wes stopped on the path. Between the barking, he could hear movement inside in the workshop. A figure appeared in the doorway holding a bulging sack and a rifle.

"Hey, who's that?" Wes shouted. The figure startled, turned and bolted for the paddock, jumping the first fence and kept running.

Wes growled. The dogs barked.

He went to the shed and looked inside. A cloud of dust hung in the air, tools and clutter had been swept from benches, tipped out of storage containers and scattered on the dirt floor. Somehow his gun cabinet had been broken open. Prised and split apart, a rifle missing. Wes picked his way through the mess, squatting to pick up an overturned milk crate filled with rags. He turned the crate over, picked through the rags, throwing them aside, looking for something. His weathered face creased, his eyes narrowed. It wasn't there.

Someone had been watching him last night.

Wes reached into the damaged gun cabinet and took out the last rifle, filling the gun and his pockets with bullets. Outside the shed, he let the dogs off their leash, one after the other, and gave a loud, clear whistle. The dogs took off towards the paddock, leaping over the fence and dashing through a dozy heard of cows. At the side of the house was the Landcruiser, the cabin inside still wet from the flooded creek crossing. Wes put the key into the ignition, his hands shaking and took off through the gates into the paddock following the voice of the two cattle dogs. Through the wiper blades and the wet and foggy windshield, the rifle beside him, a scowl on his face, Wes searched the darkness for the man with the hessian sack.

"You're not getting away from me. Not this time."

CHAPTER 15

Scrambling around in the dark, she found the phone under the bed and pressed all the buttons to shut off the sound. If it wasn't for John's mobile phone, she'd still be dreaming of Jakes. Karla woke briefly, but put her head down and went back to sleep. There was no point going back to bed. Connie's mind had already begun to fire, the memories from yesterday pouring in. John was at Wes' farm, Jakes was in her living room - he had to leave, a bunch of people were stranded in Rossville, the creek had flooded and the remains of a woman and child had been found in Black Mountain, their bones stolen from behind the bar.

She was sure Stephan had taken the skulls, and Wes had something to do with it.

As she made her way down the hall, wrapped in a

dressing gown, the mobile phone in hand, Connie heard a distant pop - a single gunshot. She stopped to listen, doubting herself. The pops started again - gunfire. She counted a dozen cracks. It was definitely a gun.

For a remote town surrounded by bush, it wasn't uncommon to hear the occasional gun shot. On the other side of Mungumby creek out near the airport was a shooting range, and from time to time, Wes had to protect his herd or put down a cow.

Connie turned into the kitchen, set the kettle to boil and settled into one of the seats at the island bench among the broken cabinets, poking at the buttons on John's mobile. She brought up the number he'd called yesterday at around ten am. It was a local number, the first three digits the same as every other number in Cooktown, the second three digits unfamiliar to her. The mobile had no reception. The landlines were out. Even if they had reconnected the phone lines overnight, it was still too early to call. That was OK. She had time.

The kettle clicked off. Her favourite mug had a chip out of the lip. John. She cursed him. The floorboards in the hall creaked, and a dark figure stepped into the doorway. It was Jakes Jenkins. The breath left her body.

"Everything alright?" His voice was deep and rough, his hair stood up, a mess and he squinted into the light.

Connie pushed back her hair.

"It's alright. You can come in. Johns not here," she said with a wry smile. He took a seat opposite her, yawning, rubbing his tattooed arms. They were nice arms. Strong. Firm. It had been a long time since she'd felt the simple, safe embrace of a man.

"Did you hear the gunshots?" said Jakes.

She nodded and offered him a coffee, more interested in Jakes than the distant gunshots.

"Sugar?" He nodded. Connie appraised Jakes' face. He was beginning to bruise and the split in his lip had dried. "You didn't fight back yesterday," she said, pushing a mug across the bench.

"I'm more of a lover than a fighter."

"What were you expecting? A conversation?"

"I got what I expected," said Jakes.

"Then why did you do it?"

"To move on. I'd like to put it behind me. Behind us."

"That was never going to happen. John hates you. He thinks you seduced me," said Connie.

Jakes sipped his coffee, put down the mug, revealing a smile.

"I did."

Connie blushed.

"You're full of shit. What's with you and Josie? You know, it isn't going to last. She's too young for you. You've got nothing in common."

"What's too young?" He asked. "Are you too young for me?"

"We're the same age. She's a kid," said Connie.

"You could be living with me right now, if you hadn't lost your nerve."

"And you settled for the next girl you came across."

Jakes drew a sharp breath.

"That hurts," he said.

"Because it's true."

"No, it's not."

The floorboards in the hallway creaked, and Josie appeared her long, legs bare, sticking out from under an oversized t-shirt. She came into the kitchen on tiptoes, making her legs seem even longer. Connie felt uncomfortable. Josie's youth and good looks threatened to derail her balanced temperament.

Jakes was looking at those long legs.

"What time is it?" whined Josie.

"Where are your pants." Jakes tone was disapproving.

"Don't stress. I'm just getting a drink," her voice was harassed. She turned to Connie. "Glasses?"

Connie pointed to a broken cupboard. Josie reached for a glass, and her shirt crept up the back of her thigh, exposing her underwear. Jakes looked away, taking a myopic interest in his coffee.

"Shouldn't you two be in bed?" said Josie.

"Sure, if she'd let me," Jakes said, flashing Connie with a cheeky grin.

Connie felt a sense of confusion. She was getting mixed information. The relationship between Jakes and Josie wasn't what she'd thought.

"I couldn't sleep," said Connie. "Usually John snores and wakes me up a few times a night. Turns out, Karla is the same. Like father like daughter, I guess." Connie smiled grim and raised a brow. "Does Jakes snore?"

"How would I know?" said Josie. She skulled her water and filled the glass a second time "I don't have a problem sleeping. Try and keep it down," she said, taking the glass with her as she tiptoed away.

Connie turned on Jakes.

"You're full of shit. You're not sleeping with her."

"I never said I was. You assumed," said Jakes.

"Is she even living with you?"

"Living and working. Sure."

"Why is she living with you?"

"She ran into trouble and needed help. I gave her a place to stay and she helps me with the business for a little cash and free rent. Turns out, she's a good worker."

"And you've never tried it on with her?"

"No." Jakes' voice pinched. "I've known Josie since

she was a little girl. I knew her parents."

The image of Jakes sharing his living space was at odds with his reputation as a bachelor. But it wasn't just a living arrangement. Josie meant something to him.

"I guess that makes you her godparent or parent?" said Connie, teasing him with a smile.

"I'm not her parent. Her Mum and Dad are in a nursing home with dementia. I'm just giving her an opportunity."

"You're talking to her like a parent," said Connie, thumbing to the place where Josie had been standing seconds ago without pants.

"Well, she's got some bad habits. I think her Mum and Dad gave her free reign. No discipline. And she's got a chip on her shoulder from when they left her, not that it was their fault. Then some other shit happened..." Jakes waved his hand in the air. "....and I stepped in to give her a hand. But she doesn't need me. Not really. She's tough. I'm just giving her a job and a place to sleep."

If Jakes wasn't trying to be a parent, he certainly had the awareness and compassion of a parent. It was endearing. Attractive.

"Both of her parents were put into a nursing home?"

"Yeah, must be over a year ago now," said Jakes.

"What sort of shit is she dealing with?" said Connie.

He told her about Josie's attitude. Connie had seen it last night when she'd almost knocked out Kipper in the bar. Connie offered Jakes some advice, and he took it like a starving man takes food.

"Have you talked to anyone about this?" said Connie.

"A little with Quicks but he doesn't say much," said Jakes.

"You're doing the right things. You'd make a good father," said Connie.

Jakes sat back and spread his hands as if he was open to the idea.

"I'm just doing my best."

This was an unexpected conversation. Connie would never have thought she'd be talking to Jakes, about guiding a young woman through life.

"Would you ever have kids of your own?"

Jakes' mouth split into a smile, and he winced, touching his lip.

"If I found the right woman. Although there's not a lot of time left."

"I don't think you're too old," said Connie, pushing back her hair.

The smile drifted from Jakes' face.

"About that night. At my place. Why didn't you stay?" he said, his eyes direct and intense.

"Because I was married."

Jake scoffed, amused.

"Your marriage was the reason you were there in the first place," he said.

There were a lot of reasons she was where she was when she got caught up with Jakes; a night out with a girlfriend, the excitement of a Saturday night off work, alcohol and, yes, her marriage.

They were at Top Pub and somehow ended up sitting with Jakes and Quicks sharing rounds of drinks, conversation and laughter. Her attention gravitated towards Jakes. He was flirting with her. She was flirting with him. She liked it. It was exciting. Her friend went home, the hotel was closing, Jakes invited her home, a big tin shed off the main street in town, and she went inside. There was a big sailboat on blocks, under repair. Jakes took her hand and helped her up onto the deck. She could feel boat swaying, gentle, drunk. Jakes was still holding her hand. Her heart was racing. This type of thing led to trouble. When he came in close and pressed his body against hers, she still hadn't made up her mind about how far she'd go. Then they kissed. His salty lips were in her mouth, the feeling was good enough to roll her eyes back into her head and cause her body to swell. With her hand in his Jakes drew her down into the hull of the boat through the small spaces, the boat seesawed. They got to the bedroom and the double bed before she stopped. She couldn't do it.

Two weeks later, a rumour surfaced that Connie had slept with Jakes.

"That was a mistake," she said.

"The only mistake you made was leaving," he said.

In hindsight, she could agree.

"How did everyone find out about it? Did you say something," said Connie.

"No. I figured there were plenty of people who saw us at Top Pub and someone just filled in the blanks," he said.

"I've spent the last eight months defending myself. It's been hell."

"You're not wrong," Jakes said.

"What do you mean? You're single. What do you care?"

"I've got a criminal record, because of you," Jakes said.

"What for?"

"Mrs Roberts, the lady who owns the corner store, heard we'd slept together. She thinks I ruined your perfect marriage. I went in there a few months ago to get some cheese. Josie wanted nachos. The old hag wouldn't serve me. So I stole a block of cheese, apparently."

"Did you steal it?"

"No. The cheese was four bucks. I gave her ten. She wouldn't take my money, so I left it on the counter and walk out. Apparently, that's theft. She pressed charges. Now, when I run out of milk, I have to go all the way across town to the Cut Price Supermarket. I blame you for that. And, I didn't even get laid that night. You're the worst affair I've ever had."

"No, I'm the worst affair you've never had," she corrected him with a smile. Jakes laughed.

John's mobile phone sat on the counter between them.

"I think John might be cheating on me," she said and unlocked the Nokia phone handing it to Jakes. "Do you recognise this number?"

The sickly yellow light from the screen coloured Jakes' face.

"Who is it?"

"I don't know. That's why I'm asking," she said.

"It's local. Have you tried calling it?"

"Not yet."

Jakes looked around the kitchen, spotted the phone on the wall and got up from his chair taking the Nokia with him. She objected. It was too early, and she wasn't ready to find out who the woman was at the other end of the phone. Jakes picked up the receiver and put it to his ear, paused, then hung up.

"It's dead," he said.

Connie was relieved.

Outside there was another gunshot, a single, soft pop. Jakes heard it too. It sounded closer than the series of shots they'd heard earlier. They hurried to the front porch of the house and looked through the morning drizzle.

"It came from the creek," Jakes said.

Others had heard it too. They shuffled down the hall like zombies, wrapped in blankets, wanting to know what was happening. There was nothing to tell.

Far off in the distance, a tight group of dirty clouds

drifted towards the hotel, bringing with them another thick sheet of rain. That rain would continue to feed the swollen creek trapping everyone in Rossville for at least another day. Connie suggested Jakes check on the creek crossing to see if he could get out before the heavy rains hit again. If he couldn't get out and they were stuck here another night, he'd have to find another place to sleep. Jakes couldn't come back to the house. She'd promised Karla.

CHAPTER 16

As soon at Jakes left, Karla burst out of Connie's bedroom two hands strapped across her mouth and ran across the hall into the bathroom. The house filled with the sound of retching. Connie pushed through the small group on the front porch and made her way to the bathroom, closing the door and holding back Karla's hair. The convulsions and gagging continued and Karla began to cry, her eyes tired and fearful. Karla was pregnant. They both knew it. Connie ran her palm up and down Karla's back. She was too young to be a mother. The doctors could fix that. Connie would be there to hold her hand, to keep Karla on track and hand out the tissues. It was a simple procedure, a little discomfort, a day or two of rest, and it would be done.

"It's going to be OK," said Connie handing Karla a hot face washer as she sat on the toilet, seat down.

There was a tap on the bathroom door.

"Connie. We've got a visitor," Sherbet Ray, whispered through the door.

Connie felt fear tug at her stomach and pulled open the door.

"Is it John?"

"No." Sherbet Ray nodded down the hall. Through the open door, she could see a white Landcruiser stopped at the back of the hotel. Leaning against the front fender, Wes waved, a cigarette between his fingers.

"He wants to know what to do with the pig."

"What pig?"

Wes was covered in mud, his hands stained with blood. He circled around the Landcruiser, dropping the tailgate to reveal the body of a large pig, in a pool of its own blood, shot through the eye.

"That's a big pig. Is it female?" said Connie. Wes lifted a back leg showing off a row of teats on the belly of the animal.

"Why does it matter if it's female?" asked Josie.

"The testosterone in males makes the meat taste funny," said Connie.

"Where'd you find it?" asked Sherbet Ray.

"By the creek." Wes leant over the dead pig and began untying a set of straps on a thick wire leading to crane arm that he would have used to lift the pig onto the tray back of the Landcruiser.

"Is the creek still flooded?" asked Emma, no doubt desperate to get home to her baby daughter.

"With rain like this, it'll be flooded for days," said Wes throwing the straps and buckles to one side. He took the hind leg of the beast and with the help of Sherbet Ray, pulled the pig from the Landcruiser. The pig hit the ground with a whomp, the impact forcing air from the lungs with a deep honking grunt. One of the waitresses squealed.

Wes produced a knife from his pocket and stuck the pig in the throat. Blood ran thick like blackberry jam into the gravel car park.

"I'm sending everyone back to the hotel," he said, throwing Sherbet Ray a length of rope. "You'll have to find another place for them to sleep. They can't stay at my place again tonight," said Wes.

"Why? Where is this coming from?" she said, thinking Wes must have been joking.

There were a dozen people staying at Wes' house, and she didn't have space for everyone.

"Evelyn Ashby's sleeping on my floor. She needs a proper bed," said Wes, helping Sherbet Ray truss up the hind legs of the pig.

"How is sending everyone back here going to help Evelyn get a bed. There'll be fewer beds if you do that," said Connie, confused.

He looked at her, serious. Unflinching.

"Tell Scratch to give her a place to sleep. He has plenty of space at his place."

Wes and Sherbet Ray pulled on the rope, dragging the dead pig across the gravel to a tree at the edge of the car park.

"Fine, I'll talk to him, but you have to take someone. You can't send them all back here," she said.

Wes threw the rope over a thick branch, and the two men pulled on the rope, hoisting the pig off the ground. The pig swung at the end of the rope, blood draining from a wound in the head, painting a ruby red pattern on the ground. Wes took out the knife, plunged the blade into the pig's groin and pulled down on the handle opening a long gash in the belly. Intestines tumbled out and slopped on the ground.

"I'm not taking anyone until Scratch takes Evelyn."

Wes wiped the blade on his pants and headed for the Landcruiser.

"Talk to Scratch," he said, pulling the door closed, starting the engine and driving back in the direction of his farm.

CHAPTER 17

In the storeroom between the kitchen and the bar, Connie took a moment to gather her thoughts. She didn't mind going to see Scratch at his house. Scratch wasn't big on handing out invitations, and Connie was curious to see beyond the galvanised fence blocking his driveway. But, Wes was forcing her to do just that. The old man wanted her to convince Scratch to take people into his home. But, Connie didn't need the extra push from Wes. She wanted Scratch to know how disappointed she was after he left without helping anyone last night. At the same time she hated the way Wes had threatened to throw everyone out. He was putting the responsibility of all these people on her, and it wasn't fair. He didn't need to do that and she didn't need the extra pressure.

Sherbet Ray had done a stocktake of the food in the

coolroom, the dry store and pantry. No one knew how long they'd be stuck at the hotel, so it was hard to say how long the food would last. Sherbet Ray could ration it out for two or three days or cut down the portion size and make what they had last a week. The dead pig would give them another day or two.

Karla was back in her own bedroom, the window locked and the blinds closed, sleeping off the exhaustion of her morning sickness. As soon as the flood cleared, Connie would take Karla to the doctors and get her tested to be sure then they'd work out a time to go to the family planning clinic.

Connie had been standing in the storeroom at the back of the bar beside a stack of beer cartons. The thigh-high stack was twisted and resting against the wall. She bent to straighten the stack and noticed a dirty boot mark on the top carton. And more boot marks were trailing in from the kitchen. Whoever had walked mud into the hotel had used the cartons as a step. Above the cartons of beer was a set of shelves. The top shelf used for the storage of spirits was empty. It had been restocked two days ago, and she hadn't served that much alcohol last night. The bottles had been taken. Stolen. She'd been robbed.

A cold feeling crept over her skin. The hotel had been locked. The only people who had access to the storeroom were the men sleeping on the floor of her hotel.

Connie marched into the restaurant, the floor dotted with sleeping men and began yelling and kicking at the bedding, and bodies searching between their makeshift beds for empty bottles, bottle caps, demanding to know who stole the alcohol. There was no evidence of the theft among them. The men mumbled and complained about the noise she was making. A pair of eyes watched her from under the sheets.

"Which one of you did it?" she demanded.

Kipper was watching her, his hollow eyes following her around the room. Connie marched over to where Kipper lay and ripped the sheet from him, his body pale, bone-thin and wearing only his underwear. Connie bundled up the bedsheet and threw it back at Kipper.

"Get out," she said. "You can all get out."

Connie felt a hand grip her ankle and tug gently at her leg. It was Fred Abe lying on the floor, foggy with sleep.

"How about you crawl in under here and keep me warm, luv."

She jerked her leg from his grip.

"I've got alcohol missing from the bar - bottles, gone, and the doors were locked last night. You were the only ones in here. Someone must have seen something."

There were whining complaints from the men - denials.

"It wasn't me."

"I didn't do anything."

"Someone must have seen something," she said, frustrated.

All of the men seemed foggy with sleep, they shook their heads. Connie felt her patience breaking, and she snapped.

"Get out. All of you," she snarled.

The men rose from their beds, stretching out their sore muscles, too slow for her liking. Kipper repositioned his underwear and took his pants from the back of one of the chairs. They looked damp. His shirt was hung out over the back of a chair, the timber floor beneath it, stained with a dark watermark.

"Why are your clothes wet?" she said to Kipper.

"What does it matter?" Kipper answered, deadpan pulling on his shirt, his face stone cold.

"Did you go outside last night?" said Connie.

"I went out for a piss," he said.

"Why didn't you use the toilets?" she said.

Kipper avoided her eyes.

"It's true," said Gunner Jones, combing his hair with his fingers. "He went out for a piss."

"I didn't steal anything," said Kipper, his voice devoid of emotion.

"None of us stole anything," said Fred Abe.

"One of you must have seen or heard something," she said. They must be all in on the theft.

Fred Abe yawned, loudly.

"I saw Kipper at the bar last night. He bought a round of beers."

Laughter rippled through the small group of men.

"I was at the bar last night," said Greenie. "You charged me a fortune."

Another round of laughter filled the hotel.

"I went to the bar-" Gunner Jones began.

"You think this is a joke? Well, you're stuck here for at least another day. You can all find somewhere else to sleep tonight. You're not staying here." Connie unlocked the front door and swung it open.

"Oh, look." Slippery Pete pointed through the open door. "It's our local playboy."

Just outside the door, Jakes arrived on the veranda, wet and breathless, bleeding from a dozen scratches on his arms and neck. He looked into the hotel at the men gathered there with eyes on fire.

"Jakes, what's wrong? Why are you wet?"

"I found someone," he said, breathless, his voice a low growl. "In the creek. They're dead."

CHAPTER 18

Jakes lead a small group in the rain along Shiptons Flat road to the creek where posts of timber, splintered, stuck out of the rushing brown water. At the edge of the creek in a cluster of debris and dirty white foam, the pale body of a young man lay on his back, feet bobbing in the water, his eyes fixed outward in a milky stare. Connie had never seen a dead body before. It was chilling. He was one of the boys who'd brought the bones back from Black Mountain. Jakes had found the body snagged on one of the splintered posts in the creek and swam in to drag it out.

A small crowd gathered around the boy. Someone suggested they call the police, but the phones were out.

Connie got closer to the body. The ground was wet, sandy and soft. This could have been John if Wes hadn't saved him. On the boys' neck, there was a small, round mark, and she squatted next to the body to get a closer look. His skin had been punctured, leaving a small, neat hole.

"Is that a bullet hole?"

Jakes and Sherbet Ray squatted over the body.

"There's another one," Jakes said.

A hole, the same size had been made in the side of the boy's chest. The rest of the body was covered in scratches.

"They look like bullet wounds to me," said Sherbet Ray.

"Why is he so cut up?" Connie asked.

Jakes lifted his shirt, his dark skin covered in small cuts.

"It's in the water. The flood is picking up stones and sticks. They're like projectiles."

"You need to disinfect those cuts," she told Jakes.

The group of people around them grew as word got around about the dead boy.

"We should get him up to the hotel," Quicks said.

"Why are you taking him to the hotel?" Connie said.

"We have to keep the body cold until the police arrive," said Sherbet Ray.

Connie could only think of one cold place big enough for the body.

"You're not putting him in my coolroom," Connie whispered. "I run a restaurant, not a morgue."

"We can't leave him outside. Think of the bugs, the flies. The smell." Sherbet Ray screwed up his nose. "Have you smelt a dead body? It's not good."

"If he goes in the coolroom, no one is going to eat out of that kitchen ever again, and you'll be out of a job."

"What other choice do we have?" Sherbet Ray said. He tried to reassure her that it would be fine. They would wrap the body. Lay down tarpaulins.

Connie didn't see that she had a choice.

The three men took the weight of the boy between them and carried him at the head of a solemn procession to the hotel. Connie went ahead and got a fresh bed sheet for them to lay him out on at the back door. People hung around, and Jakes told everyone that they would take care of the boy and asked everyone to give them some privacy. The people dispersed, leaving Connie, the Cook, Jakes and Quicks with the boy.

It was such a waste of life. The boy would have family somewhere that would cry for him, and he had friends at the hotel that they needed to talk to and give them the bad news. They agreed to tell his friends, and Tina volunteered with the support of Bev Shay and Ada Bannam, and the three women made their way down to the campground to look for the other three boys.

The light from the rising sun shone on the body of the boy, and Connie crouched beside him to inspect the two small, circular puncture wounds. If they were bullets, he'd been hit twice—one in the neck and one in the body.

Bang. Bang.

She looked up at Jakes.

"How many gunshots did you remember hearing this morning?"

"Around a dozen. Then that one shot on its own."

That's what she'd heard.

Wes was out this morning and shot the pig, bringing it back to the hotel for the Sherbet Ray to gut and butcher, the animal now hanging from its hind legs in the coolroom.

Connie looked to the Cook.

"Did you find any bullet holes in the pig?"

"One. Wes shot it in the eye. That was it," said the Cook.

"One shot?"

"Through the eye into the brain."

"That's a tough shot to make," said Quicks.

"And if you missed, the pig would run. Then you'd have no chance of taking it down. Those things are like little armoured tanks."

Connie was thinking about the series of gunshots she'd heard that morning.

"So Wes fired once at the pig. Before that there were another twelve shots," she said.

"They must've been the shots that killed this kid," said the Cook.

"And he's got two bullet holes that we can see. That leaves ten other bullets that are missing."

The crunch of gravel heralded the return of the waitresses. It had been a quick trip. Tina was shaking her head.

"They're not there. Fred Abe and his mates are already in their tents."

"Why?"

"They said they need a place to sleep tonight," said Tina.

That was true. Connie had banned them from staying in the hotel.

"Someone said they saw the four boys leaving the campground," said Tina.

"Did they say what time?"

"About two or three in the morning."

Connie had heard the twelve gunshots around seven A.M.

"They left the campground before those gunshots were fired," said Jakes.

Connie felt sick.

"Someone needs to go back to the creek and search for the others."

CHAPTER 19

Sherbet Ray and Quicks lead a search party down to the creek to look for the other boys. Jakes wanted to be part of the search, but Connie refused to let him go. He was bleeding and needed first aid to the cuts on his body. She arranged a couple of stools in the kitchen, took out the first aid kit and sat him down.

"Take off your shirt," she said with a half-smile.

"I thought you'd never ask." Jakes pulled his shirt over his head. His whole body was the same golden colour as his arms, his stomach was flat, and the tattoos on his biceps spread across his shoulders, back and chest. The cuts and scratches covered his body, some deep and long, most of them weeping.

"Risking your life to save a dead man wasn't the smartest thing you've done," said Connie.

"Maybe, I'm not as smart as you think," said Jakes.

Connie took a tube of antiseptic cream and smeared it over his cuts, her fingers brushing his warm, hard skin. Her fingers drew lines between the small cuts and scratches. Jakes went silent, enjoying himself. She was sure that if she obeyed an urge to thread her arms around his body and press her chest to his back, he wouldn't stop her.

"Do you regret coming up here, now?" she said.

"No," he said, blunt, cold.

The abrupt nature of his answer sparked her curiosity.

"You haven't told me. Why did you come here?" she said, making her question just as hard and cold.

Jakes pulled away from her, put his shirt back on and turned to face her, serious.

"After last night you should know," he said.

"Know what about last night?" she said.

Jakes thumbed his nose and cleared his throat.

"The first thing you have to understand is you can't say anything about this," said Jakes, staring her down. "The night you came back to my place and we-"

"Yes?" she said, cutting him short. She didn't need him to remind her of what they'd done.

"Someone else was there, taking photos. They took a photo of us on the boat together."

"They saw us…" she didn't want to say they'd kissed and used her hands to finish her sentence.

"Yes," said Jakes.

She knew someone had seen them together. It's how the rumour got out.

"Who?"

"Kipper," said Jakes.

Connie had thrown Kipper out of the hotel along with his friends. His clothes were wet, he'd been outside in the rain last night.

"Kipper was the one tapping at Karla's window last night," she said.

"Probably," said Jakes.

"Was he after Karla?"

"Hear me out. After you left, I caught Kipper in the workshop with a camera. Now, I've heard rumours of a peeping Tom around town. This rumour has been doing the rounds for years, and it comes and goes, but no one has seen this person. So, here I was with Kipper, and he's doing exactly what a peeping Tom does, creeping around at night, but with a camera and now he's breaking and entering. I ask him about the camera and the photos, and I can't see them. He has to develop the film, but I get it out of him. He's got his own darkroom set up at his house. So I invited myself back for a look. While he's developing the film, I have a look around. I figure if he's been out there at night with a camera, there have to be more photos, and I was right. There were albums full of them, mostly of women in different places, dressed, half-dressed, naked, close up, some really close and scared and when I say scared I mean naked, screaming terror and I recognise Josie Easten in one of the photos. As I'm flipping through I see more of Josie. He's been stalking her around town, at home on her parent's farm. He even has these weird shots that were taken inside her house. At this point, I call the police, and they start an investigation, and while this investigation goes on, I press charges against Kipper for breaking and entering to put him away while this investigation gets underway. But the investigation hit a snag. His lawyer argues that Kipper didn't take the photos. It's bullshit, but that's what they're saying, and so it's up to the police to get evidence to prove he pressed the button on the camera. No one has seen him taking the photos, so they don't have an eyewitness, and it's just our word against theirs. So they go through the photos looking for evidence, but none of the photos shows us who's behind the camera. Kipper does his time for trespassing, and his lawyer got him out of gaol yesterday."

"And, that's why you came up here, to keep an eye on Kipper," said Connie.

"Yes, and to keep an eye on you," said Jakes.

"Me?"

"Kipper had photos of you too," said Jakes.

"What sort of photos?"

"Mostly around the hotel at night or crossing the car park at the back of the hotel to your house," said Jakes.

There'd been times when she'd heard noises, and she felt like she was being watched. She felt violated and crossed her arms.

"How did you know he'd come here? I wasn't the only person he was taking photos of," she said.

Jakes cast a severe look over her.

"There were a lot of photos of you." It was the way he said it that made her shiver. "I think he used you here at the hotel as a base level for stalking. He's been doing it for years. It's dark, no street lights, you don't have any neighbours, and you and John work different shifts which means you're not always in the same building at the same time. It was sort of the same with Josie. Her Mum and Dad moved into a nursing home, leaving her on the farm, on her own. The farm is isolated, no neighbours, no street lights. She was a perfect target to take things further."

"Further?"

"That's what the police are looking into. A few weeks before I found the photos at Kipper's house, the police told me Josie had been in to see them. She'd reported someone breaking into her house to attack her. She locked herself in her bathroom while someone was in her house trying to take photos of her under the bathroom door. Josie was the first woman Kipper tried to attack and if that's true our peeping Tom is turning into to a rapist."

Kipper was out last night wandering around in the rain and dark and found his way to Karla's bedroom window.

"Did he take photos of Karla?"

She saw Jakes' eye twitch.

"This isn't about any one woman. Kipper needs to go back to gaol for as long as possible, and the case Josie has against him is our best chance of doing that."

"Did he take photos of Karla?" Connie asked again.

"This court case is delicate. The evidence I found at Kipper's house is barely admissible because they say I broke in to get it. You can't talk to Kipper about any of this."

"He could have broken into Karla's bedroom last night. What if he tries the same thing with her? No." Connie thrust herself towards the back door of the hotel and pushed her way outside with Jakes telling her to stop. But the anger burning her veins wouldn't let her stop and she marched across the gravel car park and down a grassy slope towards the open campground dotted with tents. Children were playing chase among the maze, turning the grass to mud. Canvas covers were heavy and damp, drops hung from guide ropes and the contents of each tent had been turned out and laid on tarpaulins to dry. At the edge of the cluster of poles, canvass and ropes were three small tents once belonging to the missing boys, now being raided by Fred Abe and his friends. Shakey Pete saw her coming and tapped Fred Abe on the back, pointing her out.

"Where's Kipper?" she demanded.

Greenie and Gunner Jones appeared from under the canvas flaps blinking.

"Where is he?" said Connie.

The canvas on the third tent pulled back, and Kipper emerged, his face pale and drawn, his eyes dead.

"What do you want?" he said flat.

"Get off my property," she said, drawing out an arm and pointing towards Shipton's Flat Road.

"He didn't take your alcohol," Fred Abe put his body between Connie and Kipper, his hands open.

"This is none of your business Freddie." She stepped to the side and locked eyes with Kipper. "You. Leave. Now."

Kipper's eyes drifted up to the hotel where Jakes stood, watching, arms crossed.

"There's nowhere else for him to go," said Fred Abe.

Kipper came forward and smacked a hand on the thick arm of Fred Abe.

"It's O.K. big fella. If she wants me to go, I'll go." Kipper bent his thin, wiry frame to take his damp shirt off one of the guide ropes and started walking. The other men stood their mouths open.

"You boys should choose your friends more carefully," Connie said, turning her back on them and heading up the hill to the hotel where Jakes was waiting.

"Feel better?" Jakes tone was terse.

"Don't worry. I didn't say anything about Josie. Or the photos," she said, bitter.

Kipper reached the dirt road and turned towards Mungumby Creek.

"He can't go anywhere. And he's going to be harder to watch now," said Jakes.

Sending Kipper away was the right thing to do.

"I have to protect Karla, and the waitresses and every other woman stuck in Rossville."

"Doesn't Wes live along the creek?" said Jakes, poking holes in her decision to send Kipper away. There were woman and children staying on Wes' farm.

Connie felt sheepish.

"I'll talk to Wes," she said.

"Don't say…"

"Don't worry," she cut him off. "Wes knows how to keep a secret."

CHAPTER 20

Splashing through potholes full of dirty water, the Pajero came to the end of a muddy, pitted driveway where an old, plain-looking weatherboard home faced east, the rising sun, the trees shading the winding path of the Mungumby Creek and beyond, the bumpy ridge of Black Mountain. The driveway curved around the house to where a rusty Landcruiser sat parked under the canopy of a large, dripping, white ghost gum. Connie scanned the open ground for Kipper, but there was no one around. The slam of her car door triggered barking from the back of the house. The rain had stopped, the ground was wet, and the birds were singing. She knocked on the front door.

"Who is it?" Wes' voice crackled from deep inside the house.

"It's me," said Connie, turning the knob and pushing

open the door.

The sparsely furnished house had a musty smell. In in the living room, a stack of bedsheets and pillows were piled up on one end of a large four-seat, tartan sofa and she could feel the residual warmth and stale smell of the dozen or so bodies, that had occupied the room last night. They were all back at the hotel now, eating breakfast. Wes had already cleared them out of the house.

"In the kitchen."

Connie followed in the direction of Wes' voice.

The old man sat in the kitchen with a cup of tea and a framed black and white photo laid out on the table. Behind him, leaning against the wall was the long barrel of a rifle. Connie pointed at the gun.

"Expecting company?"

"Always. Have a seat." He waved at the chair opposite.

A young cattle dog bared its teeth through the fly screen door and growled.

"Enough," Wes said, swatting the wall with a bang. The young pup settled.

The painted plywood kitchen and chrome, Formica kitchen table with matching chairs were straight out of the fifties, the paint chipped bench, worn and dented, the chrome peeling away. The only adornment on the wall was an avocado green bakelite phone.

"Where's your other dog?" she asked. The last time she'd visited the house, there'd been two dogs growling at the back door.

"Died," said Wes, dropping his head, the muscles in his face pulling back in a grimace.

"I'm sorry. I didn't know. When did that happen?"

Wes waved a hand dismissing her question and leaving silence. He didn't want to talk about it.

"Is John here?" she said.

Wes cleared his throat.

"Gone for a walk," he said.

"How is he?"

"I wouldn't know. He's not talking to me. I held him at gunpoint yesterday, remember?"

"He does realise you saved his life?"

"I'm sure he'll thank me one day," said Wes, crossing his arms.

Connie glanced around the empty kitchen, her eyes settling on a plastic kettle.

"Well, he chose to stay here so as much as he might hate you, he hates me more." She laughed, inward, her eyes welling up with shallow tears of self-pity. She swallowed them, shifting her sights to the green, bakelite phone.

"Does your phone work?"

"The line's dead. Not that that makes a difference to me. The damn thing hasn't rung in years."

There was a dead body in the coolroom. It was like holding a hot potato, and she'd feel better if she could report it to the police.

"We found a boy in the creek this morning. It looks like he was shot."

Wes' eyes shifted, his expression froze.

"Who was it?" he said.

"One of those boys who found the skulls. His friends are also missing. We've got a group searching along the creek for the others." Connie couldn't stop herself from looking at the rifle leaning against the wall behind Wes.

"You said he was shot. Why are you searching the creek?" said Wes.

"That's where we found his body."

Wes nodded, sliding the black and white framed photo to one side and sat forward.

"I heard gunshots. They came from over there." Wes

pointed, through the window over the sink towards the creek, towards Black Mountain. "I went down there to see what was going on. Drove up and down the creek a few times. The only thing I found was that wild pig," said Wes.

Connie thought about the timing of the gunshots. There were a dozen shots followed by the single gunshot that probably killed the wild boar. Wes' story matched the sounds she'd heard that morning.

"What do you think happened?"

Wes sat back and looked out the window.

"Maybe they got hold of a gun, and they were playing around when one of them got shot. It happens," said Wes.

"Except, the boy we found had been shot twice. I don't think it was an accident."

Wes continued staring out the window in stern silence.

"If they find the bullet that killed the boy they'll be able to trace it back to the gun it came from," said Connie, watching Wes.

"If they do their job right," he said, his face rock hard.

Connie dropped her eyes to the Formica tabletop and the framed black and white photo. In it, a woman was cradling a baby.

"Is that your wife?" she said, pointing at the photo, her voice soft.

Wes turned his eyes down, picking up the frame, looking into the glass.

"Yep."

"What was her name?" she said, thinking of the two skulls. She still hadn't told him that the rucksack had been stolen.

"Jane." Wes handed the photo to Connie.

Jane had freckles and dark hair. She was plain and pretty, and her eyes overflowed with love and rapture pouring over the newborn in her arms. Her love radiated out of the photo infecting Connie with warmth. She pointed at the baby, smiling.

"And this is your daughter?"

"Kate," his voice broke a little. Connie looked at the photo a moment longer before handing it back.

"They're both beautiful," she said.

Two beautiful creatures murdered, their bodies dumped in Black Mountain.

"I don't have the remains anymore," she said. "I'm sorry. They were stolen from the bar last night."

Wes frowned, his throat emitting a low, gravel growl.

"You should have given them to me."

She didn't agree with him but didn't argue the point.

"I think Stephan took them, although I can't imagine how he knew they were there." Wes' eyes twitched, and she was sure he was lying. Not lying. Withholding. She continued. "Stephan was in the kitchen or with Karla the whole time. He didn't know about the skulls. Someone had to tell him the skulls were in the rucksack under the bar. You were the only person who saw Stephan before he stole them."

"You think I took them?"

Connie sat forward.

"Before you took Stephan into town, you tried forcing me to give you their remains. When you came back from dropping off Stephan, you never asked me about them. Not once. You knew where they were. You had them."

At the threshold to the kitchen entry, behind the flywire door, the young dog growled, ears up, her head facing out towards the paddocks at the back of the house. The dog leapt up, claws scrabbling on the deck and took off into the backyard, barking. Wes got to his feet, put on his spectacles and grabbed the rifle, pushing through the fly screen door out onto the back veranda. He took up a wide stance and raised the rifle to his shoulder following the line of the cattle dog running out into the field to the figure of a large lumbering man, walking towards the house. Connie knew that walk.

"It's John. Put down the gun."

Wes lowered the rifle and continued to survey the view of yellow grass and wire fences all the way out to the bush rising up at the back of the property, grunting, satisfied.

"You two will want to talk. You can have the house," said Wes, turning inside.

Connie didn't want to talk. She didn't want to be alone with John.

"Where are you going?" she asked through the fly screen door.

Wes opened the cabinet under the sink and took out a brown hessian sack full of lumps.

"I won't be far," said Wes. Connie stepped aside as Wes came out onto the veranda.

"What's in the sack?" she asked.

Wes paused on the steps and opened the top of the sack. Inside were a jumble of bones and two skulls, the same two skulls that had gone missing.

"You were right about the kitchen hand. I paid him to take the bag," said Wes.

"I knew it. Where did the rest of the bones come from? I don't remember seeing any bones."

"That boy I drove into town last night. The one that found them had kept a few souvenirs. I had to convince him to hand them over."

Connie got the feeling that the boy never really had a choice.

"Are you going to give them to the police?"

"When I'm done," said Wes, closing the sack. There was something that didn't fit in the sack. It stuck out the top—a long dirty stick.

"What's that?" she said, pointing at the stick.

Wes held up the sack. The stick was hollow at the end, plugged with dirt and covered in rust.

"The boys found it with the skulls. As far as I can tell, that's the gun used to shoot them," said Wes.

Connie got a chill. Wes had the murder weapon. Between the skulls, the bones and the rusty gunbarrel there had to be enough evidence to find out who killed his family.

"You really need to take those to the police," she said.

"Eventually," Wes said, stepping off the porch.

"What are you going to do with them?"

Wes paused, lowered his head, scowling over the rim of his spectacles, his face colouring red.

"I'm going to catch the fucker that killed my wife and daughter." His words had a heat that frightened her, and at the same time, she felt sorry for him. He was angry and wasn't thinking straight. It had been forty years since his wife and daughter went missing. Finding their killer would be impossible without the police.

She could hear her husband's footsteps and saw him nearing the house.

Wes broke off the conversation, taking off down the path towards a big tin workshop at the back of the house. When he crossed paths with John, the two men paused for a conversation. John shot Connie a wary look. He was telling Wes that he'd seen Kipper at the back of the farm, in the bush heading into the hills and Connie remembered that she hadn't told the old man about Kipper. She couldn't tell him now. If John knew Kipper was at his daughter's window last night, Kipper would be dead within the day.

Connie looked out across the paddock towards the

bush rising up into a series of mountains each one bigger than the first stretching off into the distance. And despite the vast landscape, Kipper wasn't going far. Halfway up the first climb was a steep stone face, an escarpment, difficult to climb in the dry and impossible in the wet. The escarpment ran the length of Helensvale, and Rossville cut at both ends by the heads of two rivers. Even if Kipper scaled the cliff, he'd have a two-day hike back to the nearest main road. But Kipper didn't need to escape. He wasn't in danger. All he needed was a place to wait out the flood. Then it hit her. At the base of the escarpment was the Lion's Den tin mine, the namesake of the Lion's Den Hotel, a small, round hole cut into the hard rock and a good place to take shelter.

Wes whistled up his dog, and the two of them headed for the tin shed. John lumbered toward the back veranda, climbing the steps, slow and heavy brushing past Connie without a word.

"Are we not talking?" she said.

"I don't want to talk," he said, pushing through the flywire door that closed with a snap.

Despite herself, Connie followed him inside.

John's hair was a mess, his shirt damp with sweat and his eyes were bloodshot. He started coughing. A cough heavy with phlegm took over his entire body, forcing him to hold onto the kitchen sink. Connie didn't offer to help. She lacked the compassion to do so, and eventually, John recovered, exhausted. He searched the kitchen cabinets for a glass, taking a long drink of water.

"Why are you still here? I told you, I don't want to talk," he said, his voice rough. The coughing started again, and John moved into a chair at the kitchen table, tired.

"You should see a doctor about that when the flood…"

"Get out!" John yelled, shooting to his feet, standing over her. "I don't want to talk!" His voice filled the room, crushing. His breath hot and stale, his brow thick with anger. "Just go!" he yelled his chest heaving and rasping. His voice reverberated through her body, and her legs and arms were shaking. His hands were clenching and expanding, his shoulders hunched over her, muscles tense. He was close to violence. Through the fly screen door, she could see down to the tin shed where Wes stood in the open door, looking towards the house, the rifle in his hands.

Connie stepped back.

"OK. I'm leaving."

CHAPTER 21

The Pajero bounced down the potted driveway, and onto Shiptons Flat Road with Connie behind the wheel shaking, John's raised voice still rebounding through her body like a swarm of bees stirring anger. She didn't deserve to be treated or spoken to the way John had spoken to her. She'd done everything right. She'd worked hard and raised Karla, she'd exhausted herself for John's dream, sacrificing her own dreams and it wasn't enough for John. Fury built up inside, expanding and growing. John had let himself go, drunk too much and brought unhappiness into her life. He'd lied to her, and he hadn't made her an owner of the business. He'd kept her cut off from the business and from him, and she'd had enough of being treated like an unwanted stranger.

Anger flashed hot and exploded. A torrent of cursing bounced off the windshield, and she slapped the wheel and threw herself back in her seat. Tears came. Her marriage was over. She was leaving.

The rusty, grey tin of the Lion's Den Hotel appeared through watery tears, like a mirage. She wasn't ready to go back. She didn't want to be seen. She was a snotty mess of self-pity and smouldering hate and needed a moment to sort herself out. The Pajero accelerated past the rambling building where she'd wasted ten years of her life, sparking another flash of anger.

The muddy road continued, and the bush became dense, cool and dark, every hue of green closing in and crowding the road. The line of green bush was broken by the entrance to a driveway. Connie slowed down, pulled in and came to a stop. The Pajero was blocked by the galvanised grill of a fence clad in hand-painted signs telling trespassers would be shot and to keep out. She got out of the Pajero, engine running and rattled the gate. The chain hitched around a timber post slipped off and the gate swung open into a long driveway, overgrown, the canopy closing in overhead creating a dark tunnel into the bush.

Connie had never been to Scratch's house. He'd never invited her. He never invited anyone. The dark driveway opened into a light-filled field of tall grass and weeds, dotted with islands of old car bodies, young saplings, bits of machinery and rotting piles of refuse. On the far side of the field, where the driveway terminated, stood a worn-out weatherboard house with a distinct lean. The house was surrounded by a ring of old sinks, broken washing machines, rusty refrigerators, mouldy car doors, panes of glass some cracked and stacks of timber sprouting large lips of fungus. Connie parked beside Scratch's faded yellow Volvo station wagon and got out. The air smelt damp and stale. A hard-packed and slippery dirt path led through the maze of junk and weeds onto a creaky porch covered in stacks of newspapers growing mould, nested buckets and cardboard boxes filled with dusty glass jars. Beside the door was a large plastic pot with a dead plant.

Connie put her hand through the torn flywire screen knocking loud. Inside, came a thump and clatter.

"Who's there?" It was Scratch. She recognised his voice.

"It's Connie. And don't you dare shoot me," she said, threatening him through the door. There was a long silence. Connie couldn't hear anything inside the house. "Scratch!" She lifted her hand to knock again.

"What do you want?" The voice came at her, loud behind the door, and Connie jumped clutching at her heart.

"Scratch! Open the damn door." She belted the flaking plywood door with the heel of her hand.

"What do you want?" he repeated.

"I want to talk. Open up."

There was a snick from a lock, and the door swung open. Scratch was wearing a pair of loose shorts and a tattered white singlet pulled tight over his belly. He looked at her, then looked past her down the dirt path to the cars, his grey eyebrows twitching.

"Anyone else with you?"

"Are you going to let me in?" she said, hands on hips.

Scratch turned his attention behind him into the house. It was dark. She could see stacks of reading material, newspapers and magazines stacked on the floor lining the walls and a strong smell of vinegar wafted out of the house.

"No," was all he said. She expected as much.

Connie pulled open the flywire door stepping into his

space.

"No, please," he said, stepping back.

Teetering stacks of books, newspapers and magazines skirted the floors and cut a narrow path into a cluttered living space circled with filing cabinets and more newspapers and magazines piled up. A path through the stacks led to a coffee table littered with books, pens and balls of crushed paper, dirty bowls and mugs with dark rings. Besides the coffee table, there was a large sofa and a tall lamp. Underfoot she could feel a film of grit coating the floor. The sharp smell of vinegar stuck to her tongue and stung her nose.

Even if she could get Scratch to open his house to guests, there was nowhere for them to sleep.

"Why didn't you take anyone home with you last night? You knew people needed a bed, and you left without helping them."

Scratch waved his hand into the darkness.

"I don't do a lot of cleaning. I cleaned some of it last night, but there's too much to do, and there's not enough space for anyone."

He was right. The house was cluttered with junk; however, the hall was long, and with her eyes adjusted to the dark, she could see doors leading off into rooms. At the end of the hall, a room opened out in what seemed to be a large space. It was a big house, and she didn't believe that Scratch couldn't take at least a few people.

Scratch waddled through the maze of magazines into the centre of the living room, picking up balls of paper and stuffing them into a small bin already overflowing with trash.

"I can get help to clean and make space if that's the problem," she said, stepping into the dim living room. As soon as she crossed the threshold, Connie felt another presence in the room - that of an animal. She turned into the dark corner of the room and found a pair of eyes staring back. The beady eyes belonged to a giant Seagull, with white feathers and a yellow beak. It stood frozen and anchored to a wooden plinth with a nameplate, staring.

"What's with the bird?" she asked.

Scratch stood up to admire the stuffed creature, chest out.

"It's a nice mount, one of my best. Larus pacificus." Scratch looked around the room. More glassy eyes peered out of the darkness, animals nestled among the newspapers and perched atop metal cabinets, rats with barred teeth, lizards stalking, sparrows in mid-fight and a snake coiled, poised to strike.

There was a tightness in her temples, and she knew the credulity she felt was showing on her face.

"It's a hobby," said Scratch, moving around the room to each of the creatures. "Most of the species I have are indigenous to the area. I catch them myself. Some are introduced like the wild dog." He aimed his finger over Connie's shoulder. She turned and found herself looking into the snarling mouth of an angry canine. "I killed that myself," said Scratch, taking up an armload of dirty bowls and mugs and shuffling out of the room.

Left on her own in the living room of critters, Connie's skin crawled, and she backed out of the room turning to follow Scratch down the hall, passing open doorways into bedrooms littered with mess, a bathroom of lilac tiles and a tub ringed with dirt, a large oil painting of native bushland hanging on the hall wall, a closed door, and another bedroom with a double bed buried under a mountain of clothes.

There was plenty of room. The place just needed a clean.

The hall came out into a large kitchen/dining room where Scratch stood at the sink, running hot water over a pile of dirty dishes. Sunlight streamed in through a window lighting up a million particles of floating dust, shining on the worn and scuffed linoleum floor. The wooden cabinets were old and stained and sagging. The air stank of fat, glue and vinegar, the vinegar smell so strong it stung her eyes. She followed the smell of vinegar to a dining table where the body of a dead creature was laid out on a wooden board, cut open and cleaned out, the spine exposed, the ribs bent open like a butterfly and pinned back with small nails. Surrounding the animal were tiny blades, brushes and hooks, miniature scissors with long handles, short handles, kinked at different angles, jars of cotton balls, scalpels, tweezers and string - the tools of taxidermy. This was his hobby.

"What is that?" Connie pointed at the dead animal on the dining table.

"It's a fox."

Buried in the open flesh and camouflaged by clutter, Connie made out the shape of a long narrow snout and, at the other end, a bushy tail.

"What's it doing on your kitchen table?" she said.

"I eat on the couch," he said as if that explained everything. To Scratch, the dining table wasn't a dining table. It was a workbench.

"I didn't catch that one. I had to get it by post. Foxes aren't endemic to Queensland. They prefer cooler climates."

"You mail-ordered a dead fox?" Connie's mouth fell open. The sharp taste of vinegar hit her tongue. She closed her mouth and winced, wafting at the air. "What is that smell?"

"It's a preservative." Scratch took a glass jar from the

table and handed it to her. Inside, floating in a yellow liquid was a colourful ball of feathers with a long, thin beak.

"What is that?"

"Formaldehyde."

"Is that a bird?"

"Merops Oranatas," said Scratch. "Colourful plumage. Rare. I caught it in the garden yesterday."

"You killed a rare bird?" she said with a note of disapproval, returning the jar to the table. The bird wasn't the only thing that had been killed in the last twenty-four hours. There was a dead boy in the coolroom of her kitchen.

"Do you have a gun?" she asked.

"I don't use bullets. They make a mess. I prefer poison." Scratch reached over the table, took a cloth in his hand and used it to pick up a jar. "I make my own," he said, holding out the jar. Inside was a thick grey-green paste.

Connie wasn't interested in the poison.

"But you own a gun?" she said.

"Yes. Why?"

"We found a boy in the creek this morning. He was one of the boys who found those skulls in Black Mountain. It looks like he was shot. His friends are still missing," she said.

Scratch's eyes burned with suspicion.

"And you want to know if I shot him?"

Connie realised her mistake. She should've been more tactful and tried to steer the conversation back into safe territory.

"No. Is your gun still here? Maybe someone stole it," she said, covering her tracks.

"No. No-one took my gun," growled Scratch,

replacing the poison among the mess on the dining table.

"Then you've got a problem, Scratch. You were the only person on your own last night."

The old man lifted his head, looking out the back window of the kitchen, his eyes losing focus. Connie knew that look. She'd seen it almost every Saturday at the end of the bar when Scratch zoned out, starring into his beer. He was a strange man, a recluse, a hoarder, who killed and stuffed animals, friendly enough but never had a wife and never really had friends.

"Scratch?" she said, trying to draw him back to her.

He turned to her, his face drawn and distant.

"I didn't kill them. I didn't kill her or her kid, and I didn't kill those boys."

*****

In the car on the way back to the hotel, Scratch's words stuck with her. It seemed that she wasn't the first person to accuse him of murder, and the only other death was that of Jane and Kate and for the first time, Connie came to consider the circumstances around their disappearance. They'd gone missing in the sixties when Scratch was a young man in his teens. He must have a connection to the woman, the child or both. It was the only thing that could explain why he fought Wes for the skulls last night. He wanted to protect them from Wes, thinking Wes had killed his wife and child.

At the hotel, small social circles had formed around the tables and chairs as people talked away the hours. Connie called for everyone's attention and asked for volunteers to help clean Scratch's house. Four hands shot up. Back in the car, loaded with buckets and brooms, Connie realised her mistake. The four volunteers were local women and close friends Maggie, Vern, Francis and Kylie and they spent the short trip recalling rumours about Scratch and his unusual, private nature. Their enthusiasm to see behind the gates of his property was sickening, and their motivation for helping was for safe entry beyond the galvanised gate guarding his property. And Scratch's house did not disappoint.

"My God, It's a mess," Vern remarked, with unmasked disgust.

Scratch responded with an inward groan and a scowl.

"Look at all the dead animals. Is that a dog? Who has a dog on their wall?"

He shot Connie a look of disapproval. Connie felt to blame for the judgement she'd brought to his house and asked the women to keep their thoughts to themselves and asked Scratch to tell the women what he wanted done.

Being her second visit to the house, Connie noticed the filing cabinets, newspapers and magazines all carried a white sticker with an alphanumeric code - some sort of filing system. Scratch told the woman not to touch anything with labels and led them into the hall.

"My bedroom is off-limits. No one needs to go in there." He'd stopped at a door that was closed and gripped the handle turning the knob. It was locked, and he turned his back to the door, pointing up and down the hall.

"You can clean the bathroom and the spare room at the end of the hall."

He gave the women instructions on where to find sheets and bedding. Connie was standing in front of a landscape oil painting of amazing detail. Small strokes of the brush had created a hazy appearance of a scrubland of bluish-green hues running out to a purple haze of mountains peaking into a blue sky with vapour trails of clouds. The scene was familiar, local, similar to the bush throughout the tablelands. In the bottom corner of the painting were words in black paint: 'View from Rifle Ridge 1978' and the artist signature, comprised of two letters, 'R.R.'

While Scratch was looking away, Vern gripped the handle on the locked door.

"Get away from there," said Scratch moving in front of the door.

Vern stepped back.

"What's in there?"

"None of your business." Scratch waved the group of women down the hall.

Connie threw Vern a dirty look and wondered if yanking on her long dark hair would help the woman remember her manners.

Their entry into the kitchen was accompanied by screams of fright and delight as they gathered around the dining table noses crinkled at the smell of vinegar, fascination etched on their faces as they looked over the eviscerated fox, the jars of preserved animals and the mini surgical instruments. Their fascination in Scratch's hobby seemed to buoy the old man who puffed out his chest, enjoying the attention his work was creating.

Vern's hand wandered across the items on the table, and she picked out the glass jar with the grey-green paste.

"What's this?" she said, unscrewing the lid with her bare hands.

"You should put that back," said Scratch.

Vern put the jar to her nose.

"It smells like peanut butter and honey," she said.

Scratch took a spare rag from the table and covered his hand.

"It's an extract from the bark of the Ficus cultivars, the leaves of Rhodomyrtus macrocarpa and the berries from

Dupoisia myoporoides. I mix it with peanut butter and honey to cover the smell and mask the taste." Scratch took the jar from Vern, and returned it to the table.

"You eat it?" said Veronica sceptical.

"No, I use it to catch animals. There are very few poisons that work on such a wide range of species."

"It's a poison?" said Vern.

"And a neurotoxin," said Scratch and began to ramble on about the digestive tracts in amphibians vs birds and reptiles and mammals. The poison worked on them all.

"By mammals, you mean humans?" she asked.

"Yes. It'll kill you."

Shock registered on Vern's face, and she held her hands out from her body.

"The sink is over there," said Connie pointing with satisfaction.

Vern streaked across the linoleum floor, turning on the faucet and fumbling the soap. "While you're there, you might as well get started on the dishes," she added.

Scratch waddled across the kitchen to a set of frosted glass doors throwing them open. Bright light flooded from a white room coming in through a wall of floor to ceiling windows looking out onto a courtyard of raised garden beds, overgrown with sprawling vines and trellised plants. Among the rambling mess of green were flashes of red tomatoes, bright yellow lemon bulbs, bells of purple figs, a camouflage of avocados, bursts of blue flowering onions and pillows of orange pumpkins hiding under leaves the size of elephant ears.

Everyone was drawn towards the light and stepped into the white room. The air smelled of fresh paint. In the centre of the room stood an easel with a fresh canvas. Against one wall was a table bristling with brushes and a huge assortment of toothpaste sized tubes with colourful lids covering the spectrum of a rainbow. The linoleum floor was covered in white sheets with splatters, smears and dots of paint. Around the perimeter of the room, propped against the wall were paintings and sketches in various stages of production. The completed paintings carried a black signature, 'R.R.', the same initials on the landscape in the hall. The quality of the paintings was extraordinary.

"There's enough room in here for a mattress," said Scratch, moving the easel to one side, oblivious to the open-mouthed shock on the faces of the women, Connie included.

"You paint," said Connie, dumbfounded.

"They're amazing. How long have you been painting?" asked Maggie.

"My mother taught me in this room. She was an art teacher."

Vern stopped to pick up a small painting of a brightly coloured bird.

"Vern," Connie scolded.

"She'll learn when I cut off her fingers," said Scratch.

Vern apologised and returned the painting, pointing at a signature in black.

"What does R.R. stand for?"

"Robert Ryer," said Scratch. "That's me."

CHAPTER 22

The house was clean enough to be habitable for half a dozen people when Francis Yates dropped a glass jar with a dead rat spilling formaldehyde on the floor, her shoes and dress. The stench was overwhelming, and Scratch lost it, shouting at them to get out, and Connie left with the other women before her luck changed, and Scratch decided to withdraw his hospitality. The afternoon sun had heated the wet ground, burning off the rain from the night before making the air heavy, moist and hot. Despite the uncomfortable conditions and wearing day-old clothes, the locals, practised at dealing with sticky weather, were keeping good humour with a cool drink and a comfortable seat at the Lion's Den. When Connie walked in through the front door, the first face that greeted her was Wes. He was standing at the bar looking serious.

"I heard you've been cleaning house," he said.

Vern came in behind her.

"You'll never believe what he's got there," she said to Wes, wide-eyed and salivating at the chance to be the first to tell all. Connie rolled her eyes. Not at Vern, so much at herself for letting Vern into Scratch's house. The paintings and stuffed animals and jars of preserved creatures made it impossible for anyone, especially Vern, to keep a secret and Scratch's private life was about to go public. And it was the way Vern was doing it that jarred with Connie's sense of decency. Announcing these things, wholesale was crude. Vern framed Scratch as strange and macabre when most of what Scratch was doing was exceptional and talented. And strange. Vern talked loudly, and a group of locals gathered around to listen in. Locals, including Evelyn Ashby, the retired nurse. Without a drink or any other reason to be there, Wes moved to his table where he was within earshot of Vern.

With beds sorted for the night, Connie took a moment to relax with a reheated meal and a sneaky white wine, and she got to thinking about, John. Just the thought of him turned her stomach to knots. He'd lied to her, he'd cut her out of the business, forced himself on her and scared her. He was pushing her away, trying to get her to leave. At the same time, it seemed he wanted out. He'd tried to get out of Rossville last night and ended up drowning, almost. Pity. He was frustrated and angry and didn't want to talk to her like he was punishing Connie, but for what, she didn't know. His frustration was spilling over into her frustration and back again in a downward spiralling loop of negative feedback. John didn't sort himself out, if she couldn't do anything to change the situation, she couldn't stay. And she couldn't see things getting any better, and if that was true, her only choice was to leave him. And soon as she left she would be leaving with nothing.

The knots in her stomach tightened.

It was unfair. John had been dishonest, and it infuriated her.

Vern exhausted herself before exhausting all subject matter of Scratch's private life, and she fell quiet. But there was no shortage of conversation, and the locals turned their attention to the dead boy that Jakes had fished out of the Mungumby creek. The crowd was in no doubt that the boy had been murdered, the gunshots were a giveaway, and the person who murdered him had to be among them. And the other boys were still missing. The search conducted along the creek, earlier in the day hadn't found any more bodies or yielded any further evidence that might tell them what had happened or who did it. It was assumed that all four boys had been killed by the same person. There also seemed to be broad agreement that the murder of the boys had to be linked to the skulls found in Black Mountain.

They began to speculate on possible suspects. Vern's husband, Tim Westcott, quietly pointed out that murders were typically committed by a close relative of the victim and where wives were concerned, the offender commonly proved to be the husband. While no one spoke his name, Wes seemed to be the top suspect. Everyone knew his family had disappeared forty years ago, and the skulls had to be his wife and child. The bullet hole in the child's skull indicated they were murdered and whoever did it had never been caught.

Connie had a problem applying Tim's crime statistics to Wes. She knew the old man and didn't think he was capable of killing his family. She'd seen him with their photo, knew he had the skulls, bones and the murder weapon. He wasn't hiding the fact that he had them. And while Connie didn't share any of this information with the crowd, she did try and defend him, going over to the table and asking the crowd to talk about something else while Wes was still in the hotel. She pointed out to them that a better suspect might be Scratch. Scratch wanted the skulls for what, she didn't know. He said he wanted to keep them from Wes but who really knew why. And Scratch was the only person on his own last night. Vern Westcott added that Scratch had a morbid interest in dead things, but Connie told her she was stereotyping to which Vern retorted with a dirty look.

"Your husband was behaving quite odd last night. Violent even," said Vern.

Connie scoffed at the suggestion. John hadn't killed the boys. The only thing he'd murdered was her marriage.

"No. My husband is a lot of things, but he's not a murderer. If you're fishing for another name, take Kipper," she said explaining that this morning, Kipper's clothes were wet indicating that he'd been out in the storm. He didn't have anything to do the missing bones or the disappearance of Wes' family; however, he could have had a hand in the disappearance and death of the four boys. Several women, including Vern, agreed that Kipper was a creep and his status as a suspect was confirmed by nothing more than his character.

"Any chance of a drink?" Fred Abe interjected in the conversation. The heat had flushed his face red.

Connie couldn't see the harm in it. It was late in the day, and there was nothing better to do.

"What are you having?"

Fred Abe told her he was out of cash and Connie said she'd run a tab tallying up four beers with a marker pen on the wall of the hotel. That's the way they kept track of monies owed at the Lion's Den.

"How are you dealing with all this. Are you OK?" Fred Abe asked.

She wasn't OK. She felt short-tempered. It could have been the heat or the wine with lunch, shortness of sleep, John's temper or Karla's shock pregnancy, the surprise visit in the middle of the night, or the uncertainty of her own future.

"Why wouldn't I be?" she said.

"A bust-up can't be easy."

"Who's busting up?" she said, cold.

"I…last night…you and John…" Abe stumbled on his words.

Connie dropped four beers on the bar and aimed her eyes up at the big man.

"Married people fight. It doesn't mean they bust-up."

"No, but last night…I saw…" Fred Abe left a vacuum in the conversation. Connie wasn't interested in filling the void.

"Your beers are getting warm," she said, deadpan.

But Fred Abe didn't leave.

"You know, I'm never sure how to approach you, and I just want to say that if you're having issues you can talk to me, you know? You call me, and I'd come around, or you could come around to my place. And we could talk." His tone was soft and persistent while his cocked eye suggested Fred Abe was searching for more than just a conversation.

Connie, however, wasn't interested in Fred Abe's cockeyed conversation.

"Abe, come on, take your beers, your friends are waiting," she said, forcing warmth into her voice.

"Connie, you're a nice person, and John's John you know and you deserve someone who looks after you, and I like…"

"Abe," she cut him off with a bark. "I'm married. End of story." Wes looked up from his table by the window.

"But are you happy?" said Abe, not giving up despite her no-go signals. "What's John like at home? I don't live with him, but I know it wouldn't be easy. He's got something wrong with him. Everyone can see that. No one would blame you if you split..."

"Abe!" She put a finger in his face, shouting "You and I are not having this conversation. Ever."

A silence descended over the hotel, and everyone looked toward the bar. Over Fred Abe's shoulder, there was movement. Josie and Quicks came into the bar and behind them Jakes, looking wary, scanning the faces around the room. He made eye contact with Connie, and she felt her mood lift.

"Married." Fred Abe said, drawn-out and bitter. His face had clouded over.

Wes appeared beside Fred Abe, leaning on the bar, throwing the big man a friendly smile.

"Are you done here? I'm dying of thirst."

Fred Abe threw Wes a dirty look. If she could extend her reach far enough, she'd slap Fred Abe across the face. A beer bottle in her hand would help her close the gap and make the impact required to get through to his thick head.

Fred Abe collected his four beers in his big hands and turned out, returning sullen to his friends.

"You want to be careful around him. I've heard him talking," said Wes.

"Who, Fred Abe?" Connie's attention was on Jakes at the back of the hotel. He was with Josie and Quicks, the three of them in a huddle, leaning into each other speaking in whispers. She wanted to know what they were saying.

"Hey." Wes stuck his head into her field of vision. He was frowning at her.

"I heard you," she said.

"You're going to make trouble for yourself looking at him like that."

He was right. But, maybe Connie wanted trouble.

"I'm not staying here," Wes grunted. The old man's eyes were sunken, and he was blinking a lot. He was tired. He'd been up early that morning to the sound of gunshots. "Who am I taking home with me?"

It occurred to her that when all these people found beds, the hotel would be empty and John was away. The thought struck her with a nervous thrill. She took a paper napkin from behind the bar, found a pen and made a list of names, two lists, divided between Wes and Scratch. Wes insisted on seeing both lists and asked where Evelyn Ashby was staying. She told him Evelyn would get a proper bed at Scratch's house, just like he'd wanted.

"Why are you doing this for Evelyn?" said Connie.

Wes turned his head and looked at the ex-nurse sitting at a table in the restaurant with Vern Westcott.

"I don't want her in the house."

"Why not?"

"She was Jane's midwife."

Evelyn Ashby had helped his wife birth Wes' daughter.

"Oh, God. You should've told me." She had no idea that Evelyn was there the day Wes became a father. And now she was here just as the remains of his family had been unearthed.

Wes returned his attention to the list of names. From the back of the hotel, Jakes was on the move again, weaving his way through the tables toward the bar. Nerves stirred in her stomach.

"There's a name missing," said Wes, looking up at her raising a brow. "Where's Jakes staying?"

Connie gave the old man a sarcastic sneer and

snatched one of the napkins from his weathered hand.

"Well, I can't send him to your house," she said.

Jakes was almost at the bar when a balding head blocked her view. It was Scratch. He lifted himself into a stool while Wes stared daggers at the strange, chubby man. Then Wes reached over the bar, snatching the paper napkin from Connie slapping it down on the bar in front of Scratch making him jump. He held Scratch under a tired, burning stare.

"Don't run off this time," he said, breaking off his stare and turning toward the table by the window.

Jakes took Wes' place at the bar.

"Hi," he said, his face open and light, his voice full of interest. The nervous thrill bloomed in her stomach and throat.

"Hi."

"What's this?" Scratch leant over the napkin, scanning the names.

"That's a list of the people staying at your house tonight," she said.

"Am I on there?" said Jakes.

"No. You can stay in the hotel tonight," she said, turning her body to face him, full-frontal twisting gently at the hips. "You'll be on your own. Do you mind?"

Jakes' face lit up with interest.

"I'd prefer company," he said.

Company. She could arrange that. First, all these people had to go.

"You should get something to eat," said Connie with a sideways smile.

"Who are these people?" Scratch held out the napkin jabbing a finger at the list of names.

Connie focused her full attention on Scratch. Pointing at the first name on the list.

"You know Evelyn. She knows everyone else. Go talk to her."

Footsteps from the storeroom at the back of the bar made Connie think of her husband, and with Jakes at the bar, she had a moment of panic like she was going to be caught out. When Sherbet Ray appeared with a tea towel in hand, she was relieved.

"Ray, can you put together three more plates to feed to Josie and Quicks." She was pointing towards the back of the bar like it was some sort of sleight of hand that would make Jakes invisible.

Sherbet Ray looked worried.

"I can, but we're running out of food," he said. "We've got enough for breakfast and lunch then we're out. How long is this flood going to last?"

"It depends on the rain," said Scratch, turning back to the safety of the bar. "If it stays dry, the creek should get low enough to cross in the next day or two."

"We don't have another day. By this time tomorrow, the only thing left in the coolroom will be that dead boy."

"What about the pig that Wes shot?"

"That'll be enough for half of all the people we have. What about the other half?" said the Cook.

"Scratch has got food," said Connie. His backyard was full of fruit and veg.

Scratch was staring at the list of names, shaking his head.

"I can't take all these people," he said.

"Scratch, if you don't go home with every single person on that list, you'll never sit at this bar again."

CHAPTER 23

A blanket of calm had fallen over the hotel. Jakes, Jose and Quicks had joined the waitresses at the table by the window, talking. Fred Abe, Shakey Pete, Greenie and Gunner Jones seemed reluctant to retire to their tents. They hung back in the hotel, quietly cradling warm beers.

"Finish your drinks, guys. We're closing up."

Ada announced she was going to bed, and everyone at the table stood up to leave, except Jakes.

"Are you coming?" Josie asked him.

Jakes shook his head.

"Do you want us to wait for you?" Tina asked Connie.

"No, I've still got to lock up. I'll be a while," she said.

Josie, Quicks and the waitresses said good night and left through the kitchen, the swinging door creaking.

"I'm not sure about staying in these tents," said Gunner Jones.

"The last people who slept in them died," said Shakey Pete. "Why didn't we get a proper bed like everyone else? Can't we stay in the hotel?"

"No, you can't."

"There's got to be some spare beds at your place," said Greenie.

"There aren't."

These men were protecting the person who stole the alcohol from her last night, and although she was sure it was Kipper who stole from her until they told her who it was, none of them were staying in the hotel.

"That's not true. I hear there's a spare place next to you," Slippery Pete said. The other men laughed.

"You better be fast. That spot will fill quick," said Greenie.

"I think it's already filled. You like a warm bed, do you Jakes?" said Slippery Pete, malice in his voice.

He had a right to be angry. Jakes had slept with his wife.

Jakes opened his mouth to say something back, and Connie cut him off.

"We're not having this conversation. It's time you all left."

The men got to their feet and sauntered towards the door. Fred Abe looked hurt and angry. He was still seething from her rejection, while Slippery Pete directed his hate at Jakes.

"The next bed you sleep in will be six feet under," he said and stepped out into the night.

Connie locked the door behind them.

"Would you like a drink?" she went to the bar and poured two glasses of wine. Her nerves were rattled, not from what had happened, but for what was about to happen.

Jakes picked up his glass and took a sip.

"I'll get you some sheets." Connie went into the back

of the hotel, checked the lock on the back door and found fresh bedding and pillows.

Back in the bar, Jakes had cleared an area in the middle of the room. In the windows, she caught her reflection against the darkness outside.

"Move into the corner, against the wall," she said, her voice dropping to a whisper.

The air between them was electric, their movements restrained as they rearranged the furniture and laid out the bedsheets, her hands shaking, heart racing, head dancing.

Jakes brushed against her arm. It felt electric. There was movement at the window. Her reflection stared back, judging, and she pulled away from Jakes.

"What's wrong?" he asked.

"Wait here." She started for the back of the hotel, reached inside the swinging door to the kitchen and switched off the lights. In the pitch-black Connie wove a path through the tables and chairs, blind. She didn't need to see where she was going. She found Jakes by the sound of his breathing and took him by the hand, pulling him with her into the blind corner of the bar. They dropped to their knees. Her heart hammered in her ears like someone was banging on the door to get in, but there was no one there. It was just her and Jakes, kneeling on the hard floor facing each other in the dark.

Jakes placed a hand on her hip, pushed her hair back from her face.

"I've thought about this moment for a long time," he said, his words echoing her thoughts. Ever since that night in his workshop, she couldn't remember a day she didn't think of Jakes.

She kissed him, soft and warm, the pressure of his body on hers, radiating heat. The excitement built in her body, and she dug her nails into his skin, took his bottom lip between her teeth and bit down, soft. He responded, pressing her harder into his body, his hands gliding around her and grabbing her arse squeezing hard and pressing her hips into his. She could feel him swelling.

They didn't have a lot of time.

She clawed at his shirt, pulling it up and over his head and ran her hand down his chest over his tattoos, stomach to the top of his pants working the button, her hands shaking. He pushed her hands away, pulled open the button himself then cuffed her wrists with one hand and lifted her arms uplifting her blouse over her head and down the length of her arms, his hands on her skin. They came together again, kissing, pushing and squeezing. His hands found the back of her bra and flicked the hook. The straps loosened and he chased them down her shoulder with his lips until her bra fell away. He cupped her, brushing her nipples with his hands, and kissed them before coming up and kissing her, their bare skin, chest to chest, warm.

Desire buzzed in her head, driving her mad. She forced an arm between them and pushed a hand into the front of his pants, finding him hard and wet. Jakes responded to her hand with a long groan and ran his own hand over her shoulders, breasts, down her stomach and between her legs, squeezing and rubbing.

She pushed his pants below his hips, revealing the curve of his white cheeks. Jakes pulled away, stripping off his pants, down to bare skin. She did the same, pulling open the button of her shorts and stripping off, her body on fire. They came together again, skin on skin, naked, hard, smooth and warm. She could smell his sex and felt his mess, wet on her stomach.

Jakes ran two fingers down her pelvis, through her hair slipping between her legs, between her skin, his hands firm, pressing her buttons. Her mouth opened, letting out a soft cry and her fingers curled over his chest clawing at his skin. He kept moving his fingers. She leant back presenting him with a firm nipple that he took between his teeth. Her soft cries became a steady, rhythmic moan. A gentle shove from Jakes and she was lying on her back. He raised himself over her, his lips on hers, his hands on her hips and lowered himself between her thighs, pressing into her, dividing her swollen flesh, sliding over her and lighting small sparks of pleasure. Her lips parted in a smile. She reached out and pulled him closer, forcing him into her. He pulled back, and she pulled him forward, deeper again until they met at the hip, and he pressed his pelvis into hers grinding against her, sending pulses of warm electricity up her stomach and chest and down into her legs. He kept pushing and moving harder and faster. Shock waves ricocheted inside her, dividing and multiplying, reaching every finger and toe. A pressure was building, pressing against her skin, filling the space inside, crushing her lungs, shortening her breath until she stopped breathing holding on. A small explosion rippling up from between her legs like a searing hot flush releasing sweat and fluid and a quiet scream. At the same time, Jakes released a deep groan, his face tightened with the pain of pleasure, and his body shook. He pulsed inside her, and she felt a warm gush. They held onto each other as the aftershocks reverberated through their bodies. She held on and laughed quietly, the tension releasing from her body. He was lying on top of her, warm and heavy, breathing in her ear. She stroked the back of his head, tracing her fingers down his neck. She was smiling. She felt free.

"I've wanted to do that for a long time," her voice was barely a whisper.

He lifted his head, and she could make out the lines of his face.

"I…" his voice fell away. They were nose to nose, his eyes dancing in the dark. She stroked the side of his head. His eyes shifted side to side, and there were deep lines across his forehead.

"What is it?" she said. "What are you thinking?"

His eyes fixed on hers.

"I want to know, how I can spend the rest of my life with you?"

CHAPTER 24

She didn't want to leave, but she couldn't stay, and Jakes came with her in part. The smell of him clung to her skin and the memory of his weight and warmth had imprinted itself on her body. She took it with her out of the hotel and into the cool night air. Gravel crunched, loud, jarring her ears, bringing her out of a waking dream. She was halfway across the car park when she heard the feet behind her, approaching fast, and she spun around.

A tall, dark figure, a heavyset man reached out and grabbed her by the arm. Fear filled her body and poured out her mouth, and she screamed.

"Hello, Connie." The voice was deep and sluggish pulling at her arm, and she thrashed against the vice-like grip.

"Who's that? Fred?" Connie matched the voice, his

size and shape to Fred Abe. And there was another voice, another dark figure.

"Did you two have a nice time in there?" He was a man of regular shape and size-Slippery Pete.

Fred Abe had a tight grip on her arm.

"What's going on?"

Connie's heart was thumping in her chest, her body tense. She tried to rip her arm from the grip. He wasn't letting go.

"Get off me," she yelled.

"Good, let her scream" whispered Slippery Pete, turning to the hotel where two more figures were crouched in the dark at the back door to the kitchen. The door rattled, the lock clicked open. The men readied themselves, poised to attack.

The door opened, and Jakes burst out.

"Jakes, look-out," she screamed.

The men pounced. Their bodies hit Jakes in a full tackle, knocking him over.

"Hold him down," said Slippery Pete, balling up his fist. He landed the first blow in Jakes' stomach.

Jakes groaned.

Connie screamed.

Slippery Pete swung a boot at Jakes' ribs.

"No," Connie screamed again. Fred Abe put his arms around her body, clamping her to his chest and clapped a big hand over her mouth.

"Let's go somewhere quiet," said Fred Abe, lifting her weightless off the ground. Those words scared her. Fred Abe was crushing her in his arms, his strength frightening. He carried her toward a thick stand of trees beside the hotel.

From the back door of the hotel, Jakes screamed out her name and she could hear the thud of boots and fists, kicking and punching.

The dark undergrowth loomed ahead of her and she knew, if she went in, she'd never come out the same. Every part of her body went cold with fear. She bucked against the strength of Fred Abe's arms, in vain. The trees drew near. Panic filled her body. Straining her neck, Connie pushed her face forward against his meaty hand and opening her mouth, taking in the flesh of a single fat finger and bit down. Fred Abe cried out, yanking away his hand. Connie screamed, wriggled and dropped, her feet slipping out from under her and she fell sideways onto the sharp gravel, knocking the air from her lungs and she lay on the ground, winded, unable to move. Then she felt a hand grip her ankle. Fred Abe pulled her feet first, dragging her by one ankle through the gravel towards the trees. Air returned to her lungs, and she screamed, kicking at her own ankle, kicking at his hand. Her shoe clipped his fingers, and Fred Abe cried out in pain, his grip loosened and Connie pulled her leg free, flipping onto her stomach and crawling fast, gravel digging into her hands and knees, scrambling to her feet and running for the house.

The light on the porch came on, the front door swung open and Sherbet Ray, Quicks and Josie ran out.

"Help Jakes!" screamed Connie, pointing toward the men at the back of the hotel.

Josie ran at the men screaming, and they scattered without a fight.

At the edge of the car park in the dark undergrowth, the hulking figure of Fred Abe slipped into the shadows.

"Cowards," Josie called out after them.

They took Jakes limping into the house blood running from his nose and mouth.

"You're bleeding," said Jakes, pointing out the cuts on Connie's hands, elbows and knees.

"What happened?" Karla was dressed in pyjamas, looking wary.

"It's O.K. Karla.

"Go back to bed," said Connie.

"Are you O.K.? I heard you scream," said Karla.

"We're all fine now," she said.

Karla threw a frown around the room before leaving and returning to her bed.

"That was my fault," said Jakes. I should've walked you home."

"It wouldn't have made a difference," said Connie. Slippery Pete had been there to get his revenge on Jakes for sleeping with his wife. "There were too many of them. Besides, I think Fred Abe was after me."

She explained how Fred Abe had taken her and showed them the mark of his hand on her arm and ankle.

Sherbet Ray wanted to get out his kitchen knives and hunt Fred down.

"Leave it to the police. It's assault. He'll go to gaol," she said.

Despite the attack, Jakes couldn't stay at the house. They'd slept together. It wouldn't be right, and Connie sent him back to the hotel.

Lying in bed, her body throbbing with pain, Connie felt unsafe. She'd never picked Fred Abe for a rapist. Maybe that was his first attempt and lucky for her it hadn't worked out the way he'd planned. If it wasn't for Quicks and Josie and the others, it could've turned out different, and she shuddered at the thought.

Then it occurred to her that a similar thing had happened to Josie except Josie had been on her own at her parent's farm, her attacker in the house on the other side of the toilet door. It would have been frightening. Connie could understand why they wanted to put Kipper in gaol for as long as possible. She wanted the same for Fred Abe.

"Fucking men," she said, and in her mind, she made some sort of allowance for Jakes. He wasn't like Fred Abe or Kipper or John.

A fog fell over her eyes, and her mind settled on Jakes. But her thoughts were interrupted by visions of Fred Abe in the dark. She became unsettled, getting up to check the lock on her bedroom window peering behind the curtains, through the glass to the dark outside. He was out there somewhere. The thought made her uncomfortable. Once more, Connie rechecked the lock on the window, then the lock on the front door before returning to bed, telling herself she was safe. Eventually, with her body exhausted, her mind foggy, Connie drifted into a half-waking dream. She was weightless, floating, the room spinning, tumbling end on end, dizzying and out of control.

CHAPTER 25

The smell of pancakes drew Connie out of bed and into the kitchen where Sherbet Ray stood, spatula in hand over the cooker.

"You're up," he said with a wry smile.

In the sink was a stack of dirty plates, several chairs had been left askew and crumbs lay scattered on the island bench. Connie rubbed her eyes.

"I didn't hear anyone. I must have slept heavy."

"You look better for it. I would even say you're glowing." The Cook gave her a cheeky smile and handed her a stack of fresh pancakes. "I'm sure you worked up an appetite last night."

Connie threw Sherbet Ray a look of warning.

"Shouldn't we be rationing out the food?" She took

one of the pancakes, folding it and stuffing it in her mouth.

"Not if you raid Scratch's garden today."

Connie chewed and swallowed.

"Hmmm. I forgot about that. Where is everyone?" She pointed at the mess and the empty chairs.

"They're out searching for Fred Abe and the others."

"What for? What are they going to do?"

"Nothing, Jakes wants to keep an eye on them. I like him. He's a better man than John."

"Ray, can we not do this? I'm not ready to go public with this. And, I don't want it to get to Karla."

Sherbet Ray poured the last of the batter into a pan.

"I've been thinking about those skulls. Do you think Fred Abe and Kipper took them?" said the Cook.

"I know who's got the skulls," said Connie speaking around another pancake.

"Who?" Sherbet, Ray looked indignant.

She swallowed.

"Wes. And it's not just the two skulls. The boys found some bones and an old gun barrel. It's got to be the weapon used to shoot them. Wes showed me yesterday."

"What's he going to do with them?"

"He wants to use the skulls to catch the killer."

Sherbet Ray scoffed.

"Unlikely."

"I know. I'll call the police as soon as the phones are working. They can sort it out with Wes."

Sherbet Ray waved the spatula over the pan.

"The police are going to have to deal with the dead kid in the coolroom, Fred Abe and those skulls. They're going to have their hands full." He shook his head, turned back to the stove and poured out another pancake. "Who do you think shot the kid?"

Connie chewed another pancake.

"I've got a feeling Scratch has got something to do with it," she said. "I think he lied when I asked him about the gunshots. He said he didn't hear them, but I don't believe him."

"Have you asked Wes about it?"

"Wes heard the shots from his house and went down to the creek, but when he got there, no one was around. He didn't see anyone."

They heard the front door open and footsteps coming down the hall. Jakes appeared. She smiled. He didn't smile back and looked around the kitchen then checked the corridor.

"What is it?" said Connie, putting down her knife.

"Where's Karla?" Jakes said, whispering.

Connie felt a cold snap of panic.

"Why? Is she missing?"

"She's still in bed," said Sherbet Ray.

Whatever was going on, it wasn't about Karla. Connie felt cool relief.

"What's wrong?" she said.

"It's John. He's at the creek. There's another body. You'd better come with me."

*****

Her first vision was of John's body caught in the weeds, floating face down in Mungumby creek. It wasn't to be. The floodwater had eased, the waterline dropped, exposing the banks of the creek and John stood at the edge of the floodwater, his shoulders slumped, head bowed over a dead body.

All the waitresses were there with Quicks, watching from behind a screen of dense bush. In the trees around them, debris hung from branches like cobwebs in a

164

haunted house.

"Who is it?" asked Connie.

"It's one of the missing boys," said Jakes in a whisper.

"Do you know how he died?"

Jakes shook his head.

"John won't let anyone near the kid."

"Why?"

"We don't know." Emma was seated on the trunk of an uprooted tree, legs swinging. "He's been staring at the body for a while now," she whispered.

"Has anyone tried talking to him?" said Connie.

"We tried, before, and he got angry," said Tina. "Then he asked for you."

Connie looked at John, trying to judge his mood from his demeanour. He didn't seem angry. John was quiet, solemn. A few years ago when a friend of John's died in a motorcycle accident, they'd been to the funeral and John had stood over the open casket, head bowed; staring in the same way he was staring at the boy. Except, John didn't know the boy, and this show of sentiment seemed misplaced. Either way, John didn't seem to be a danger.

She looked at the boy. His body lay still. If a bookie was taking bets, she'd wager the boy had been shot, the same as his friend in the fridge. Although Connie suspected Scratch as the killer, she didn't know for sure, and John's strange behaviour led her to think that maybe John had something to do with it.

She ran over what she knew. When the gunshots had been fired, John was at Wes' house. He had his own bedroom there, and it would have been easy for John to climb out the window and get away without anyone knowing he was missing. When Connie had turned up at Wes' farmhouse, yesterday, John had been out for a walk. That was unusual too. John didn't exercise, and she wondered if there was some other motive for leaving the house. Maybe John had been down to the creek, covering his tracks and disposing of dead bodies? Either way, John didn't seem like a threat right now. Besides, there were people around, watching.

"I'll talk to him." As soon as she said it a wave of guilt washed over her as Connie realised she was about to face her husband for the first time since she'd slept with Jakes. She forced the thought from her mind.

"You don't have to do this," Jakes whispered.

"This would be easier if you weren't here," she told him.

"Look," Tina whispered, pointing.

John was moving, circling the dead boy, his feet splashing at the edge of the water. He bent down and took the boy by the wrists, dragging him out of the water and lay the boy's arms down before crouching beside the body, staring, grimly at the corpse.

Connie stepped out of the scrub.

"John," she whispered his name, trying not to startle him. He glanced at her, eyes devoid of emotion then dropped his head again to stare at the boy. Connie came closer. The water in the creek was moving quickly, hissing and gurgling around a long, smooth bend. The boy lay on his back, his body wet and sprinkled with sand, his milky eyes open, staring at the sky. Below one eye, his cheekbone had collapsed inward and in the centre of the depression was a small dark circle - a bullet hole. He'd been shot in the face. Despite the disfigurement, she recognised the boy. He was the oldest of the group of friends.

"I tried to…" John started, his voice trailing off, staring at his hands. "I couldn't bring him back." He looked up at her. John's face was ashen. A crust of sand and saliva encircled his mouth. A similar circle traced a line around the boy's mouth, and Connie realised, John had tried to resuscitate the boy. It would have been in vain. The boy was pasty white and waterlogged his skin unnaturally smooth and tight - clearly, lifeless. For whatever reason, John must have thought he could bring the boy back from the dead. And now John was breaking down, sniffing and sobbing, tears forming in his eyes and running down his face. Connie was sure John was losing his mind, and she felt a mix of repulsion and compassion. She wanted to reach out and put a hand on John's shoulder to offer comfort and stopped herself. The time for mercy had passed. Still, she couldn't leave. This was Karla's Dad.

Connie let John cry and shifted her focus to the surroundings. The floodwater hissed around the curve of the creek. The sand under her feet was the same sand on John's mouth and the same sand covering the boy's body. Like the boy, Wes had been covered in sand, dripping wet when he'd returned from town. He'd been here after the bridge had collapsed. He'd been looking for John and found John drowned. Then it all made sense. This was where John had drowned. If it wasn't for Wes, John would've died. It explained John's morose mood. He wasn't crying over the boy, he was crying for himself.

This was self-pity. Shallow. Selfish. Connie felt a pang of anger and took John by the elbow.

"Come on, let's take a walk," Helping John to his feet, Connie guided him upstream away from the body.

As they moved off the bank, and through the bush, there was movement behind her. The waiting group came out of hiding and surrounded the boy on the bank, no doubt working out how to carry the dead weight to the cool room to be with his friend. Two bodies both had been shot. And, two boys were still missing, their killer unknown.

Their slow walk led them to the crossing and the splintered remains of the bridge. John stopped on the road and looked across the creek. The trees on the other side swayed in the wind, the water bubbled and hissed. He seemed to straighten and took a breath. His eyes regained focus.

"I'll come home," he said.

Connie's stomach dropped. That wasn't what she wanted.

"John, we've got to talk about this."

"I'll sign the documents. You'll be an owner. You can have the whole business for all I care. I just want to come home." John's ruddy red eyes seemed sincere, a complete contrast to the animalistic eye's she'd seen in the bedroom.

She thought of Jakes. She thought of the business papers with her name on them. These were the things that meant a lot to her, the things she wanted. Having John in the house, in her bed, didn't fit. It wasn't right.

Still, she needed her name on those papers.

"Give it a few more days. Wait for the flood to go down, and we'll talk."

"What's there to talk about?" he said.

"What you did the other night scared me. I need more time," she said.

"I didn't mean that. I don't know what I was doing."

"It's not just that. You need to tell me what's been going on in town. Where do you go? Are you seeing someone?"

John clenched his jaw, his neck turned red. She'd struck a nerve, and he frowned.

"I want the truth too," he said. "About Jakes. Maybe you didn't sleep with him, but something happened." John's anger came through in his voice. It was there but under control. He was trying.

"I told you already. I kissed him. We held hands. That was it. Nothing else happened," she said. "And, I still came back to you," she added, trying to make him feel better. Or make her actions seem better - maybe both.

"Do you still love me?" he asked.

"Not right now."

Silence fell over them. John dropped his head and stared at the road. Over his shoulder, on the far side of the gushing creek, the trees swayed in the wind, a movement at ground level caught her eye and Connie caught sight of a figure moving off the road and disappearing into the trees.

A moment of fright stopped her heart and she took a sharp breath.

John looked up at her, and seeing her expression, turned to face the same direction.

"What is it?"

"I thought I saw someone," she said. The figure had a hunch and white hair and moved, slow and balanced. "An old person. A man, I think."

John stared for a while then took in a deep breath, sighed, starting down the dirt road, bushing past her.

"Where are you going?" she asked, concerned that he was heading for the hotel.

"To think," he said and kept walking.

Maybe he was going to think about filing for divorce, although that seemed doubtful. If anyone was going to do anything about their marriage it was Connie. Only she would have the guts to pull the trigger, and she'd only do that when the time was right. In the meantime, she'd do her best to get her name on the business papers.

On the far side of the creek, the road was empty, and the bush seemed to be staring back. She didn't want to stay here on her own. Then Jakes came out of hiding, pushing through the branches and joining her on the road.

How'd you go?" he asked his voice soft.

She was pretty sure Jakes had heard their conversation.

"The same way it always goes," said Connie, falling silent.

Jakes shuffled his feet in the sulphur-yellow dirt.

"They took the body back to the hotel," he said.

Connie looked into the fast-flowing waters. There were still two boys missing.

"You'd have to think the other two boys are in the water too," she said.

"We checked all the way down to the Anan River. The water there is even thicker and higher. If they got that far, their bodies could be washed out to sea by now."

Connie faced upstream, north towards Wes' farm, the origin of the twelve gunshots.

"Has anyone searched upstream?"

*****

Connie led the way, off the road and into the bush upstream, the soil still damp from receding floodwaters. Large nests of knotted debris gathered around the base of trees, and stringy bits of grass hung from branches. They walked in silence, scanning the banks and the murky water and the white foam bobbing at the edges of the creek. Jakes seemed distracted, keeping his distance. It was an after-effect of her conversation with John, although she couldn't tell if Jakes was being cold or just giving her space.

The bush thinned out further upstream and opened into a small clearing cut off by a post and wire fence. On the other side of the fence was a carpet of new, green grass dotted with grazing cattle, heads down, eating. Beyond the paddock stood a large tin workshop and a white weatherboard house - Wes' farmhouse.

The fence bordering the farm ran parallel to the creek, and on the other side of the creek, the dark boulders of Black Mountain peaked over the treetops. In her head, Connie drew a line from Black Mountain to the farmhouse, and the line ran right through the place where she stood.

"This is where Wes said he'd heard the gunshots. This was where the boys were shot," she looked at the soggy bank of the creek only a few meters away. "And this must be where they were dumped in the creek."

Jakes and Connie scanned the banks of the creek for another body but found nothing. On the ground along the creek, the earth had been raked in one direction by the flood. Connie walked up the bank to the highest point where the grass stood up. She was close to the fence line and thought to search the ground when a crunch came out of a thick cluster of trees nearby. The tight-knit of trunks and bushes stood on the fenceline to the farm. Jakes had heard it too - the crunch of dry leaf litter. He came to her side, and the two of them stood in the clearing, staring at the stand of trees.

"Who's there?" Connie shouted.

A crashing sound came from the trees, and a body shot out of the shadows, running away down the fence line, feet thumping the ground. Connie ran after them, circling around the stand of trees and saw a short, rotund figure disappearing into the bush.

"Scratch. What is he doing here?" Her heart beat out of her chest, and she turned back to the stand of trees, sticking her head between the trunks. It was cool in the shadows. The earth had been trampled, and there were shoe prints in the dirt. Stepping inside the stand, Connie looked out at the landscape around her. She could see Jakes, the creek, the fence line, the paddocks, the big tin workshop and the weatherboard house. It was the perfect vantage point to watch everything, without being seen.

"I think he's been watching Wes," said Connie coming out into the sun.

Jakes was at the fence line and waved her over.

"Look at this." He pointed at a mound of freshly dug earth the size of a bed pillow.

"Someone buried something," she said.

"One of the missing boys?" suggested Jakes.

"No. It's too small." Too small for a grown male, anyway. A small child, perhaps, but a child hadn't gone missing.

Whoever dug the hole was in direct sight of the farmhouse. If they didn't want to be seen burying whatever was down there, they could have dug the hole somewhere more discrete, like the bush nearby. But, they'd chosen to dig here, exposed and in the open.

"Wes must have dug the hole."

"What do you think is down there?" asked Jakes.

Connie looked around for clues. The hole was above the high point of the flood. It had been dug in the last few days, Wes must have lost something. Something worth burying.

She snapped her fingers.

"It's his dog."

CHAPTER 26

They were back at the hotel. Half the tables were full of people whispering about the second dead boy, worried that the killer was among them. At a table by the window, drinking iced water, Sherbet Ray, Quicks, Josie and Jakes were the only few who knew about the grave they'd found by the creek.

Yesterday, Connie had found out Wes' dog had died. Wes was emotional, and it appeared to her that the dog had died, recently, perhaps that morning. The mound of earth on the grave was fresh. If the dog had died yesterday, then Wes had been at the creek burying the body around the same time the boys had been murdered. But she already knew that. Wes had been upfront, saying he'd gone to the creek to investigate the gunshots and hadn't seen anyone. Maybe that's when he'd buried his dog. She'd seen him hours later and the emotions for his dog dying would have been so raw, that he didn't say anything. He didn't want to talk about it. That was understandable. What she couldn't comprehend was the possibility that Wes was lying and he'd killed the boys.

"What about Scratch. What was he doing down at the creek?" asked Sherbet Ray.

"I'm pretty sure he was watching Wes' house," said Connie.

"Why would he do that?" said Josie.

"He wants the skulls and thinks Wes has them."

"Does he have them?" asked Josie.

"I don't know." Connie looked at Sherbet Ray with a straight face. She'd told the Cook that Wes had the skulls, but didn't want everyone knowing.

The Cook's eyes bored into her.

"I think Wes shot them," said Sherbet Ray, convinced of Wes' guilt.

"I don't know. I've got a feeling about Scratch," said Jakes.

Connie had a feeling about Scratch too.

Sherbet Ray stretched and yawned.

"You have to go over there anyway. We need food for tonight unless you want all these people to starve."

Connie looked at Jakes.

"Do you want to come with me?"

*****

Scratch's yellow Volvo had been parked in the driveway at the front of the crumbling old house, the engine cold. Connie led Jakes through the junk and weeds to the front door, knocking. No-one answered. Jakes tried the door. It was open, and he pushed it back, stepping

174

inside.

"Scratch, are you home?" Connie called out.

Again, there was no answer.

"What's that vinegar stink," said Jakes going through into the living room.

"Formaldehyde."

It was Jakes first time in the house. He was enthralled by the clutter, the stuffed animals, the stacks of magazines. Down the long hall, Jakes peered into every room, except one, the door locked. In the kitchen, Jakes couldn't help being drawn to the table with the dead fox, the small surgical instruments and the jars of birds, rats and snakes. He picked up a scalpel and tested it on an envelope, impressed by the sharp blade. Putting it down, Jakes began picking up each of the jars bringing them to his eye, peering through the bent image of the dead animals inside. When Jakes reached for the pot of greyish green goo, Connie stopped him.

"That's poison," she said.

A loud thump came from inside the house. They both stopped to listen. It came from the hall. Jakes crept back the way they'd come checking the rooms as he went, stopping at a locked door.

"What's in here?" he asked.

Connie shrugged and tapped the timber door with the knuckle of her finger.

"Hello? Is anyone in there?"

There was no answer.

"It could be those missing boys," said Jakes. "Is there a key?"

"Not that I know of."

Jakes looked at the lock then backed up against the wall opposite the door.

"Stand back."

"What are you doing?"

"I'm going to kick it in." Jakes shifted his feet to get a grip.

"No." A voice from the other side crackled like a warm flame. "Don't kick it in." It was a woman.

"Who's that?" said Connie.

"I'm coming out."

They heard the scrape of metal on metal, the click of a lock and the door opened.

A woman with silver hair and skin like filo pastry stood in the doorway.

"Evelyn?" It was Evelyn Ashby, Cooktown resident and retired nurse hiding in the room. "What are you doing in there?"

Evelyn looked up and down the hall.

"Is Robert back?"

"Scratch? No."

"Good. I'm glad you're here, Connie. You should probably take a look at this." Evelyn stepped aside, waved Connie into the room and flicked a switch on the wall.

Light exploded from an exposed bulb in the centre of the ceiling illuminating a dozen tall cabinets, the shelves bowing under the weight of hundreds of books. And every book was the same cardboard-colour, every spine marked with black, permanent ink and stitched together with heavy red and black twine.

Jakes wandered up to one of the bookshelves and selected a book at random. Evelyn put out a hand and took the book, smiling at Jakes.

"Would you mind watching the front door?" she said sweetly.

Jakes shrugged and left the room.

"What am I looking at?" asked Connie.

Evelyn took a book from the shelf and handed it to

her.

"They're drawings," said Evelyn.

Connie split open the book and found herself looking at a small, yellow bird with a long, needle-like beak penetrating a pink flower. The detail was amazing.

"Did Scratch draw this?"

Evelyn pointed a crooked finger at text written across the bottom of the page. 'Phylidonyris Novaehollandiae, New Holland Honeyeater'. Next to this, in the bottom right corner were the initials RR. The same initials she'd seen on the paintings.

It was Scratch.

The book contained a menagerie of birds, small and big, in browns, greys and blacks from a candy-coloured dove to a crow.

Connie scanned the rows of books.

"Are they all birds?"

Evelyn moved down one line of shelves, pointing.

"No, they're split by fauna and flora and arranged alphabetically. Amphibians, Arthropods, Birds, Fish, Marsupials, and..." The silver-haired woman stopped, took out a book, opened it and handed it to Connie. "Mammals."

It was a drawing of inside the hotel, tables and chairs, mostly empty with artefacts and objects hanging from the ceiling and walls. The accuracy and details were astounding. Steaming plates of food were being served at a table of three, by a woman with dark, blonde hair.

"That's me."

Evelyn reached over her and flipped the page.

There were more of these lifelike images of Connie doing ordinary, everyday things; taking out the garbage, standing behind the bar, walking home at night from the hotel. Her skin crawled.

"He's been watching me."

"Don't feel special. You're not the only one he's been watching." Evelyn took out another brown, hand-bound volume and stood beside Connie, flipping through the pages, stopping at a full-colour sketch of a dusty streetscape lined with single-story, colonial-style buildings. At the centre of the image was a blue and white shop front with a painted sign that read 'Butchers'. On the dirt pavement at the front of the shop were two people, arm in arm, the young woman in a pleated pink dress standing on tiptoes stretching to kiss the lips of a tall bearded man in a striped apron. It was a touching image of a loving moment.

Evelyn was beaming at the drawing.

"January fourteen, nineteen fifty-five, the day after we got married."

"That's you?" Connie pointed at the young woman in the pleated dress.

"We never had a honeymoon. Eddie couldn't get away from the business. But we had a good life. We raised four children. I did my time as a nurse at the old hospital and Eddie ran the shop until the day he died." Evelyn's eyes watered with pride.

Connie would never look back on her marriage with the same warmth and love.

"May I?" said Connie, taking the book from Evelyn, pinching the page between finger and thumb, tearing it from the spine. She handed the leaf of paper to Evelyn.

"You should have it," she said.

Evelyn flashed a cunning look and took the image in her crepe skin hand.

The book revealed another drawing. A newborn had been pictured, bundled up in a sheet, her head in the crook of a woman's arm, breastfeeding.

"I know this image. That's Wes' wife and daughter."

Connie had seen the image as a photo, framed and laid out on Wes' kitchen table.

Evelyn lent in nodding with a sad smile.

"That's Jane and Kate. She was lovely. I always thought she'd run away. To think they were killed..." Evelyn shook her head, tutting.

"Do you think Wes killed them?"

"Maybe. I don't know."

Connie turned the page.

A woman was hiking through the bush, a walking stick in one hand, the other supporting a heavily pregnant belly. It was another image of Jane. She looked small, healthy and fit, the type of woman Connie would've liked as a friend.

She turned the page.

It was another image of Jane bushwalking. This time a child was strapped to her chest, and Jane was looking back, over her shoulder as if someone was following.

"Do you know what these are?" Evelyn pointed to several markings on the back of the previous drawing. There was a blue stamp indicating that the drawing was the property of the Queensland police. A red stamp showed that the drawing had been admitted to evidence. At the bottom corner were faded letters and numbers in grey, graphite.

"The police must have had an interest in the drawing."

Connie turned the page back to the drawing of Kate breastfeeding. It was an intimate moment captured by a young Scratch forty years ago.

The police stamps were on every image of Jane, and there were quite a few images, leaving Connie with the impression that the police had, at some point, taken the drawings from Scratch's collection and returned them at a later time. Connie also noticed that the alphanumeric code in graphite on the back of the drawings was not exclusive to the ones with the police stamps. Every drawing had an alphanumeric code.

"Scratch must have made these markings," she said.

In the gap between the two images of Jane bushwalking, nestled against the inside spine was the rough edge of a torn stub of paper. It wasn't from the image Connie had torn out and given to Evelyn. That was a few pages back. It was a missing page.

There was a noise in the hall. Connie closed the book. Jakes appeared in the doorway, swung himself inside the room and closed the door.

"He's here," Jakes whispered a finger to his lips.

Evelyn flicked off the light, and the room went dark. The floorboards in the hall were creaking, the sound getting louder. Connie held her breath. A shadow came over the door. She could hear laboured breathing on the other side, and the door rattled.

Connie jumped with fright.

"Who's there?" The voice in the hallway sounded weak.

Then a something hit the door, slid down the face and hit the floor. The house went silent.

Evelyn moved towards the door.

"Hello? Robert? Are you there?" There was no answer.

Evelyn pushed Jakes out of the way and pulled the door open.

On the floor in the hallway, Scratch lay unconscious, covered in blood.

CHAPTER 27

Evelyn pressed two fingers against Scratch's neck. The blood was coming from his upper arm beneath a tourniquet made from shredded cloth taken from Scratch's pants. His face was pale, and his breathing shallow. The ex-nurse removed the tourniquet from his bicep revealing a small round puncture wound.

"He's been shot. I need more room. Move him into the kitchen," said Evelyn. Jakes picked Scratch up by the ankles and dragged him down the hall, leaving a trail of blood. Evelyn followed, stepping over a bulging hessian sack. Connie picked up the sack and looked inside. It was the bones, the skulls and the gun barrel.

In the kitchen, they lay Scratch out on the linoleum floor. Connie placed the hessian sack on the table with the eviscerated fox.

"It's the bones. Scratch must have stolen them from Wes. I'm guessing Wes shot him. And Wes is going to know where to find them. We need to lock the doors."

Jakes went to the front of the house while Connie headed for the back door. As Connie reached for the laundry door, she saw the knob turning, and the door inched open. A shadow appeared through the crack.

Her stomach dropped, and she threw herself at the door, slamming it closed.

"No. Get out." She took hold of the knob, fumbling with the snib, locking the door. Beneath the rapid beat of her pulse, Connie heard the thump of running feet growing distant. She lent around the door and peered out a side window. At the back of the courtyard past the vegetable beds, Connie saw a thin, pale figure disappearing into the line of trees.

"What's going on?" Jakes appeared in the laundry, panting.

"Someone was out there. They've gone now."

"Did you see who it was?"

The height and shape of the thin, pale figure were fresh in her mind.

"I think it was Kipper," she said.

Jakes put his arms around her in a crushing embrace that seemed to pull her shaken nerves together, and she felt better. He let go, and she pulled him back, kissing him.

"We should help Evelyn," she said.

Evelyn had laid out several small surgical tools beside Scratch's unconscious body, and she'd cut off the arm of his shirt, exposing his shoulder. Beside her was a bowl of clear water and she was cleaning the wound with a fresh sponge.

"Is everything alright?" she asked without looking up.

"Yeah, we're fine," said Jakes. "The doors are locked."

Scratch looked pale.

"Is he going to be O.K.?" asked Connie.

"The bullet went straight through. There's not a lot of blood, and it doesn't look like it hit anything important. He must be in shock. Can you get me a blanket?" She directed her question at Jakes.

Jakes took off down the hall and into one of the bedrooms.

Evelyn directed Connie to a large, curved needle.

"We need to sterilise it. Heat the needle over the stove." Jakes returned with the blanket and covered Scratch up to his wounded arm. Connie ran the needle through a gas flame and handed the needle back to Evelyn, who threaded the needle with a fine string. The ex-nurse put the needle to the wound, piercing the flesh and drawing through the thread. Connie's stomach turned, and she looked away, focusing her attention on the bulging, brown hessian sack.

From the time the bones turned up at the hotel, Scratch had wanted them. Scratch moaned, his eyes opened, and he cried out in pain, his arms thrashing the air, the needle and thread dangling from his skin, the wound spilling blood.

Jakes rushed in and held Scratch down.

"Relax. We're looking after you. Evelyn is going to stitch you up."

Scratch looked around the room, searching every face before he calmed and lay back, pale and exhausted.

Connie came forward.

"Who shot you?"

"Wes." Scratch turned his head sideways to look at the hole.

"Do you think you can get into a chair?" said Evelyn.

"I'm not sitting on the floor to do this if I don't have to."

They put Scratch into a chair at the dining table and a chair beside him where Evelyn sat.

"This is going to hurt."

But, Scratch barely flinched as the needle pierced his skin.

"Someone followed me back here, through the bush," he said through clenched teeth.

"Kipper. He tried to come in through the back door," said Connie. "Why would Kipper follow you back here?"

Scratch shook his head, jaw clenched.

"What were you doing in my drawing-room?" said Scratch, locking his eyes on Connie.

"You've got an amazing talent, Robert," said Evelyn, pulling through the thread, pulling the skin around the wound together. "You shouldn't keep it hidden."

"I'll do what I want with it. How'd you find the key?"

"Keep still. And stop complaining. You're lucky to be alive," said Evelyn. "A little closer to your chest and you'd be lying in the coolroom with those two boys."

"You found another?" said Scratch. He didn't seem shocked or surprised.

"Did you shoot those boys?" said Connie. Scratch glanced, and gritted his teeth and kept his thoughts to himself.

"I saw you at the creek," she pressed the old man. "You were hiding at the exact place where the boys were shot."

"And if you hadn't turned up, I would've had the skulls sooner, and maybe I wouldn't be sitting here with a hole in my arm."

"What about the boys? What happened to them?"

Scratch looked between Connie and Jakes.

"It's not my fault. Wes wasn't keeping those skulls, and

I couldn't do it on my own. I was going to pay those boys to take the skulls. I never thought he'd shoot them."

"Wes shot them?"

Scratch nodded.

"Shot them and dumped them in the flood."

Connie registered shock. She'd known Wes for years and trusted him, and he was a killer. Maybe he'd killed his wife and daughter too.

"How?"

"When the bones went missing from the bar, I knew he'd stolen them somehow. I went to his farm and watched him take the rucksack with the bones and some other things out of his car and hide them in his workshop. I couldn't go in there and take them. Not with his dogs chained up outside. So I went back to the campground, got those boys out of their tents. I told them what I wanted and offered to pay them. They didn't have to do it. I drove them down to the creek and told them what to do, and off they went while I stayed by the fence and watched. They were in an out pretty quick, and they had the bones, but the dogs were barking, and Wes came out of the house and caught one of them running off. Well, he set his dogs onto them and followed in his car. The dogs caught the boys at the creek. The four of them hid in that group of trees. I was further down the fence, and I saw what happened. Wes turned up with his headlights on, and he had a gun. He threatened to shoot them if they didn't give him the skulls. Wes wasn't kidding. He fired on them and kept firing until he was out of bullets. The boys didn't have a chance. Then he took the skulls back and threw the bodies of the four boys into the creek."

Connie looked a Scratch trying to see into his soul. He didn't appear to be lying. If she was going to believe him, everything she knew about Wes had to make sense.

"What about the dog? Did you see him bury it?" said Connie.

"You know about the dog?" asked Scratch.

"Jakes found the grave," said Connie looking around for Jakes. But, Jakes was gone. She peered down the hall and saw him disappearing into one of the rooms. Connie turned back to Scratch. "Do you know how his dog died?"

"That was the boys. That's how the shooting started."

Connie's brow creased with confusion.

"The boys shot his dog?"

Scratch wincing as Evelyn drew another suture through his skin.

"Wes sent his dogs in to flush out the boys. I'm not sure which one of them fired the gun, I couldn't see, but the boys fired first. It was horrible. I kill animals all the time, but I hate to see them in pain. When they shot, the thing didn't die right away. It was howling. The noise was horrible."

Connie imagined the scene, thinking what it would have been like from Wes' vantage point from behind the headlights, the rain streaming down. She could see the stand of trees, heard the sound of a single gunshot, and saw the old cattle dog jerked back by the bullet, yelping and pawing at the air, howling. The shock he would have felt was real. So too was the rage and Connie lifted the rifle, took aim at the trees and pulled the trigger.

"Done." Evelyn sat back and admired two lines of stitches – the entry and exit wounds, on Scratch's arm. Jakes was still missing.

"Jakes?" Connie called into the hall.

"Just a minute."

Evelyn took a bandage and began wrapping Scratch's arm.

Wes had lied about shooting the boys. He'd told her

he'd heard the gunshots but didn't see anyone down at the creek. The lie wasn't surprising. She couldn't expect him to admit to murder. And, he'd also told her he was using the bones to catch the killer. Perhaps that too was a lie. Maybe he was trying to throw her off the trail to hide the fact that he'd killed his wife and daughter. But, if Wes was trying to cover up their murder, he should've done a better job at hiding the bones. Or even better, he should've destroyed the bones. A sledgehammer would do it. Instead, he was keeping the skulls close enough to catch and shoot a thief. Scratch had been caught in the trap. He'd taken the hessian sack and got away with it. Maybe the trap was for Scratch and Scratch was the killer. And there were the drawings from the locked room that didn't reflect well on Scratch; drawings of Jane walking in the bush, pregnant, breastfeeding Kate, Jane holding her baby. Scratch had been interested enough to draw her. In some of those pictures, she was sure he'd been there, with her in the bush, watching. The police had looked into it. They'd taken the drawings from him as evidence, and Scratch must have been a suspect in their disappearance.

"I asked you about the gunshots yesterday, and you told me you didn't hear anything. Why'd you lie?" asked Connie.

"Hey, I didn't kill them. Wes did that. I just asked them to do a job. They took the gun. They shot his dog. I didn't do anything wrong, and I don't want anything to do with it."

Scratch was trying to separate himself from the shooting and disown himself from the whole incident, but he knew he was one who instigated the entire thing. He didn't want to take responsibility for it.

Evelyn had finished with the bandage and stood up.

"You should rest. Keep an eye out for any sign of

infection."

Footsteps approached from the hallway and Jakes appeared a brown, hand-bound book in his hand. He held the pages open, showing Scratch an image of Connie and John on the couch at home, watching television.

"How did you draw this?" asked Jakes. There was a harsh edge in his voice.

Scratch's eyes dropped again.

"You drew this from a photo, didn't you?" Jakes' eyes bored into Scratch.

Scratch touched the bandage on his arm and checked his range of movement, wincing and cradling his arm.

Jakes got in his face.

"Who gave you the photo?" said Jakes.

Scratch eyeballed Jakes, shifting in his seat.

"I've seen the photo. Tell me, who gave it to you?"

Scratch sniffed and lifted his head.

"I got it from Kipper."

CHAPTER 28

"The police said Kipper was involved with someone else. It was you," said Jakes pointing the finger at Scratch. "You're working with him. You've been creeping around, looking through windows, haven't you?"

"No." Scratch sat in the chair in the kitchen, a fresh bandage on his arm, staring back at Jakes with hurt in his eyes.

"Did you go to Josie's place? Were you there when Kipper attacked her?"

"I don't have anything to do with him anymore," said Scratch.

"How did you get the photo?"

"He gave me the photo," said Scratch.

Kipper had given Scratch a photo of Connie and John on the couch watching TV. That meant Kipper had been watching her through the window of their living room.

Connie felt uneasy knowing she was being watched, photographed and traded.

"That's perverted, Scratch," said Connie. "Why'd you take the photo from him?" asked Connie.

"I didn't take it. Kipper gave it to me. I'm not like him," said Scratch.

"And what's he like?" asked Jakes.

"He's a peeping Tom." Scratch's eyes darted around the room.

"Why didn't you say something to the police if you knew he was a peeping Tom?"

"Kipper threatened me. Said if I told anyone he'd tell them I was in on it. I wasn't."

"I'm not convinced."

"Look at me. I'm old. I can't get around like I used to."

"You just walked from Wes' place to here through the bush bleeding from a bullet wound," said Connie.

"So you're saying you used to be a peeping Tom?" said Jakes.

They were closing in on Scratch, threatening.

"No, it's different. I do it for the drawing. It's capturing people when they don't know anyone is watching. It's the same with animals, birds and the like. If no one is there, you see them for what they are. I saw Kipper for what he was. I just saw it too late. The first photos he'd bring me were pretty ordinary. I'd paint them, and that was it. Then the photos became more graphic. He showed me photos of women in their bedrooms, half-naked. I told him I couldn't do it anymore. I said he should stop. I threatened to call the police. He said if I did, he'd tell them I paid him to take the photos."

"Do you still have this photo?" asked Jakes, holding up the book with the drawing.

Scratch got up from the chair and stumbled.

Jakes caught him.

"Take it easy," said Evelyn.

Scratch regained his feet and led Jakes down the hall into the cluttered living room. They wove their way through the stacks of magazines and newspapers to the filing cabinets lined up at the back of the room. Scratch picked up a mounted snake, put it to one side, extracted a red account keeping book from a stack of red books and opened the pages. Inside were lines in tight rows and columns filled with entries in blue and black pen. He ran his finger down the page and stopped at a row then snapped the book closed. Replacing the book and the dead snake on top of the metal cabinet Scratch reached between the cabinets and felt about, coming out with a set of keys. He selected one of the cabinets and opened a drawer, sifting through the hanging files and lifting out a manila folder. With the buff coloured folder in hand, Scratch shuffled to the couch, sat down and opened the folder on the coffee table. Inside were several leaves of loose paper and a small rectangular photo that he handed to Jakes.

The photo was a darker, grittier version of the drawing. A film of dirt on the window filtered the view of the living room. The view inside was further obscured by the reflection of a ghost-like image. Jakes brought the photo closer. Connie lent in. She made out the dark circle of a camera lens and behind it, a pale, ghostly face.

"Kipper," said Jakes, his voice exploding. "We've got him. This is the evidence we need. This photo is going to put him in gaol."

Connie was still looking into the photo, past the ghostly reflection into the darkness beyond.

"Was there anyone else working with Kipper?" she asked Scratch.

"He never mentioned anyone else," said Scratch.

"I need you to talk to the police about this," said Jakes. "You need to make a statement about Kipper and what happened."

"As long as it doesn't come back on me. I didn't do anything wrong. I didn't take the photo. I just drew it."

"It won't come back on you," promised Jakes.

Connie turned to Jakes.

"Wes is going to come for the skulls," she said.

"He's not taking them back," said Scratch.

"He's killed those boys, and he's already tried to kill Scratch. If Scratch tries to stop him from taking the skulls, Wes will kill him, and you'll lose your witness." She could see Jakes thinking, his eyes darting between the photograph in his hand, Scratch and the front door.

"We need to keep Wes away from here," said Connie.

"The easiest thing to do would be to give him back the bones," said Jakes.

"You do that, and I'll go straight back there to get them," said Scratch, closing the filing cabinet and replacing the keys.

Connie frowned.

"I know you want to protect Scratch, but the bones don't belong with Wes. What if Wes killed his wife and daughter. He could cover up their murder. The bones need to go to the police."

Scratch pushed past her waddling through the stacks of newspapers towards the corridor.

"What do you want to do?" asked Connie.

"I think we should take the bones back to Wes. At least then we won't end up with another dead body in the hotel."

Scratch left the room and took off down the hallway.

"Where's he going?" said Connie.

"The bones," said Jakes, running after Scratch.

They caught up with him in the kitchen, clutching the brown sack in his arms.

"You're not taking them," he said.

"It's for your own good," Jakes said. "Wes is going to come after you."

"There's a mother and a child in here who also need protection. Wes is a murderer. He's not getting these bones."

Jakes lunged for the hessian sack. Scratch pulled away, and a scalpel appeared in his good hand, pointing the sharp instrument at Jakes.

"I can take care of myself," said Scratch, his eyes narrowing. "Get out."

Connie put a hand on Jakes' arm. Scratch had taken a bullet to get the bones. He wasn't about to let Jakes take them without a fight.

"Maybe there's another way."

*****

Evelyn was in the back seat of the Pajero with Connie at the wheel and Jakes beside her.

"I'll talk to Wes," she said. "Maybe I can convince him to leave Scratch alone."

"I'm not sure this plan of dropping in for a chat is a good idea," said Jakes. "He just shot Scratch, and he killed those four boys."

"Those boys shot his dog and think about the boar he shot. He killed it with a bullet through the eye. If he wanted Scratch dead, he would have shot him proper. And I don't think he killed his family. I know Wes, he'll talk to me. Maybe we can work something out."

"If you're going to the farm, I can't go with you. John's there."

Jakes was right. If she had a choice, she'd take him with her. But she couldn't. John and Jakes were like oily water on a flame.

"I'll drop you off at the hotel," she said, pulling up in the front car park.

Evelyn opened the door to get out and stopped.

"Um, I think we've got a problem," said Evelyn,

pointing down the length of the dirt road. A tail of mud shot up from the back of a white, rusty Landcruiser as it sped towards them. On its approach to the hotel, the four-wheel drive didn't slow and passed them at speed, Wes behind the wheel, firing off a look of warning as he flashed by.

Connie swore, putting the Pajero in reverse, pulling out and finding first gear, spinning the wheels and went after Wes.

"When we get there, don't go rushing in. He's probably got a gun," said Jakes.

They returned along the muddy road turning in to Scratch's driveway through the galvanised gates, to the old weatherboard house. The yellow Volvo was there and so too was Wes' Landcruiser, the door open, keys swinging in the ignition.

Jakes threw open his door and ran for the house, ignoring the advice he'd given her, not to rush in.

"Jakes!" Connie called after him.

Jakes made it to the front porch, pulled open the door and went inside. Connie pushed her door open then paused to look back at Evelyn.

"I'll wait here," Evelyn said.

Connie hurried to the house, her feet slapping on the hard dirt path up onto the front porch, stopping at the open door. She could hear voices, shouting and entered. The hallway was clear, the voices were coming from the kitchen, and Connie walked quickly down the corridor, picking up on the smell of fresh toast.

"Where are they? Where are the bones?" Scratch lay on the laminate floor on his back, eyes wide with fear staring up at Wes, the farmer standing over him, a rifle in his hand, yelling. The state of the kitchen had changed in the short time they were gone. The table had been swept clear, a wet, stinking pile of broken glass, sharp tools and the dead fox lay in a heap on the floor, the clutter replaced with two plates, one with crumbs, the other with a piece of half-eaten toast. One of the chairs had tipped over.

Wes was still shouting for the bones. Jakes knelt and placed a hand on Scratch's chest.

"Scratch, can you talk?"

There was no response. "Somethings wrong. He's awake and breathing, but I don't think he can move."

A gurgling sound came from Scratch's mouth. His hair and clothes were a mess, and the bandage on his arm was loose and spotted with blood.

"What have you done, Wes?"

Wes turned on her, his eyes ablaze.

"I shot him. He's lucky to be alive." Wes turned on Scratch, shouting, "Where are they? Where are the bones?"

The bones.

Connie scanned the pile of mess on the floor, looking for a brown hessian sack. It didn't appear to be there. "I don't see them. They were here before, on the table."

"Look at his bandage." said Jakes, facing Wes. "Did you do that?"

The fresh bandage Evelyn had wrapped around Scratch's arm was damaged and bloody.

"Yes, I shot him in the arm."

"No, did you mess up the bandage?"

"No, I found him like this on the floor," said Wes.

"Did you make this mess?" asked Connie.

"No."

Connie looked at Jakes.

"Someone else was here."

Jakes shook Scratch.

"Scratch, can you talk?"

There was no response.

Whatever had happened to Scratch had happened fast. In the time it took them to drive to the hotel and back there'd been a fight and Scratch had been laid out on the floor, his bandage messed up. And they'd had time to make toast. There were two plates on the table - one for Scratch, one for the thief. When they were here last, she'd stopped an intruder at the back door. That same person had followed Scratch back to the house and would've got in if she wasn't here. Connie went through to the laundry and found the back door wide open. Outside, the garden was quiet. She pulled the door closed and locked it.

"Someone was here," she said back in the kitchen. "See the two plates? Wes must've scared them off. They left through the laundry."

"Evelyn. She's in the car," said Jakes. "I'll get her."

Jakes got up from the linoleum floor, disappearing down the hall.

"Lock the door when you come back," said Connie, taking Jakes' place beside Scratch. The old man's breathing was shallow. A sheen of sweat covered his skin, and he was pale.

"Scratch. Can you hear me? Can you talk?"

Desperate eyes locked on hers but he said nothing. Except for those eyes, Scratch was unresponsive. He couldn't move his arms, legs or head.

Behind her, a cupboard door slammed, and she jumped. Wes was going through the cabinets.

"What are you doing?" she said.

"Looking for the bones."

"I don't think they're here. I think whoever did this stole bones. Look." Connie pointed at the kitchen table. "Two plates. Two people. The chair, the mess on the floor and his bandage. Someone's been here, and the bones are missing."

There were hurried footsteps down the hall, and Evelyn appeared. She saw the mess on the floor.

"Oh."

"Something is wrong with Scratch."

"Oh." Evelyn knelt beside Connie and addressed the weeping bandage with a frown, unwinding the cloth from his arm. "The stitches are broken," said Evelyn. "That would have been painful." The ex-nurse continued to examine Scratch, pulling back his eyelids, looking over his skin and opening his mouth, making a concerned noise.

"I don't know. It's like he's had a stroke. Or he's taken poison."

Connie got up from the floor, went to the table, picking up the leftover piece of toast and put it to her nose. The grey-green paste smelt like peanut butter and honey.

"It's poison," said Connie. "Scratch has been poisoned."

CHAPTER 29

"What type of poison?" Evelyn asked.

Connie had an idea of what it would be. Looking through the clutter on the kitchen floor, she couldn't see the jar of green goo.

"It's homemade. Scratch makes his own."

Evelyn rolled Scratch onto his side, tilted his head back, opened his mouth and put her fingers down his throat.

Nothing happened.

"His gag reflex isn't working. I need warm water, a jug with a spout, a funnel, mustard, salt and eggs." She barked the orders at Wes, who was still searching the kitchen cupboards. Connie went to the pantry and found powdered mustard, eggs and salt. Wes found a jug and they mixed everything together producing a lukewarm, off-yellow, pungent-smelling liquid.

Evelyn took the jug and pulled Connie to the floor.

She told Jakes to sit him up then they propped Scratch against Connie, his back to her chest and she held him there limp and heavy.

"Hold him up." Evelyn stuck her fingers between his teeth and prised his jaw open, placing the funnel in his mouth. She gave the jug to Jakes.

"Pour it in. Do it slowly. Wait until he exhales."

Jakes positioned the jug at the funnel. The smell of the yellow liquid wafted into Connie's face stinging her nose. Evelyn gave the command to pour. Jakes splashed the yellow liquid into the funnel and Scratch began to gurgle.

"He's not swallowing," said Jakes.

Evelyn stopped him, pushing the jug away, removing the funnel and turned Scratch's head to one side. The yellow liquid dribbled onto Connie's legs, warm and wet.

"This poison is strange. Scratch is awake. His eyes are open, but his body isn't responsive. He's paralysed. And it must be strong," said Evelyn, her voice wavering, worried. "Let's try again."

Jakes repositioned Scratch against Connie, and she placed one hand on Scratch's forehead, holding his head back against her shoulder, his mouth hinged open. With his face next to hers they were eye to eye, his pupils large, alert and full of fear.

"Come on Scratch," she whispered into his ear. "You've got to drink this stuff. I know it doesn't taste nice, but you've got to swallow. Try and swallow."

Jakes placed the funnel into Scratch's open mouth holding the jug in position.

Scratch took a rattling breath in. His chest rose to a peak, and Evelyn gave the command to pour. Jakes filled the funnel and kept filling until a trail of yellow liquid ran down Scratch's cheek and neck.

"That's enough," said Connie.

But Jakes had other ideas. He discarded the funnel, thrust the jug at Evelyn and clapped a hand over Scratch's mouth, pinching his nose.

"Stop. What are you doing?" said Evelyn.

Jakes shot Evelyn a hard stare.

"It's not coming out this time."

"You'll kill him." Evelyn yanked at Jakes' arm. Jakes had clamped hard onto Scratch's head and wasn't letting go.

"This is the only way. If he doesn't drink this, he's going to die." Jakes said, the muscles in his arms tense. He was right.

Evelyn dropped her arm, letting Jakes alone, and a deathly silence crept into the room.

Jakes stared into Scratch's face.

"Swallow. Come on."

Connie put her arms around Scratch, willing him to swallow. But, nothing happened, and his face turned crimson. The stinking yellow liquid seeped from his nose, staining Jakes' fingers.

There was a deep gurgling noise.

Connie felt hope rise and looked at Evelyn for confirmation.

"Did he swallow?"

Evelyn's eyes remained low.

"No, it's going into his lungs."

Scratch was drowning. Connie felt her throat constrict.

"Jakes' stop," she said. "You're killing him."

"No." Evelyn placed her hand over Jakes' hand, covering Scratch's mouth.

"He's right. If the poison doesn't come out, he'll die."

All three of them held Scratch in position with Wes watching, from the kitchen sink. Scratch's face turned purple. His pupils began to shrink, and a few seconds later, he passed out. Connie felt it happen. His muscles lost all tension, and his body went slack. A dark patch appeared in his crotch. He'd wet himself.

Evelyn removed her hand.

"That's enough."

Jakes' relaxed his grip and peeled his hand away from Scratch's mouth. As he did this, they heard a sucking noise followed by a wet gulp. The lump in Scratch's throat dipped.

"He swallowed," said Evelyn, surprised.

Jakes looked into his open mouth.

"It's gone. There's no liquid."

"Put him on his side," Evelyn said.

They lay Scratch back on the floor. Connie's heart was racing. Nothing was happening. She looked to Evelyn for direction.

"Put your fingers down his throat."

Connie pulled Scratch's jaw open, took two fingers and pressed them past his teeth, into his soft pallet and down his throat. His body jerked, and a gush of warm liquid hit her hand, splashed up her arm and projected out onto the linoleum floor in a lumpy stream of yellow-green.

"Yes." Jakes was jubilant.

Connie shook her hand, flicking off a string of goo and bits of bread.

"We're not out of the woods yet. He's not breathing," said Evelyn slapping Scratch hard on the back. The slapping produced another flush of bright yellow fluid. Evelyn called for a cloth. Wes threw her a tea towel, and the old woman wiped at the mess on Scratch's face, took a breath and put her lips to his blowing, putting breath in his body. His cheeks expanded, his chest rose and fell. Evelyn repeated the action, cycling oxygen from her body into his. Scratch convulsed. He drew a wet, sucking breath—a sign of life.

"Put him on his side." Evelyn wiped her mouth.

They flipped Scratch to his side. He convulsed then vomited. His eyes fluttered opened, spinning around the room, semi-conscious then rolled up into his head, and he passed out, unconscious, breathing. Scratch was alive.

CHAPTER 30

Connie washed the poison from her arms in the kitchen sink with Evelyn beside her cleaning her lips and rinsing her mouth. Jakes was in a pair of rubber gloves cleaning the vomit from the linoleum floor while Wes sat at the table. He looked tired and troubled and watched over Scratch with concern. He didn't look like a man who'd killed four boys.

"Is he going to be alright?" asked Wes.

Scratch's colour had returned to a whiter shade of pale.

"We'll have to keep a close watch on him. The poison is still in his system," said Evelyn.

"I need those bones back. Why would anyone want to take them?" said Wes.

"Maybe there's someone else out there who thinks you shouldn't have the bones. Maybe there's someone out there who thinks you killed your wife and child," said Connie, a note of bitterness in her voice.

The rifle Wes had brought into the house was leaning up against the wall by the hall.

"Is that the gun you used to shoot those boys?" said Connie.

Wes' head shot up, and his eyes narrowed. A growl formed in his throat, but there were no words.

"Scratch told us what happened. He was there when you shot them. He saw you dump their bodies in the creek."

Jakes moved gave Connie a look of caution and positioned himself between Wes and the rifle.

Wes' old face turned hard.

"Of course, he was there. He was trying to take the skulls. Did he tell you they shot my fucking dog! They took my family, broke into my shed and stole my gun. They used my gun to shoot my fucking dog!" Wes was shaking with rage. "And I'll go to gaol for it. I don't care. But I'll be damned if they put me away before I find the arsehole that killed my wife and daughter." Wes paused, looked down at Scratch and took a shaky breath. "I need those bones."

Connie considered Wes trying to decide if he was talking shit, trying to determine if he'd killed his own family or if he was telling the truth and there really was a killer, unknown.

Scratch made a deep, wet, sucking sound.

"Do you think Scratch had anything to do with the murder of your wife and daughter?" asked Connie.

"The police questioned him. They searched his house. But they did the same to me. I don't know. They never laid charges. Not on me and not on him.

"How old was Scratch when they disappeared?"

"About twelve. Old enough to pull a trigger," said Wes. "But, getting their bodies into Black Mountain. That's hard. Harder for a twelve-year-old to lift a fully grown female," said Wes.

"You said whoever did this to your family would come for the bones. When Scratch sent the boys to steal the bones from your workshop, he stayed behind in the bush. Let's say you didn't catch the boys and Scratch got the bones back then Scratch kills the boys himself. No one would know who had the bones. Scratch comes back home, destroys the bones. Without the bones, you're back to where you were a few days ago; no evidence, nothing to test. You'd never find out who killed them. Maybe that's what Scratch was trying to do."

"And, he was hanging around your wife before she disappeared," said Evelyn, drying her hands. "I've seen the drawings."

Wes frowned.

"What drawings?"

*****

Evelyn lay into Wes' hands a brown, hand-bound book open on the drawing that mirrored the black and white photo of his wife and daughter breastfeeding. But, Wes didn't seem surprised to see the drawing.

"Scratch's mother took this photo. She took a lot of photos. She probably gave it to Scratch to draw. His parents were good friends of ours until the accident."

"What happened to them?"

"Their car went off the road at Rifle Creek Ridge. They died instantly. Scratch was at home with his grandmother. Jane had to give them the news."

Connie flipped the pages showing Wes the drawing of

Jane walking in the bush, a baby-sized bundle strapped to her chest. Her head turned back, looking over her shoulder, her face hidden by her long, dark hair.

"Have you seen this one?"

"Yes, the police showed them to me during the investigation. Did Scratch draw this?" asked Wes.

Connie pointed at the initials.

"Robert Ryer," said Wes. "I didn't know he drew this. I thought they were some sort of police sketch. Did he draw this from a photo?"

"I think he was there," said Connie.

"This was the day she went missing. See what she's wearing? And look close." Wes pointed at Jane's waist. Hidden by her body was a long stick."

"A walking stick?"

"A rifle," said Wes. "She never went walking with a gun. There was no need. She took the rifle because she knew she was in danger. And see the way her head is turned? Someone was following her. That's why the police thought it was a murder; only they couldn't find their bodies."

"Where were you that day?" asked Connie.

"I was at a cattle auction in Mareeba." Wes scowled at her. "I had several witnesses. If Scratch was there and saw this, that means he was the last person to see Jane and Kate alive."

Connie stared at the picture. It was eerie knowing this was the last time they'd been seen alive. She could make out the shape of Kate's head resting on her mother's breast. If she had been shot where she stood, there was every possibility that the bullet went through Kate's skull and into Jane's heart. One bullet. Two lives.

Wes lifted the book to his eye then ran his fingers down the spine.

"There's a page missing," said Wes. It was the same stub of torn paper Connie had seen with Evelyn. Wes flipped back and forward through the pages. As he flipped, Connie watched the alphanumeric code on the back of each page change. She remembered Scratch taking one of the drawings to the filing cabinet and finding the corresponding photograph.

"I think I might be able to find that picture." Connie took the book from Wes, flipping back a few pages, pointing at the alphanumeric code, reading it aloud. The next page had a similar code, with only one digit higher than the last. The numbers changed in the same increments as she flipped forward. When she reached the torn stub, the alphanumeric code skipped a digit.

"We're looking for E, three, twenty-seven," she said, putting down the book and leading the way to the metal filing cabinets in the living room. Her stomach growled. She was hungry. Starving. The others back at the hotel would be hungry too, and they still hadn't picked any vegetables from the garden. Connie put her hunger out of her mind and focused on the cabinets.

Each cabinet had letters and numbers but nothing that matched up with the alphanumeric code for the drawing. Then she remembered the stack of red books under the dead snake. It was the first place Scratch had gone to find the photo of Kipper's reflection.

Moving the dead snake aside with a shiver, Connie chose the first red book from a stack of red books. It was in a relatively new condition compared to some of the older books that were falling apart. Inside were pre-ruled lines filled with small, handwritten entries. The first column showed a list of alphanumeric numbers similar to one she'd seen on the drawings.

"This is it," she said, running her finger down the list.

But, none of the codes seemed to match the one from the missing drawing. The reference numbers were, however, similar in structure. Like the codes on the back of the drawings, all the codes in the book started with a letter, followed by two numbers. In the adjacent column to the alphanumeric numbers was a list of locations.

"What if we try and find something in the book, just to test the system?" she said.

Jakes leant into her and pointed at the last entry on the open page.

"How about this one?"

The description for the entry was 'Trifolium repens in situ'.

"What is that?" he asked.

"No idea, but the date shows the entry was made only a few days ago. It should be easy to find."

Connie read out the alphanumeric code and Jakes, Evelyn and Wes began searching the crammed living room for matching letters and numbers.

Jakes was the first to find it.

He held up a magazine.

"What's a fight-ol-ogist?" he said.

The glossy cover of the 'New Phytologist' showed a hand-drawn, colour image of a pink, star-shaped flower. The drawing style looked familiar. She took the magazine and opened it to the inside cover. At the bottom of the page, she found the title 'Trifolium repens in situ' and the name of the cover artist. Robert Ryer.

"Shit. Scratch drew this," she said, admiring the cover. Suddenly, the stacks of magazines and papers made sense. "This is all Scratch's work," she said her arms out, circling the room.

"So, that's how he makes his money," said Evelyn.

"Alright," said Wes with a growl. "What about the

missing drawing,"

The entry for the missing drawing didn't belong in the red book in her hand. The dates were too recent while the drawings were much older, so Connie swapped the red book for an older, faded and batted version with dog-eared, yellow and lose pages. Despite the difference of decades, the book had the same pre-ruled lines and small handwriting.

Connie ran her finger down the column of alphanumeric numbers, looking for a match and found it.

"E, three, twenty-seven. Got it."

"What's the location?" asked Jakes.

The location code had been struck out and replaced with another line that had also been struck out.

"Hang on." Connie focused her eyes on the small, writing. 'C'twn Pol St'. But, all these markings left no room for a current location, and she followed the line to the end where a small mark had been made in black pen. "Try M, three, twenty-five, C," she said.

"Does it tell you what we're looking for?" asked Evelyn, searching the room.

Connie read the description aloud.

"Bodies. Crossing over." she said. The search in the living room paused, and they all looked to her. Connie felt a chill and looked again at the entry. Next to the description was a single word in small capital letters—'COPY'.

The search led Jakes to a grey filing cabinet. It was locked. Connie did as Scratch had done and reached between the cabinets, felt a hook with the keys that opened the cabinet. Jakes sifted through the hanging files, checking the labels, picking out papers and putting them back, eventually producing an old manila folder.

He opened it. The file was empty.

Connie gave a disappointed sigh. Her stomach ached with hunger.

"This is a waste of time. I need to get back to the hotel with food for everyone."

Evelyn volunteered to help pick the vegetables and told them she'd stay with Scratch to make sure he recovered.

"I'm staying too," said Wes. "I want to be here when he wakes up."

"You two get started in the garden. I'll put everything back in its place," said Jakes.

As Evelyn and Wes left the living room, Connie followed, but Jakes grabbed her arm and pulled her back, one finger to his lips, indicating for silence. He waited until Wes and Evelyn were out the back door.

"The file wasn't empty," he said, producing a single sheet of paper.

Police stamps blotted out a blurred black and white image, a photocopy of the original drawing, and a bad copy at that. The quality was so poor it was difficult to make out any defining features in the dim light.

"What is it?" she asked.

Jakes shook his head.

"I don't know."

CHAPTER 31

By the time Connie had eaten, it was dark outside, her feet hurt from standing and her body felt heavy with sleep. Half of the people had already gone to bed, and the other half hung around, bored and talking, biding their time with nothing else to do. There was speculation that tomorrow the creek would be low enough to cross for those with the right vehicle and everyone believed it because they wanted to believe it. It gave them hope. They'd spent the past two days cooped up at the hotel, sleeping on couches and floors, wearing the same clothes. Talk of a creek crossing tomorrow had injected anxious anticipation into the small crowd.

Jakes was seated across from her at the table by the

window in the bar. He was showing Josie and Quicks the photograph of Kipper in the reflection of her living room window. The three of them shared a vindictive joy. When the flood subsided, the three of them weren't planning on going home. They would take the photo straight to the Police Sergeant, Andy Cross and get Kipper arrested. He would be taken off the streets, put on trial and sent to gaol.

Connie didn't share in any of the excitement. The thought of everyone leaving Rossville made her nervous. Without all these people around her, Connie would be left with John to face her messed up marriage. John would want to come home, and Connie couldn't put him off forever. She didn't want him in the house. She couldn't sleep beside him. It wouldn't be right. Her only option would be to leave, and when she did leave, she would be going with very little and would have to start again. It was a crushing thought. Worse still, she'd be leaving Karla behind when Karla was pregnant and needed Connie the most. The timing of it all was terrible.

There was a part of her that wanted to stay. Connie wanted to keep Karla and the hotel. She'd raised Karla from a little girl, and she'd built the business to where it was today. Connie had worked the floor, the bar, the kitchen and maintained the gardens. She washed the linen, served locals and managed the staff. She'd given her breath, body, and life to the hotel and the hotel was part of her; an extension of her body, her protective shell. Without it, she was incomplete and unprotected. If she left, she would be exposing herself to a mountain of dangers and uncertainty.

There had to be a better way. She needed to take with her a form of protection. She needed money, lots of money and the only way she would get that was to take her share of the hotel.

And she could do it.

At the creek today, John had promised to give Connie her share of the business. It was a big carrot to dangle. Maybe he knew she wanted to leave and perhaps he was doing it to keep her, and it might work until pen touched paper. When John signed over her half of the business, Connie would begin the big finale. It was a fantasy she'd dreamed of many times over. Connie would be in the hall, bags packed, and John would enter. He'd look at her confused. She'd tell him she was leaving, see the shock on his face and know that John had finally realised he'd fucked up.

However it ended, Connie still had to play John and make him think that there was a chance this would all work out. She'd have to live a lie.

It wouldn't be too hard to fool John. He was a mess. At the same time, she didn't want to drag it out, for John's sake. She didn't want to cause more pain than necessary. And, for her sake, she had to be smart and tough and couldn't let John drag it out, either. Being entangled with John for any length of time would threaten her chance at a relationship with Jakes, and the longer this went on, the more chance there was that John would get the upper hand. He'd probably use the signed papers to negotiate his place back in the bed beside her. That couldn't happen. Even if they didn't have sex, which they wouldn't, sleeping in the same bed as John didn't sit well with her, and it wouldn't sit well with Jakes.

The ending had to be quick. Connie just needed John to sign the papers. That would take half an hour of administration and a trip into the post office on Charlotte St to see that the paperwork got posted this time. Then a short wait of a few weeks for confirmation that she was the owner. She could get away for two weeks to avoid

John and even use the time to take Karla to the family clinic in Cairns for the termination. Then Connie could leave, for good, and she wouldn't have to start from broke. She could take John to court and get half of what she'd earned.

That's how it had to be. Connie had to sell John the lie. She'd tell him to stay at the farm with Wes, and he could only come home when he made her an owner. But with the paperwork done, John could come home, and Connie would be gone. The next time he'd hear from her, would be through her lawyer. Until then, Jakes would have to stay away. She'd explain it to him. She was sure he'd understand.

Jakes was looking at her from across the table, saying her name. He touched her arm, gently bringing her back to the conversation. It was a public gesture of affection, and it was dangerous. It would only spark rumours. Connie pulled away.

Jakes didn't seem to mind.

"Show them the drawing," said Jakes, waving at her pocket beneath the table.   Connie produced the photocopied image Jakes had found in Scratch's house and placed it on the table.

"What is it?" said Josie.

Connie had already gone over the image with Jakes when they'd returned to the hotel. The paper was a blotted image, a bad copy of another sketch by Scratch. They'd identify some of the lines and shading. The darker tone of the drawing indicated that it was dusk or dawn. There were shadowy trunks, limbs and branches in a semi-dark landscape. In the background was a dark mass.

"That's Black Mountain," said Connie, pointing. In the mid-ground was a white line snaking across the page from left to right. "And that's Mungumby Creek in the dry. You can see the pebbles on the creek-bed," she said. In the foreground were the sketchy outlines of shrubs and tufts of grass and standing among the grasses was a strange shape. It had a soft curve at the top with three or four limbs of varying thickness trailing down.

Quicks pointed at the strange, alien shape.

"What's that?"

Josie tilted her head, squinting at the image.

"It looks like a giant jellyfish," she said with a snort.

A plate of food fell slid onto the table, and Sherbet Ray fell into a seat with a sigh of exhaustion.

"Do I get paid for working the last few days?" he said to Connie.

"No, you're doing it out of the goodness of your heart," said Connie.

Sherbet Ray grumbled, unfolded a parcel of steamed veg wrapped in baking paper and tossed the paper onto the table.

"What are you looking at?"

"Scratch drew it. We think it's got something to do with the murder of Wes' family," said Connie.

"It looks like an inkblot test," said the Cook, stuffing his mouth with a fork full of greens.

"What's an inkblot test?" asked Josie.

The Cook swallowed.

"It's a test to see if you think like normal people or if you're a sad, emo, serial killer type."

"How does it work?" said Josie.

"You put ink on a piece of paper and fold it in half. Normal people see a tree, or a house or a man."

Connie pointed at the strange shape in the centre of the drawing.

"Alright, Doctor, what do you think that is?"

"My professional opinion; it's not a house, which

makes it either a tree or a man," he said with inflated confidence and a slather of jest.

Connie turned the image around and stared at the alien shape. In the centre of the table, the baking paper Sherbet Ray had used to steam his veg crinkled and opened like a flower, falling over the photocopied drawing. It gave Connie an idea. She got up and went to the bar. Taking a pencil from beside the till, Connie went through to the kitchen, returning to the table with a roll of baking paper. Tearing off a clean sheet, Connie placed the baking paper over the photocopied image and used the pencil to trace the outline of the three-legged jellyfish. Ignoring the grass and bushes, Connie extended the three lines to the ground and appraised the simple outline. It didn't look like anything familiar, and Connie tore off another sheet of paper, trying again. This time she played with the different lines, extended only the middle line, to the ground. It was thick. Too thick to be anything other than a tree, so she split the object into two separate legs. It seemed to make sense.

"That could be a man," said Josie.

The strange shape had a bump on top with an outer ring and, assuming the bump was the crown of a head, Connie sketched in the ring as the brim of a hat.

"Wes wears a hat," said Sherbet Ray, raising a suspicious brow.

"Anyone can wear a hat," said Connie, annoyed.

"It kinda looks like a man," said Josie. "and they're carrying something."

Connie traced the blurred lines over each of the man's shoulders then stopped to see what she had, comparing the original sketch to the tracing. The sketch suggestion the location of joints; an elbow and a knee. She drew them into her rough illustration. The joints led to a shoulder, a neck, a head and a torso, hanging over the man's shoulder.

"It's a dead body. He's carrying a dead body," said Quicks.

Connie took out a fresh sheet of baking paper and started again, drawing in the man with the hat and the body of his shoulder, arms and head limp, legs dangling. Everyone at the table drew a breath.

"That's got to be the killer," she said.

"It still looks like Wes," said the Cook.

Connie lent over the photocopied drawing again, studying the blurred lines. If Scratch had seen what he'd drawn, he's seen the killer side-on, striding through the trees with a clear view of Jane, dead, the face of the killer hidden by her torso. There was no way to tell who the killer was.

"If that's the woman, where's her kid?" said Quicks.

Jakes reached out and placed a finger at the man's midsection next to a dark object blending in with the background.

"That the kid."

Connie squinted at the dark blob. It was the size of a small child, and she could make outlines, like tiny limbs. Her heart broke.

"That's Kate."

The image became clear. It was a window into the past, a snapshot of a killer disposing of two bodies to cover up a double murder. Connie's insides turned stone cold. She was holding her breath as if hiding behind the bushes, staring into the semi-darkness, the killer with the bodies walking by. He was heading for Black Mountain, climbing down the bank crossing the dry creek bed and stepping onto the boulders of Black Mountain. She could see him climbing, searching the dark voids between the rock for a gap big enough and deep enough to make the bodies disappear.

"Scratch saw this," said the Cook. "And even he thinks Wes did it. You've got to stop defending Wes."

Connie pointed at the stamps blotting out the weak facsimile.

"The police had the original drawing. They interviewed Wes and couldn't prove anything. You can't tell from the drawing, who it is and the police couldn't either. And, I'm not defending Wes. I'm just saying this isn't absolute proof."

"It's got to be Wes," said the Cook, adamant.

Josie pointed at the red evidence stamp that held a signature and a name.

"Ask Andy Cross, who he thinks did it. That's his initials," said Josie.

"That's not Andy Cross," said Quicks. "Look at the dates. Andy would have been a kid at best. Those initials are from Andrew Cross, his Dad."

"His Dad was a policeman?"

"He was the Sergeant before Andy."

With the skulls and bones from Black Mountain and the weapon used to kill Jane and Kate, the police would have a fighting chance of finding the killer and that killer was looking more and more like Wes.

Connie conceded that it wasn't looking good for Wes. It was looking more and more like he'd killed his wife and child.

"I just can't believe Wes would kill his family," said Connie.

"Why not, he killed those boys," said Jakes. "And he shot Scratch. He hasn't got a problem killing people."

"Should we be worried about Evelyn?" The old woman was at Scratch's house with Wes, watching over Scratch.

"As long as she doesn't get between Wes and the bones she'll be fine," said Jakes.

Even if Wes hadn't killed his family, the old farmer was facing his last days of freedom. He would know that. As soon as the floodwaters subsided, the police would come and put him behind bars. And, at his age, Wes was going to die in gaol. And he deserved it. The shooting at the creek had been brutal. Their families would want justice. The people in the community who'd seen the bodies would need closure. And if he'd killed his family, it would be a fitting end for the old farmer.

Oddly enough, it didn't seem like a fitting end for the man she thought she'd known for ten years. He'd been a friend and a good man. The murder of the four boys was out of anger, and any suggestion that he'd killed Jane and Kate sat at odds with everything she knew about Wes.

The sketch lay on the table, the outline of the two bodies unmistakable.

"I saw someone at the creek today. On the other side," she said. "I think it was an old man."

"Did you talk to them?"

"No, they hid in the bush."

"It could be the killer," said Josie in an overly, dramatic voice and a wry smile.

A few chuckles went up around the table, but Connie wasn't laughing.

Sherbet Ray gave off a loud yawn, standing and picking up his empty plate.

"I'm dead tired. Is anyone coming back to the house with me?" He landed Connie with an intense look. As much as she wanted to stay with Jakes again, Fred Abe had soured last night's experience. That and she was tired. Tired enough to ruin good sex and she didn't want to disappoint Jakes or herself. Besides, it was getting too dangerous. She'd already spent last night and most of the day with Jakes. People would begin to talk, and if John knew she'd slept with Jakes, he'd never give up half of the hotel for her. But all this was temporary, and she was patient. She'd give up Jakes tonight for the hotel, and when she got the hotel, she'd get Jakes too. In a few weeks, a month at worse, she'd have everything she wanted.

"Are you going to be OK?" she asked Jakes.

Jakes' smiled a sad smile, his eyes full of longing.

"For now."

The corners of her mouth turned down, and her heart hurt.

"Sorry," she whispered before stepping away. At the swinging door into the kitchen, she stopped, smiled back at Jakes and waved goodnight.

CHAPTER 32

A ringing sound separated her from her dream, and her body woke feeling heavy, her head disorientated. The sound came from the kitchen. It was the landline ringing, and Connie fell out of bed and threw on her dressing gown. The phone hadn't rung for days. By the time she pulled open the bedroom door, the ringing had stopped, the sound replaced by the voice of Sherbet Ray, talking. She went into the kitchen and found the Cook with the handset to his ear.

"We found two in the creek," he said.

"Is that the police?" she whispered.

Sherbet Ray nodded.

"We put them in the coolroom in the kitchen at the hotel." A pause. "When can you make it up here?"

There was the sound of movement from the living

room, and Josie, Quicks and the waitresses shuffled into the kitchen looking dozy.

"The skulls?" said Sherbet Ray. "No, someone stole them." A pause. "I don't know where they are. No one knows. Scratch had them at one point, and they were stolen a second time. And Scratch got poisoned. No, he's still alive. No, I don't know who did it."

The conversation wound up, and Sherbet Ray ended the call.

"The police are coming up. They think they can make the crossing and start getting everybody home. We should be able to get out of here today," said the Cook.

A mix of relief and joy filled the room. For Connie, however, it was different. She was home, and when everyone left, it would be her, Karla and John. The thought of John injected her with a pang of despair. She hadn't spoken to Jakes about her plan, yet and needed to talk to Jakes before he left. He had to know that she couldn't go back to town with him. She had to stay at the hotel until John signed the business papers.

The phone rang again. Connie picked it up.

"I need your help." It was Evelyn. There was panic in her voice. In the background, the deep, broken voice of a man was screaming.

"What's going on?"

"It's Scratch. He's hallucinating. I can't control him. I need help."

"What about Wes?"

"He's gone. You need to get here now." There was a crashing noise in the background.

"OK, I'm on my way," said Connie.

"Hurry, and bring help," said Evelyn, hanging up.

Emma came forward.

"Can I use the phone? I'd like to call home," said the

young waitress.

Connie stepped aside, giving Emma access to the phone.

"Scratch is awake," she said to the Cook. "Evelyn needs help. I'll take Jakes." The short trip to Scratch's house would give Connie time to talk to Jakes and tell him what she'd planned to do.

Connie dashed down the hall past Karla's door and into her own bedroom, dressing quickly before rushing out the front door across the car park towards the hotel, the keys to the back door in hand. But she didn't need them. The back door to the hotel was ajar.

She felt uneasy and pulled open the door stepping into the commercial kitchen. It was quiet, empty, clean. She pushed through the swinging door into the restaurant. In the blind corner of the bar were a set of sheets, crumpled. She called out to Jakes. There was no answer. She checked the toilets and did a sweep of the hotel. The place felt empty, and it worried her. At the same time, she was worried about Evelyn, and she couldn't keep searching for Jakes.

As Connie headed for the back door, she stopped in the kitchen. Her eye had caught sight of a plate left out with a piece of bread on it, half-eaten. Beside it was a piece of paper. She walked over to it and read the note. 'Breakfast. Made with love.' The handwriting was her own, signed with a heart. She'd written the note for John three days ago.

Confusion compressed her brow.

The bread on the plate had several bites missing, and she could smell sweet and savoury, peanut butter and honey. The paste on the bread was a greyish colour. Her stomach sank. At the bottom of the fresh black bin liner lay a familiar-looking jar of grey-green goo. It had been taken from Scratch's house and brought into the hotel, spread on a crust of bread and laid out with the note; and someone had eaten it.

"Jakes." Connie breathed his name. Her stomach pinched with panic. "Shit."

Jakes had eaten the poison. He needed her help. She'd seen how fast the poison had worked on Scratch. If Jakes didn't get help right away, he was going to die. The panic washed over her body and into her brain, kicking at her chest, shouting at her body. 'MOVE!'. She wanted to run around screaming but knew it wouldn't help.

"Think"

Connie forced herself to focus on her surroundings. The back door to the kitchen had been left open. She'd searched the hotel. Jakes wasn't here, and he wasn't at the house. She tried to think where he could have gone and put herself in his shoes. If someone had poisoned her, the first thing she'd do was get help, and the only person she knew who could save Jakes was the same person who'd saved Scratch.

"Evelyn."

CHAPTER 33

Connie ran from the kitchen, heading for the Pajero. As she pulled out onto Shipton's Flat Road, she looked for Quick's silver sedan. It was missing. Jakes must have taken it to get himself to Scratch's house and get help.

She drove fast.

At some point, Jakes would begin to feel the effects of the poison. He would lose sensation in his body, lose control, unable to move or speak. At the same time, Jakes would remain conscious, to a point, aware that he was going to die, terrified. How long that would take, before Jakes died, Connie didn't know. For Scratch, it had taken the poison maybe twenty minutes to disable him, but Scratch had eaten a whole slice of bread, maybe more. It was a lot more than the two bites Jakes had taken, and her only hope was that a lower dose of the poison would be slower to take effect.

Connie felt a flush of anger, thinking of all the enemy's Jakes had, trying to pick one that would want him dead.

There were several; Fred Abe, Slippery Pete, Kipper and John. It had to be John that left the poison. John was the only one who knew about the note. But how did he get the poison from Scratch? If he was the one who took the poison, was he the one who also poisoned Scratch? And why would John take the bones? John had no interest in the bones, no reason to kill Scratch. There had to be someone else involved.

Connie thought she'd seen Kipper at the house and there was a good chance, that after they left, he'd come back and poisoned Scratch. He'd done something to Scratch's wounded arm, to break the stitches. Evelyn said that breaking the stitches would've hurt and it seemed that Scratch had been tortured – forced to eat the poison. But why?

Kipper wanted something from Scratch.

The photo of Kipper's reflection was the evidence the police needed to put Kipper in gaol. Kipper would have known that. He'd given the picture to Scratch and Scratch had kept it in his files. Kipper had just got out of gaol. If he was going to stay out, he had to get that photo back, and he must have tortured Scratch to get it. But Scratch couldn't give it to him. Scratch didn't have the image. Jakes had already taken it from him.

That made Jakes the next target.

It was beginning to make sense. Kipper had taken the poison from Scratch. Somehow, he'd crossed paths with John who had the note Connie wrote, and the two of them had got together to kill Jakes.

But murder seemed extreme, even for John who'd given Jakes a sound beating. For John to go this far, he must have found out Jakes had slept with Connie.

Connie's insides deflated like a sinking sponge. She felt terrible. If she didn't find Jakes, John would kill him, and

Connie would lose everything, including Karla and the hotel.

Guilt and anger mixed with fear as Connie steered the Pajero down the driveway, pulling up outside Scratch's house. The yellow Volvo was there, but there was no silver sedan, and Wes' white Landcruiser was missing. Connie got out, running along the hard-packed dirt path to the front porch where Evelyn was seated on the steps, looking exhausted.

"Is Jakes is here? He's been poisoned."

Evelyn, dressed in men's clothes twice her size, rose from the steps, her expression turning to alarm.

"Poisoned?"

"The same as Scratch. Is Jakes' here?"

Evelyn shook her silver head.

"No."

Connie glanced around the yard as if she was going to find Jakes hiding in the junk. But, she didn't have time to search the countryside. Jakes didn't have the time.

"I need to use the phone."

Connie hurried past Evelyn and into the house. The acidic smell of diarrhoea punched her in the nose, and she raised a hand to cover her face.

"What is that?" said Connie, barely breathing.

"It's Scratch. The poison is working its way through him."

"Where is he?" said Connie, checking the rooms as she started down the hall.

"In the bathroom. He's passed out again."

Connie reached the bathroom door and saw Scratch passed out in the bathtub, wet, covered with a towel and breathing.

"He should be in a hospital," said Evelyn. "He needs fluids."

Connie thought of Jakes facing a similar fate or worse if she couldn't find him. She continued down the hall into the kitchen.

"Where's Wes?"

Evelyn hitched up her oversized slacks.

"As soon as he found out who took the bones, he left."

Connie stopped and turned to face the old woman.

"Who took them?"

"Kipper."

Connie was right. Kipper was involved.

Kipper was a peeping Tom, a voyeur who'd tried to rape Josie and kill Scratch. She glanced at the dining table where Kipper had tortured Scratch, pressing the bullet wound, breaking the stitches and forcing Scratch to eat the poison. He was after the photo of his reflection, but Scratch didn't have it. Jakes had the photo. Then, for some reason, Kipper took the bones.

Connie turned to Evelyn.

"What would Kipper want with the bones?"

"I don't know. Wes asked the same question," shrugged Evelyn.

The only connection between Kipper and Scratch was the photographs they shared. The bag of bones had nothing to do with that.

But it didn't matter. All that mattered was finding Jakes.

Connie picked up the phone and dialled Wes' number. Wes' farm was the only other place she could think to find Jakes. He couldn't be anywhere else. The phone rang. She tapped her nails on the Formica bench, impatient. If Jakes was at the farm, he was there with John, which couldn't be good. She saw the keys to the Volvo. The phone rang out. Just because no-one answered didn't mean no-one was there.

"I'm going."

"What about Scratch? He needs a hospital."

Connie took the keys to the Volvo and handed her own keys over to Evelyn.

"Take my car. It'll get you across the creek. Call the hotel if you need help. I have to find Jakes."

CHAPTER 34

The Volvo bounced along the dirt road, throwing up a rooster tail of mud as she sped away from Scratch's house. The farm was the only place she hadn't checked. Jakes had to be at the farm.

The hotel came into view. Four-wheel drives loaded with people were leaving for the creek. Connie pulled into the car park as the last four-wheel drive took off, the wispy blonde hair of Quicks behind the wheel, the waitresses in the back, squealing with joy as they headed for home.

The squeals faded, the sound of the engine died, and Connie plunged into a silence she hadn't heard for days. She had to get to the farm, but needed to be thorough and checked the hotel a second time for Jakes. But, like her first search, the hotel was empty. A quick check of the house and she'd move onto the farm. Connie pushed through the back door of the hotel, heading across the carpark and saw Wes' old Landcruiser parked beside the house.

Connie looked around for Wes. The proximity of the car to her home suggested Wes was inside the house. She thought of Jakes and ran for the house, climbing the steps and pushing open the front door.

"Wes? Are you here? Jakes?"

No one answered.

The hall was quiet, and the kitchen was empty.

In the living room, bedding had been folded and stacked on the couch. Everyone had packed up and left.

Connie called out to her stepdaughter.

"Karla?"

There was no answer. Connie had a bad feeling.

From the front of the house, came a dull thud of a car door followed by a second, similar thud and an engine started, wheels churning gravel. Connie ran the length of the corridor through the front door, out onto the porch and saw Wes' white Landcruiser pulling out onto Shiptons Flat Road, heading for the farm.

It was strange. If Wes were here, he would have responded to her calls. If Karla were here, she would have called back. Connie turned back into the house and stopped at Karla's bedroom, hammering on the closed door. Still no answer. She pushed open the door, and a fresh breeze brushed her arms. The room was chaotic. The bedside table was leaning to one side, the lamp had fallen off, and a breakfast bowl was upside down in a soggy mess on the floor. On the bed, sheets had been stripped back and dragged in the direction of the open window, the curtains billowing in the wind.

An unnerving chill spread through Connie like a contagion and she ran to the window leaning out. On the ground outside, lay Karla's quilt.

"Karla!"

Her stomach sank. Someone had been here, and they'd

left, taking Karla with them.

Connie ran from the house around the outside of the hotel, to the yellow Volvo, jabbing the key into the ignition, hands shaking. The car started, and Connie kicked at the pedal, the Volvo spraying mud and shooting down Shiptons Flat road. She watched the road ahead, searching for the white Landcruiser, convinced that whoever was driving had taken Karla.

It wasn't Wes. He wouldn't do anything to Karla. It had to be Kipper. He was a peeping Tom, he'd stalked Josie and taken photos of Connie. The night of the storm, Kipper had been at Karla's window, and now, he'd come back for Karla. Connie felt sick. She'd been so busy looking for Jakes she'd left Karla on her own.

The driveway onto Wes' farm came into view. Connie had to make a decision. She couldn't see any trace of the Landcruiser and couldn't tell which way they'd gone. If Kipper really did have Karla, he wouldn't take her to the creek where everyone was crossing. He'd look for a quiet place where no-one could disturb them.

Connie yanked on the wheel, turning onto the farm and shot along the driveway, angry, her eyes welling up with tears. She was going to get Karla and God help anyone who tried to stop her.

Wes' Landcruiser appeared at the front of the old house. Connie pulled up and got out, running for the house, her hands clenching, nails hungry for flesh. A gunshot stopped her in her tracks, and she dropped to her heels, her head scrambling. Panic threatened to drive her back to the car, but couldn't go back. She had to get Karla.

Dropping to a stoop, Connie ran to the house, pressing herself against the siding by the door. A high pitched scream came from inside - Karla. And Karla was yelling, "Get away. No. Leave me alone." Thumping sounds from inside told Connie, they were on the move towards the back of the house.

Cold fear melted in the radiance of rage, and Connie moved to the front door. It was open, and she stepped, cat-like through the entry. Smoke floated around the ceiling, and the air was acrid and dry with the smell of gunpowder. She followed the smell into the living room. Furniture had been knocked over, and cushions from the couch were scattered around the room. A white patch of dust covered the floor, and above it, the ceiling had a puncture mark – a hole from a single bullet surrounded by tiny flecks of blood. From the kitchen came a moaning sound. Wes was lying on the linoleum floor, ankles and wrists bound with tape, his hands and face sheathed in blood, writhing in pain. He saw her and startled, frightened.

"It's OK," she whispered, rushing to his side, unwinding his bonds. There was a deep laceration to the top of his head - the skin split open, exposing the white bone of his skull. Blood poured from the wound.

"What happened?"

"Kipper. He's got Karla," said Wes, slurring his words.

Connie sat him up, freeing the old man's wrists from his bonds when his body slumped over, passed out. She pulled a tea towel from the oven door and twirled it into a band, wrapping it around Wes' head, covering his wound.

A shrill scream filled the house, and Connie's blood ran cold. She got to her feet, legs shaking and followed the screaming into the hall. There were several doorways into bedrooms and bathrooms, some open, some closed. The sound of a sharp crack came from behind one of the doors, and the screaming stopped. Her heart was racing, rage boiling as she gripped the knob, throwing open the door and rushing into darkness. With the lights out, the curtains closed she couldn't see a thing. Then her eyes adjusted and there was a bed with a figure tied to the frame. It was Karla. She was bound and gagged with silver tape, her eyes wide with terror, staring past Connie into the corner of the room. The hair on Connie's neck stood up, and her stomach sank. As she spun around, Connie heard something moving through the air and saw a dark object swinging in from the corner of her vision. The blow caught her in the side of the head, the room tilted, and the shadows around her turned to black.

CHAPTER 35

Connie woke up on the floor of the bedroom head throbbing, mouth sealed up, breathing through her nose and a warm trickle running through her hair. Her arms were locked at the wrists behind her back, and her ankles were bound together. A figure knelt over her grinning, and her eyes came into focus on the pale face of Kipper.

"Two for one," he said, discarding a roll of grey tape.

Karla was kicking and writhing on the bed, straining against the tape around her wrists and ankles, her mouth gagged, her screams muffled.

Kipper's dark eyes scanned Connie, drinking in her body. Her stomach flipped, sick. Her wrists hurt and she tried to pull them apart, but couldn't move. Kipper had her trussed tighter than a Christmas Turkey. She was cooked. He placed a pale hand on Connie's ribcage, soft and gentle, and she cringed at his touch. Terror rose, pumping blood, her head throbbing.

Kipper grabbed her breast and squeezed, rough, delight lighting his face.

Connie screamed into the tape over her mouth. Her head exploded with pain.

Kipper put his hand under her chin, gripping her jaw and forced her to look into his cold, dead eyes.

"We're not going to fight. You're going to play nice. Got it? Otherwise, I do her…" He pointed to Karla.

A mix of fear and anger spread through her body. He was going to rape her or rape Karla. Despair fell on her like an iron blanket. There was nothing she could do.

Kipper grabbed the inside of her thigh, hard and Connie jumped, instinctive.

"Fine," Kipper growled. He pulled away, stood up and crossed the room, kneeling on the edge of the bed, leaning over Karla. Karla began to writhe and scream in terror.

Connie went into a frenzy, bucking and kicking at her restraints, oblivious to the pain in her body, screaming into her gag, "No."

Her throes drew Kipper's attention back to the floor, and Connie lay still, obedient.

"Last chance," said Kipper, lifting himself off Karla. Oxygen pumped through her nostrils, her head throbbed, dizzy. Kipper took Connie by the ankles, pulling her around into the middle of the room, dropping her feet and placed both hands on the inside of her knees, forcing her legs apart. This time she lay still, wincing as the tape around her ankles pinched.

Connie put the pain out of her mind and lay still, sucking air through her nose, her mouth taped shut. Pops of colour flashed across her vision. She needed more oxygen. She was going to pass out.

Karla whimpered from the bed in full view of Kipper, unbuckling his belt and pulling open the front of his pants, rubbing himself, staring at Connie, gagged and terrified.

Kipper reached out and clutched at the front of Connie's jeans, pulling open the button and sliding back the zipper exposing her underwear. Her muscles twitched, repulsed. She wanted to lash out and fight back, but she couldn't. He would only hurt Karla.

Then he lowered himself over her pressing against her, rubbing. Tears came to her eyes, and Connie, turned her head to hide her face from Karla. Kipper's head was buried in her shoulder, stinking of alcohol, excitement on his breath.

Through the tears in her eyes, Connie could see the bedroom door, open. She wanted to leave. By a timber dresser was a rifle, the weapon used to injure Wes and knock her unconscious. The gun was out of reach.

Kipper grabbed at her body, breathing into her neck as Connie lay, helpless. No one was coming through the open bedroom door to save her; Wes was unconscious, Jakes was missing, and John wasn't there.

She was on her own.

Kipper was thrusting and grabbing, his excitement growing, his breath punctuated with horrible gasps.

She wanted to hurt him. He wasn't a strong man. If her hands weren't tied, she could fight him off. The side of Kipper's head moved up and down, and his hand slipped down the back of her pants.

Terror gripped her. She needed to breathe.

Connie stretched her jaw, spitting into the tape over her mouth, lubricating the glue. The tape loosened and came off her jaw. Cool air flowed into her mouth. She could breathe. The dizzy feeling faded. The pain in her head still intense. Connie felt her weight and the weight of

Kipper on her arms and legs. He wasn't heavy.

Kipper's head continued to bob up and down next to hers, rubbing against her, his face buried in her shoulder. When he was done with her, there was nothing stopping him from doing the same to Karla. Fury burned away her fear. She couldn't lay still and let this happen. Connie turned her head to face Kipper, looking at his ear. She opened her mouth as wide as she could, bared her teeth and took in a mouth full of Kipper's ear, biting down - hard.

A burst of warm blood filled her mouth with the taste of iron.

Kipper screamed, thrashed about, kicking and hitting and clawing, his ear clamped between her teeth. With her legs bent and her feet beneath her, Connie thrust her hips up, lifting Kipper and throwing him off balance. He fell to one side. His weight off her, her teeth still in his ear, Connie lowered her shoulders sliding her bound wrists, down her back and under her bottom and got stuck. She couldn't get past the back of her knees. Despair swept over her.

Kipper was still clawing at her face, trying to get his ear free of her teeth. Connie needed more space. More time. She clenched her jaw, her head searing with pain. From between her teeth, she felt skin tearing, and gristle popped. Kipper screamed. A piece of his ear separated from his head and fell into her mouth. Kipper rolled away, writhing in pain, his hand on the side of his head, blood streaming through his fingers.

Connie spat out the ear, lifted her knees to her chest, tucking her bound ankles over the bindings on her wrists, bringing her hands to the front of her body.

Kipper's pained cries turned to angry grunts as he rolled to his knees, cursing.

Using her fingers, Connie pulled at the tape around her ankles.

Kipper raised his head and gripped the dresser, rising from the floor with a murderous glare. But instead of coming for her, Kipper turned for the rifle. Connie's body tensed, she rolled to her knees, ankles bound and threw her body at Kipper. They collided, Kipper knocking the rifle to the ground and Connie got a hand to the gun as the two of them grappled for the weapon. As they wrestled for control, Connie found her feet, and she stood, pulling Kipper up with her. He had the butt of the gun, and she had the barrel. As they pushed and pulled, the barrel swung around, pointing into her stomach. Kipper got a hand free and reached for the trigger. As his finger curled around the trigger, Connie pushed the barrel aside, and the rifle went off with a loud crack. A bullet punched a small hole in the wall beside the bed and Karla screamed into her gag. Connie still had the barrel in hand and felt the heat, searing her hands. Still, she held tight, fighting for her life and gave the gun a yank. Kipper's bloody grip slipped, and he released the weapon, stumbling back into the open door. Connie fell back onto the bed - onto Karla holding the wrong end of the rifle, her wrists still bound. Kipper steadied himself. Connie spun the gun around, sliding the bolt back to load another bullet and lowered her aim at Kipper. She pulled the trigger. Kipper leapt into the hall as the rifle kicked and the door jamb exploded in a shower of splinters. Between the ringing in her ears, Connie heard the sound of feet pounding down the hall.

Kipper was gone.

She ripped the tape from her wrists and ankles, pulled away Karla's bindings and the two of them hugged.

"Stay here." Connie took the rifle and ran from the room, down the hall, through the living room into the kitchen, stepping over Wes' body, the old man moaning, and pushed out the back door. Kipper was already over the first fence and running through the paddock heading for the tree-covered mountains at the back of the farm.

Connie lowered the rifle, took aim and fired. The bullet missed. Regardless of her aim, Kipper wasn't coming back. She lowered the rifle and turning to go inside, caught her reflection in the window. She looked wild, hair a mess, clotted with blood, tape hanging from her wrists, a rifle in her hands and anger burning in her eyes.

Karla's voice called out to her.

"I'm in the kitchen."

Karla was helping Wes to his feet, groggy and moved him into a chair, the blood on his head dry.

"Kipper's got the bones," said Wes.

"I know. Have you seen Jakes?"

Wes shook his head and winced.

"What about John? Have you seen John?"

Wes shook his hand - No. The old man was pale. He needed a hospital.

Connie found a first aid kit and gave it to Karla, telling her to bandage Wes' head, then headed back into the house searching the rooms looking for any sign of Jakes.

The last bedroom at the end of the hall was closed. She pushed it open.

A foul smell wafted out of the room; a potent mix of body odour and stale alcohol. The room was a mess. The bedsheets were crumpled, and there was a dip in the centre of the mattress where the body of a large man had laid. Beside the bed were a stack of dirty dishes, wads of tissues and several empty scotch and vodka bottles. There were more empty bottles standing on the floor beside the bed. The bottles looked familiar. They were the alcohol stolen from the bar.

The room belonged to John. John had stolen the alcohol.

But there was more here than one man could drink - even John. Then she remembered the intoxicated breath of Kipper against her neck. Kipper hadn't been anywhere near the hotel. He had to get his alcohol from someone and must have got it from John.

Like the poison used on Scratch that had been taken to the hotel and put together with the note she'd penned for John two days ago, the empty bottles of alcohol shared among the men suggested a connection between Kipper and John.

But John was missing and so too was Jakes.

Connie's chest tightened.

She had the feeling that John had tried to poison Jakes, and he'd been successful in some measure. If Jakes was still alive, John would be with him, if only to make sure that Jakes died.

If she found John, she'd find Jakes.

Connie returned to the kitchen. The rifle lay on the table with the keys to the Landcruiser. Karla was tying off the bandage around Wes' head. Connie found Wes' spectacles on the floor, the lens cracked and broken and gave them to the old farmer.

"We need to get you to the hospital."

Wes stood up stumbling, woozy against the refrigerator. Connie took his arm and led him out of the kitchen.

"Karla, bring the keys to Wes' car. You're driving."

Karla took the keys to the Landcruiser and followed them outside.

"Go to the hotel. Pack some clothes and call Dawn Kirby. Ask her if you can stay there tonight. Then get to the creek. If someone is there, get them to drive you into town. Take Wes to a hospital. I'll try and get into town later."

They reached the Landcruiser, but Wes fought Connie, refusing to get in the car.

"No. I need the bones. Kipper has the bones," said Wes, hands shaking. He was weak, and Connie forced the old farmer into the passenger seat.

"Don't worry. I'll get the bones back," said Connie. "You need to get to the hospital."

Karla was in the driver's seat, the engine running, crunching the gears. She looked out of the driver's window, her brow creased.

"What about Dad?"

"Don't worry," said Connie, looking towards the mountain behind the farm. "I'll find him."

CHAPTER 36

Connie took the rifle from the kitchen table and took the Volvo, driving through the paddocks at the back of the farm, cows bellowing, Black Mountain and Mungumby creek to her left. Where the fences ended, the land rose, and the bush became thick. Two days ago John had seen Kipper in this bush. At some point, the two men had shared alcohol, shared their hate for Jakes and combined together the jar of poison with the note she'd written and come up with a plan for murder. Kipper was the key. He was her last hope to find Jakes. If she found Kipper, she would find John, and hopefully, John would have Jakes.

But hope was fading. A solid hour had passed since Connie had found the poison and Jakes was still missing. Her chances of finding Jakes alive were unknown.

The Volvo stopped at the final fence line, and Connie

got out with the rifle. She slipped through the barbed wire into the long grass and followed the fence line searching the dense bush for a way in and found a path, overgrown where the long grass had been trampled flat by recent traffic. Listening and looking through the trees, Connie entered the bush. Brown and silver trunks and dark green foliage became her world, dense with shadows, rich with the smell of decay and eucalyptus, full of the song of birds and insects. This was the bush where Jane had been shot, her baby strapped to her chest, their bodies carried downhill, across the creek and into Black Mountain. But, Connie wasn't going to end up like Jane. She wasn't going to disappear. She was going to find Jakes and get out of this alive.

The bush track became steep, her head throbbed, flies attacked the blood in her hair, her legs ached, and the rifle weighed heavy in her hands. It would be easy to give up and go back to the hotel, to pick up Karla and Wes and Scratch and see them safely to the hospital. But, hate drove her on. John's involvement maddened her. He'd caused so much damage. Fred Abe and Slippery Pete must have told John she'd slept with Jakes and John had poisoned Jakes out of jealousy.

The sound of voices flowed downhill through the trees and stopped Connie in her tracks. She listened and searched the trees ahead for some show of who was behind the voices, and the urgent, raised tone between several deep male voices suggested an argument.

The voices became louder, and Connie stepped off the path into the bush, hiding behind a large tree.

"You can't come with us," said one of the male voices.

"Why not?" Connie recognised the booming voice of Fred Abe.

"What were you doing with Connie the other night?"

"I was getting her out of-" Fred Abe started, and another voice cut him off.

"Don't Bullshit, Abe." I know what you were trying to do and we weren't there for that. And, tell us what you've been doing with Kipper before he went to gaol? We know someone's been looking through windows. That's you, isn't it?"

Connie peered around the tree getting a glimpse of four men; Gunner Jones, Shakey Pete, Greenie and Fred Abe.

"Good-bye, Abe. You can find your own way home," said Shakey Pete.

The men separated from Fred Abe, moving downhill, towards Connie. She pressed herself against the tree as they passed by with their heads down following the path.

Connie remained hidden. She could hear Fred Abe making short, sharp movements before he moved off into the bush. She waited for the sound of Fred Abe to die off and looked around the tree.

The coast was clear, but she'd been rattled. Following Kipper into the bush didn't seem like such a good idea. If Fred Abe caught her out here, she was toast. The silence of the bush weighed heavy on her indecision.

She began to move her legs and arms and find her way back onto the path still undecided on her direction when another noise approached, from downhill, and a figure appeared, climbing the path towards her.

Connie lifted the rifle.

The figure lifted his head, and she saw Wes, his head bandaged, hat on, blinking at her through broken spectacles.

"What are you doing here?" she whispered, hoarse.

Wes clutched at his chest, touched the bandage on his head, wincing in pain.

"I need those bones."

"Where's Karla?"

"At the hotel. Did you find them? The bones?"

"No. Go back. You shouldn't be here." Connie still had the rifle pointed at the old man, her finger on the trigger, her body tense.

Wes regained his breath and straightened.

"I'll go back when I have those bones. Besides…" said Wes, approaching and pushing the gun aside. "…you look like you could use the help." Wes stepped around her and took the lead. Every nerve in her body felt taut and ready to snap.

"Are you coming?"

The track led uphill through the bush and ended at a sheer grey granite wall several stories high with deep cracks. At the foot of the cliff, the ground was covered in fallen stones, small and large with sharp edges. This was the escarpment. Somewhere along this long cliff line was the Lions' Den Tin min and the place where Kipper had been hiding out.

Wes turned following the line of the cliff climbing over the rocky ground. Connie followed, gun in hand, legs aching searching the path ahead. She heard them before she saw them; a voice echoing off the hard rock surface.

She grabbed Wes by the elbow, stopping him and waved him down off the rocks and into the line of trees below the cliff. The voices were coming from further down the escarpment and Wes forged forward, weaving through the tall trunks, drawing level and, taking up a position behind a large boulder.

From behind the boulder, they could see Kipper and John standing among the stones at the base of the cliff in a heated conversation. Among the rocks were broken bottles – more alcohol stolen from the hotel. Behind the two men, at the base of the cliff was a small, round hole tunnelling into the earth - the entrance to the old Lion's Den tin mine.

John was standing, hands on his hips, head bowed staring at the rubble at his feet.

"He's still breathing," said John.

"Then do something about it." Kipper went to the mouth of the small tunnel and disappeared inside.

John began pacing up and down while staring at the same spot on the ground among the rocks.

Connie stretched her neck to see over the boulder. Laying among the broken glass and rocks was the body of Jakes Jenkins.

Connie felt a surge of relief.

Jakes' chest rose and fell, and his eyes were open, following John's movements. He was alive, but he appeared to be affected by the poison, conscious and unable to move.

Connie dropped behind the boulder.

"Can you see the bones?" Wes whispered.

Connie shook her head. She wasn't interested in the bones. She had to work out a way to help Jakes. Connie rose up again to watch.

John bent down, taking Jakes by the wrists dragging his limp body across the uneven ground and placed Jakes' head on a large, flat rock. Jakes' face fell to the side, and his eyes found Connie. There was no expression in his face, and a pale, grey tinge of death coloured his skin.

Connie's heart broke for Jakes. John had done this. Anger poured into her veins, setting her body on fire, and Connie weighed the gun in her hand. She had to get John away from Jakes, even if she had to threaten her husband at gunpoint.

From behind the boulder, Connie fingered the trigger

and took a breath looking up. In the shadow of the cliff, John had dropped to his haunches sliding his hands beneath a large chunk of quartz the size of a four-slot toaster. Straining under the weight of the stone, John stood up, lifting the rock, to his waist. At his feet lay Jakes. John lifted the quartz stone to his chest and pressed it above his head, eyes down, arms shaking - aiming the stone at Jakes' head.

"No." Connie jumped out from behind the boulder, brandishing the rifle, screaming John's name. "Put it down, John."

They locked eyes down the long barrel of the gun, John's face red, straining, Connie's eye on the target.

At the mouth of the tin mine, Kipper emerged, a hessian sack in his hand. He saw Connie with the gun and froze.

"Don't do it, John. Step back. I swear, I will shoot you." Connie's voice crackled like wild electricity, alive with rage.

Hatred swum in John's eyes. He shook under the weight of the stone, spit projecting from his mouth. His eyes dropped to Jakes, his feet shifting, taking aim at Jakes. Rage filled her eyes and John came into sharp focus. She aimed her rage at John and released, pulling the trigger. The rifle gave a satisfying kick, and the bullet left the gun, thumping John in the chest. His face registered shock and pain, his body jerking back, and the lump of quartz slipped from John's hands.

CHAPTER 37

The quartz rock slammed into the ground with a clack, missing Jakes by inches. John lay on the ground, on his back staring at the sky, blood flowing from the wound in his chest.

A smoke haze billowed out at the end of the rifle, the smell of burned gunpowder and blood mixing like a cocktail, bitter, dry and metallic. A mix of relief and shock whirled about in her chest and stomach. She'd saved Jakes, but she'd shot John.

"What have I done?"

Wes came out of the bush shouting at Kipper, "Where are the bones!" Kipper turned and with nowhere to run, disappeared into the mouth of the tin mine.

Connie felt a hand on her arm. Wes was pulling gently at the gun. She gave it to him, and he went after Kipper ambling over the rocky ground into the mouth of the tunnel leaving Connie with her dying husband and lover.

She got to John in time to see the light go out in his eyes. She'd killed him. Karla's Dad, her husband was dead, killed by her own hand. She felt guilt for herself and sadness for Karla. She deserved to get locked up and probably would. Despair filled her body with darkness.

Laying among the rocks, Jakes was taking shallow breaths, still alive. She went to him and took his head in her hands, the hands that had killed a man wanted to save another. Jakes' eyes were half-open, his pupils reduced to small pinpricks. But, he was breathing.

"I'm going to get you out of here. Just stay with me," said Connie, her tears falling onto Jakes' face.

Jakes wasn't a big man, but he wasn't so small that she could carry him out on her own. Connie needed help, and the only person there to help was Wes, and he'd gone after Kipper. Connie got off the ground, legs shaking and ran to the mouth of the tin mine after Wes.

Stooping to step inside, Connie found herself in a dark circular tunnel, the air cool, damp and musty, the walls scared with the marks of picks. Connie called out to Wes, and her voice echoed back. She took a step forward, unwilling to go too far and leave Jakes. Her eyes adjusted to the low light and she could see the round mine shaft ran in a dead straight line down into the earth.

"Wes, come back. I need you," her voice echoed, desperate.

"Go back," a voice crackled out of the dark and Wes appeared shuffling towards her, doubled over, grunting, the rifle in his hands clattering against the tunnel wall. "There's another tunnel. Kipper took another tunnel. He's getting away."

Connie backed out into the light, and Wes came out

after her turning back and looking up at the cliff face waving the rifle around, squinting through his broken spectacles.

"Do you see him?"

"We have to get Jakes to the hospital. I need your help,"

But Wes wasn't listening. He was scanning the face of the escarpment searching the cracks and crevices. A rock the size of a melon came loose and fell, smashing into the rubble at their feet.

"There." Wes was pointing at the place from where the rock had fallen. A dirty hand appeared from a small hole, reaching out and clutching at the cliff face searching for purchase. More dirt and rocks showered down, a head emerged from the cliff face, and Kipper was birthed from the earth. He wriggled his way into the sun, clinging to the steep, rocky surface, bringing with him a brown hessian sack and, hand over hand Kipper began to climb.

"Throw down the bones, or I'll shoot," said Wes, shaking the rifle, squinting up at the cliff face.

"Please, Wes, we've got to get Jakes out of here. He needs help." If Jakes died, she'd killed John for nothing.

But, Wes had his focus on the rifle, the butt to his shoulder, winking up along the barrel pointing up at Kipper. The gun kicked and cracked, and the bullet hit the rock, spitting chips and kicking up a small cloud of dust.

"Did I hit him?" he said, adjusting his glasses. "I can't see a thing."

"Wes, don't worry about Kipper. We have to save Jakes," she said, shouting over the ringing in her ears.

Wes lowered the rifle and shoved the gun into her hand.

"You wanna get out of here. I need those bones," he said, pointing at Kipper. "Shoot him."

She'd already killed one man. The last thing she wanted to do was shoot another, even if it was Kipper.

"I can't shoot him," she said, pushing away the rifle.

But, Wes wouldn't take the gun.

"He saw you shoot John. If he tells the police you're going to gaol. Shoot him, and I'll take the blame. I'll tell the police I shot them both; Kipper and John."

"Wes, I can't."

"And when you go to gaol, who's going to look after Karla?"

The question gave Connie pause to think. Connie looked up at Kipper climbing slow and steady, hand over hand, the bag of bones dangling from one fist. She balanced the gun in her hands, thinking about Kipper in the bedroom at the farmhouse. And he was getting away with the remains of Jane and Kate. Kipper didn't deserve her sympathy.

Connie lifted the rifle and steadied her shaky hand, putting Kipper in her sights. The gun jumped and cracked. The rock above Kipper exploded, showering him with dust. Kipper stopped, shook the dust from his face and reached up again for another handhold.

"You missed," Wes said. "Go again."

The rifle cracked. The rock beneath Kipper's hand exploded, his hand slipped, and he lost his footing, his body tipping backwards and he fell turning in mid-air until he shot screaming, headfirst into the ground with a wet thud and the loud crack of bones breaking. His body bounced once and settled into the rocks. It was a gruesome sight; arms and legs twisted at unnatural angles, the stones around Kipper's body spotted with blood. It was too much for her. Connie dropped the rifle, bent over and vomited.

Wes picked up the gun and crossed the stony ground, bending over Kipper's body, reaching into the tangled mess and grabbed the hessian sack, pulling. A soft high pitched moan came out of the broken body. Kipper was alive. Barely. Shards of broken bones had punched through his skin and his breath, wet and rattling, carried the sound of impending death. He moaned, a high pitched and primordial sound that penetrated her body and filled her stomach with hot needles.

"Stop it," she said, covering her ears and sinking to her knees, her eyes blurring with tears.

Wes put the hessian sack to one side and picked his way through the rocks, circling the twisted body. He found a clump of blood-soaked hair among the twisted limbs, standing close and spreading his feet Wes took aim and with a click, snick, clack of the rifle, he cocked the bolt and pulled the trigger.

The bullet kicked Kipper's head, and the crack echoed off the cliff.

"Awful business," said Wes, picking up the hessian sack with the bones and started walking.

"Where are you going? What about Jakes?"

"I can't lift him, and neither can you. I'll get help." Wes said, shouldering the hessian sack and heading back along the rocky escarpment. "Stay with him. Keep him alive."

"Hurry," she yelled after Wes. Jakes was still breathing. "Please hurry," she whispered, exhausted and confused—none of this made sense. There were two dead bodies, blood on the rocks, John and Kipper were dead. She sat with Jakes, lifted his head into her lap and waited.

CHAPTER 38

The birds sang from the bush. Connie sat with Jakes', his stare weak, his eyes hooded, breathing shallow and his skin was cold and clammy. Connie felt like a mess. Her heart was pounding, her nerves frayed, and she felt sick and uneasy. She spoke to Jakes in encouraging words telling him help was coming, running her fingers through his dark hair. When his stare wandered, she called him back.

"I'm here. Stay with me."

A few meters away, Kipper's dead body settled into the earth, his blood trickling from the splits and holes in his skin, flies swarming around the bullet hole in his head. John was the same. Connie looked away and tried to distract herself from the sound of the files.

She wasn't sure if she could trust Wes to return. He had the bones and Connie still couldn't decide if Wes had killed his family. And now she'd seen a side of Wes she'd never seen before. He was brutal. He'd killed those boys, shot Scratch and killed Kipper – all for the remains of his wife and child. There was a single-mindedness to his actions, and now he had the bones, Connie couldn't be sure that Wes would afford her and Jakes, any more compassion than he'd shown Scratch or Kipper or the four dead boys. The old farmer was more interested in using the bones for God-knows-what. He's told her he would use them to catch their killer, but if Wes was the killer, he wasn't going to hang around and wait for the police. Now the creek was down, and Wes could leave and go anywhere. He could disappear.

The buzz of the flies grew intense, and she couldn't hear Jakes' breathing. Wes wasn't coming back.

Connie stood and tried lifting Jakes but lacked the strength. She tried dragging him and made it a few meters before her head began to throb, and she had to sit down. It was hopeless. She came to save Jakes, and she couldn't do it – not on her own. She cried, fell apart and pulled herself together again. Jakes needed help. She would have to leave to find someone who could help get Jakes a hospital.

The crack of a twig came from the bush below the rocks. Connie looked up, her heart pumping, head throbbing. She couldn't see anyone.

"Who's there?" The drone of the flies hampered her hearing.

Then a movement caught her eye. Except, it wasn't in the bush. From the far end of the escarpment, a figure came out of the trees. He was tall, wearing a hat and moved into the shadows beneath the cliff, skipping across the rocks, jogging towards her. He was moving too fast for it to be Wes.

Connie got to her feet, uncertain, ready to run, unwilling to leave.

"Who's there!" she called out to the figure.

Then she heard it again - a crack from the bush and a large man, burst out of the trees. It was Fred Abe. He ran at her, bounding across the rock, his huge body filling her vision, his arms outstretched, his face twisted with a hungry desire.

Connie ducked and stepped sideways. Fred Abe's fat fingers, grazing her shirt front as she pulled away, out of his reach and she ran, downhill towards the bush. From the far end of the escarpment, the man with the hat was shouting from the shadows, a revolver in his hands, pointed in her direction. The weapon fired, and Connie hit the tree line, leaping into the thick scrub, pushing through the undergrowth with the branches and shrubs ripping and whipping her face and arms. Behind her, she could hear more shouting, and another round of gunfire and all she could think of was Jakes, lying helpless on the ground. There was no going back. Jakes was going to die, and she'd lost her chance to save the man she loved.

CHAPTER 39

Crashing through the bush, Connie stumbled onto a dirt path that led her downhill to a barbed-wire fence. On the other side was an open field; the farm. She looked along the fenceline and saw the Volvo parked nearby. Next to it was a police vehicle. But there were no police around, and the blue and white four-wheel drive was locked. Maybe Wes had sent the police to help her. Her faith in Wes returned. The man she'd seen in the shadow of the cliff wearing the hat must have been the police.

The presence of the police brought mixed blessings. On the one hand, they would get Jakes the help he needed. On the other hand, they would find John, dead and start to ask questions – questions Connie wasn't ready to answer.

Connie had to get moving. She got to the Volvo and

drove, leaving behind the police, Fred Abe, John, Kipper and Jakes. If the police found out she'd killed John, she was going to gaol, and Karla would become an orphan.

She'd have to tell Karla her dad was dead. Connie felt terrible. The guilt of taking Karla's dad from her weighed heavy on her heart. But if she got caught for what she'd done, it would be worse. She couldn't leave Karla on her own. She had to fix it.

Wes had promised to take the blame for shooting John, and she had to know if she could trust the old farmer to keep his promise. She had to talk to Wes before the police got to him and the two of them had to get their stories straight.

Wes' weatherboard home came into view, and Connie pulled up at the front of the house. There was no Landcruiser, and she ran through the house, calling out, but the place was empty.

In the kitchen, a pool of drying blood caked the floor. The Bakelite phone rang, loud and Connie jumped. She reached out to pick up the handset and stopped herself. She didn't want to talk to anyone except Wes, and she couldn't risk answering the phone. Whoever was calling would become a witness, pinning her down to a time and a location. So, Connie ignored the ringing and pushed through the flywire door onto the back porch. Over by the large tin workshop was the rusty Landcruiser. Her hopes lifted. The tin door into the workshop swung open, and Wes came out, a rifle in one hand and the hessian sack in the other, his dog beside him. The dog spotted Connie and ran at her barking. Wes stopped the dog, calling it to heel. From inside the house, the phone kept ringing.

"We need to talk," said Connie.

"You look like death warmed up. Where's Jakes?"

"He's still up at the tin mine. Did you send the

police?”

Wes, had one hand on his cattle dog, the other on the gun, his eyes drifting past Connie to the house.

“Who do you suppose is calling?” Wes said as if talking to the dog.

“Did you talk to the police about John?”

Wes approached her, coming close and held out the hessian sack.

“No. Hold this.”

Connie took it. It was the remains of his family, the hessian sack stained with the blood of Kipper.

“Why are you giving this to me?”

“I’m not.”

Wes dug one hand into his pocket and removed a set of keys. He handed Connie the keys and took back the sack, turning and heading towards the Landcruiser.

“You can drive,” he said.

“Where are we going?”

“You want to talk. I need a drink.”

*****

The bones rattled, knocking together as they drove, Wes in the passenger seat with the hessian sack on his lap, Connie steering for the hotel.

“Were you serious when you said you’d take the blame for John?” Connie hated herself for asking, but Wes was the only person who could keep her out of gaol.

“Don’t worry. You’ll be fine,” said Wes.

His words weren’t enough for her. She didn’t need to know she was going to be fine. She needed to know how to stay out of gaol. They needed to get their stories straight so that whatever lie they told to the police couldn’t be torn apart when scrutinised.

Connie pulled up at the front of the hotel, the car park empty.

"What do we tell the police?"

Wes pushed open the car door.

"Tell them I did it," he said, climbing out and heading for the entry into the bar.

Connie still wasn't satisfied. She needed to if Wes was going to talk to the police and if he did, what he was going to say. If their stories didn't match, she was going to get caught in a lie.

But, Wes seemed distracted. His eyes were scanning the area surrounding the building, and he stopped the entrance to the hotel, peering through the door before going inside.

Connie followed and caught sight of her own reflection in the window; a bloody, matted, scratched and dirty woman with wild eyes.

"How about that drink?" Wes called out from inside.

The hotel felt strange. Every space in the place held memories of John. Some good. Some bad. He was never coming back. John was dead.

Wes was seated at his table, the hessian sack on the table and the rifle standing against the wall. He faced the window looking out onto the car park with a clear view down Shiptons Flat road.

Wes' didn't seem to understand how desperate she felt. He didn't want to talk about the police. His hand rested on the hessian sack, and his eyes were fixed on the window - on the road leading to the Lion's Den.

Connie hurt. She was tired and drained. Pity welled up inside her and flooded her eyes as she broke down.

"Hey." Wes' had turned to her and put on a soothing voice, "It'll be OK."

Connie didn't feel OK. She was angry.

"Why are you still here?" she said, wiping tears from her dirty face. "What is going on? Why did you bring those?"

Wes lowered his eyes to the hessian sack. When he looked up, he's face had set hard as stone.

"I'm going to meet the bastard that killed my family."

CHAPTER 40

"Wes, you can't be serious?"

"Dead serious."

Connie threw her hands up. Now she really needed a drink. She took a full bottle of whisky from behind the bar and two clean glasses, placing them on the table in front of Wes.

"Shooting John was the right thing to do," said Wes as Connie sat opposite him. "There'll be times when you won't be sure. Just remember, I was there, I saw what happened, and I'm telling you it was the right thing to do."

"And Kipper?"

"Good riddance."

"The police saw me up there," she said. "Who was it?"

"Andy Cross," said Wes.

She knew Andy and he knew her. The local Sergeant

would often visit the hotel on his rounds of the community to pick up on any news that had passed over the bar.

"I don't know what to tell him." said Connie, despair in her voice.

"Keep it simple. Just tell him I shot them. I shot John and I shot Kipper. That's all you need to say. Let me take the blame."

These were the words Connie needed to hear, and she felt a mix of relief and guilt.

"Thank you," she said.

Wes raised a hand and pointed out the window, squinting through his broken spectacles.

"Who's that?"

On the road to the hotel, a white and blue four-wheel drive came into view. It appeared to be the same police vehicle she'd seen in the back paddock at the farm. Dread began swirling in her stomach.

"That's Andy."

Wes reached for his rifle.

"No, Wes. Put the gun away."

Wes ignored her, one hand on the gun, scowling through the window.

The vehicle pulled up, and Sergeant Andy Cross got out wearing a broad-brimmed hat, and a utility belt sagging under the weight of handcuffs and a revolver. The Sergeant moved to the back of the vehicle, opened the rear door and lent inside.

"Do you see anyone else?" growled Wes, squinting, his glasses broken.

"No, it's just Andy."

The Sergeant came up, struggling under the heavy weight of a body slung over his shoulder.

Connie's heart swelled.

"Wait. He's got Jakes." She leapt from her seat and

raced out the front door.

"Is he alive?" she called out from the front of the hotel, tears filling her eyes.

"Barely." Andy grunted as he carried Jakes into the hotel and laid his body on the floor of the bar. "I've called for a Paramedic. What's wrong with him?" said the Sergeant.

Connie knelt next to Jakes and put her ear to his mouth. She could hear his shallow breathing.

"He's been poisoned," she said.

Jakes' eyes were heavy, barely open, his pulse was weak, and his skin was red and hot.

Wes shifted in his seat, facing the Sergeant.

"Hello, Andy."

Andy jumped and saw Wes for the first time, his head wrapped in bloody bandages, the rifle pointed up at the tin roof. "Anyone else with you?" asked Wes.

Andy's hand drifted to his side over the service revolver.

"Who are you expecting?" said Andy.

Wes stared at the Sergeant through his broken spectacles, silent.

Every muscle in Connie's body had tightened.

Andy's eyes settled on the table, and the hessian sack.

"What's in the bag?"

"Jane and Kate," said Wes, laying a hand on the bones.

There was another short silence.

"I'm glad you found them," said Andy. "How about I take that rifle off your hands?" Slow and steady, Andy moved forward, Wes eyeing him off. Gradually, the Sergeant closed the gap between them and reaching out, wrapped his fingers around the butt of the rifle, lifting it from Wes' weathered hands. The gun exchanged, Connie relaxed and Wes turned his back on Andy to face the window.

With the tension in the room dissipated, Connie got to her feet, heading for the bar.

"Where are you going?" The Sergeant stopped her with a suspicious look.

"I'm getting water. For Jakes," she said. "The poison is in his system. The water might help to flush it out."

Andy followed her to the bar, watching as she filled a glass with water.

"I saw you at the tin mine. What happened?"

She wasn't ready for questions.

The Sergeant searched her face and hands – looking for signs of guilt – and the moment she said something wrong, she'd be in cuffs.

Wes remained at his table, staring out the window, watching the road, uninterested in the conversation at the bar.

"We can talk later. Help me with Jakes."

Andy worked with her, holding Jakes upright while Connie poured small amounts of water into his mouth. But, Jakes wasn't swallowing. His eyes were almost closed and distant.

"Jakes. Stay awake. Stay with me." Jakes didn't respond. "Jakes, don't you die on me," she put her fingers into the glass and placed water onto his lips.

The Sergeant's eyes were needling her skin.

"Who poisoned him?"

"John or Kipper. I don't know. Maybe both of them. Scratch made the poison but not to kill anyone. Someone stole it from him and fed it to Jakes. I don't know who did it."

"Was it an accident?"

"No, not a chance."

"And you think it was John?"

"And Kipper. Both of them, I think."

Jakes' throat dipped, and he made a gulping sound.

Her heart leapt.

"He swallowed." She put the glass to his lips, splashing water into his mouth. Jakes swallowed again. She wanted to cry. "It's going to be O.K. You're going to be O.K., Jakes. Just stay awake. Stay with me."

"What about John? Do you know who shot him?" The Sergeant's question filled her with shame. Once again, Connie looked to Wes. The old man promised to take the blame. He said she could tell the police he'd done it, but it was hard to tell a lie and betray a… She wondered what Wes was to her. A friend? More than that? Either way, she couldn't do it. Wes would have to make his own false confession before she said anything.

Andy followed her gazed to the table by the window.

"Wes? What happened up there?" he said.

Wes brought his attention into the hotel.

"Sure, I'll tell you." The old man lifted himself out of his seat, steadying himself on the table then took a fist full of the hessian sack and stumbled forward across the timber floor. "Come with me. I'll show you the bodies."

He was heading for the kitchen.

"Wes, stop." Andy got to his feet, the rifle in hand. "Bodies. What bodies?"

"The two in the coolroom."

Andy looked to Connie for confirmation, his face full of disbelief.

"Two boys," she said. "We found them in the creek."

"Drowned?" said Andy.

Connie looked at Wes.

"Shot," said Wes.

"Who shot them?" said Andy.

"One of the locals," said Wes turning towards the swinging door. "I'll show you."

Connie wasn't sure why Wes wanted to show Andy the bodies, but they weren't getting in without the key.

"The key for the padlock is on the shelf above the sink," she said as Wes held open the swinging door, waiting for the Sergeant.

Andy came level with the old man and held out a hand, asking for the hessian sack in a soft, but firm voice.

"Let me carry them."

With a small hesitation, but without complaint, Wes handed the bones to the Sergeant. Finally, the bones were finally in the hands of the police.

The two men stepped into the kitchen, the swinging door closed behind them and the hotel went quiet. In the silence, Jakes' laboured breaths gave her hope. She put water to his lips and he swallowed. Things were getting better. She could cry.

From the kitchen came a loud thud and shouting. Someone was thumping the walls. There was more shouting and thumping and the short sharp clash of steel on steel like an angry dog jerking a chain.

Connie frowned. Rising up, she drifted across the floor and pushed on the swinging door.

*****

At the front of the hotel, a silver four by four pulled in beside Wes' rusty Landcruiser, the driver, a dark silhouette behind the windshield, ratcheting on the handbrake. The vehicle sat for a few seconds, the occupant watching, the engine cooling with a rapid tic before the door opened, and two feet in tan boots touched down. The quiet surroundings broke with the double crunch of a pump-action shotgun, the door closed and the tan boots kicking at the gravel advanced on the entry to the Lion's Den Hotel.

*****

Behind the dull, stainless steel benches at the back of the kitchen, Wes had his shoulder against the coolroom door, the door jumping, rattling the thick metal handle. In one hand, Wes held a padlock, trying to steady himself and locate the padlock in a hole in the coolroom latch.

"What are you doing?" said Connie.

The padlock dropped into place and Wes pinched it closed with a click.

"Wes?!"

The old farmer stood up watching the coolroom. The door jumped and rattled. The padlock held. From behind the thick white door, Andy's voice was shouting abuse.

"Let him out," said Connie.

"Do you have a gun?"

"No. Where's yours?"

Wes thumbed at the coolroom door.

"In there with the bones. I need a gun," said Wes, pushing past Connie to the swinging door and disappearing back into the restaurant.

Connie crossed the kitchen to the coolroom and pulled on the heavy handle. The padlock was jamming the action. She pulled on the padlock. It was fastened closed. The key on the shelf was missing. Wes must have taken it with him.

Crossing the kitchen to the swinging door, Connie was about to push through when she saw, through the window, Wes with his hands in the air. Standing opposite him, shotgun in hand, was a silver-haired man with a stoop, the shotgun aimed at Wes' stomach. Their voices reached her through the door, but she couldn't make out the words. Then the silver-haired man uttered a command, the gun jerking sideways, and both men moved into the bar and out of sight.

Connie heart was hammering. In her head, she played back the scene she just witnessed. In the ten years she'd been running the hotel, She'd seen a lot of faces. This old man with the stoop was not one of them. He was the same age as Wes, a little older perhaps, and there was something in their brief conversation, the body language of the two old men that made her think they knew each other.

Connie looked into the restaurant again. There was no way of telling if they were still in the bar or if Wes had been marched out of the hotel.

At the corner of the bar, Connie could see Jakes feet. She had to get to him. At the same time she didn't want to walk into the wrong end of a shotgun.

Andy rattled the coolroom lock, shouting from behind the thick door. She couldn't stay in the kitchen and wait to be found. She couldn't run and leave Jakes do die. Andy said the paramedics were on their way. If the man with the gun was gone by the time they arrived, they could get to Jakes and save him.

Creeping quietly across the kitchen, Connie held her breath and slipped through the storage room in a low crouch and into the bar.

CHAPTER 41

Hunched behind the bar, taking shallow breaths, Connie heard the rasp of an old voice.

"Is there anyone else here?"

"You and me. That's all that matters."

"Where's Andrew?"

"In the kitchen. Locked in the coolroom. I can let him out if you like?"

There was a short silence.

"What's his problem?" rasped the old man.

"He's drunk."

Connie guessed, the two men were talking about Jakes.

"Are you going to shoot me?" said Wes. He sounded angry.

"Sit." The voice crackled, commanding.

Chairs creaked as the two old men took seats nearby; probably at Wes' table. With the armed man settling into the bar, there was no way she could get to Jakes without being seen.

She heard the sound of liquid being poured and the chink of glass on glass. Someone was pouring whiskey. There was a loud sip.

"Why'd you kill them," said Wes.

"Where are they?" rasped the old man.

"Where's what?"

"The skulls. I know you've got them. Where are they?"

Connie was getting dizzy and needed to breath freely. She crept back to the kitchen, her mind racing.

She never believed Wes. She didn't think it was possible that the person who killed his family was still alive and that he could be found, but, he was alive and sitting with Wes in the bar of her hotel. Wes had never given up on his family. When the skulls were found, he had one thing in mind. Revenge. He'd used the bones, set a trap, hoping the killer would turn up. Or maybe it wasn't hope. Maybe Wes knew all along who did it. Eitherway, the old farmer had got what he wanted, except his trap had backfired and Wes was looking down the wrong end of the gun.

And Jakes was trapped there with them.

The frustration and anger of it all was getting to her. She wanted to go out there and end it and get Jakes the help he needed.

She looked around the kitchen for a weapon. There were knives, and rolling pins, mallets and pots. She could sneak up behind the old man and clock him on the head. A nasty surprise. But, if she got caught, a rolling pin would be no match for a shotgun.

The sweet smell of peanut butter and honey wafted out of the bin. It was mid-afternoon. Lunch was overdue. And so, Connie did what Connie had always done.

CHAPTER 42

Pushing through the swinging door into the restaurant armed with a smile and plate, Connie carried two crusts of bread into the restaurant, announcing her arrival in a loud, friendly voice.

"I'm so sorry that took so long. You must be starving." As she rounded the corner of the bar, the two old men came into view. Wes was seated by the window, the man with the silver hair sitting opposite, the shotgun in his hand, the barrel aimed at Wes. Connie ignored the gun. "It's not much, but it's all we have left after the flood." She smiled and put the plate in the centre of the table looking to Wes. "Who's your friend?"

"He's not my friend," said Wes.

Connie got a good look at the man. He had cold, blue eyes beneath a crop of silver hair and a strong chin. There was something familiar about that chin.

"Who are you?" rasped the silver-haired man.

"I own this place," she said. "Who are you?"

There was a pause. He had a mean face and waved the shotgun at her.

"Sit."

Connie stiffened and dropped into a chair next to Wes. This wasn't some game. The gun was real. On the table between them was the bottle of Whiskey and two glasses. The old man took a sip and set the shotgun and his eyes on Wes.

"Where are the skulls? Tell me, or I'll shoot her."

"Like you shot Jane and Kate," said Wes.

"You shot his family?" Connie said with mock surprise.

The old man gave her a cold stare.

"Shut up. Where are the skulls?"

"I know about the skulls," said Connie, drawing the old man's attention. "I was here when they came in. The kids that found them also found the rifle used to kill them."

The shotgun swung across the table, the old man taking aim at her chest.

"Where are they?" he said.

"Shut up or you'll get yourself killed," said Wes. "Ignore her. Tell me why you did it, and I'll tell you where to find everything. The skulls, the bones. You can have them all and fuck off. I just want to know why."

Jakes lay on the floor in front of the bar, unmoved. The sweet smell of honey and peanut butter wafted into the air. The eyes of the silver-haired man dropped to the plate. He reached out to the whiskey bottle, splashing a measure of the spirit into his glass, returning the bottle to the table and taking a drink.

"Fine, I'll tell you. But you're not going to like it."

His arm extended across the table again and this time he took a piece of bread, and a bite, chewing on the poison.

It had worked. She'd poisoned the old man. Connie's heart tumbled through hope and despair. If it worked, she'd get to Jakes and if the old man died, she'd have to explain it to the police. She tried not to think about that. All she needed to do right now was stay alive long enough for the poison to take effect.

CHAPTER 43

"What is this?" said the old man, scrutinising the bread.

"It's homemade," said Connie.

He took another bite, put down the bread and adjusted the barrel, locking his aim onto Wes.

"I didn't mean to kill the girl. That was an accident."

"It doesn't look like a fucking accident." Wes bristled with anger. "You shot my daughter in the back of the head."

"Shut your hole. If you wanna hear this, you'll calm down and listen. Jane had the girl strapped to her chest. I shot Jane from behind. The bullet went through her, through the girl's eye and out the back of her head."

Wes' body tensed.

"Murderer. Why?"

"We were sleeping together. She was going to tell you."

"Liar!"

"That's the truth. If Jane had said anything, she would've ruined my family."

"So you ruined mine."

"Be honest, Wes. You and Jane weren't doing well." The silver-haired man held Wes in a hard stare. "She was lonely. She felt trapped up here. You'd take off to the cattle yards every month and leave her at home, so I'd come up and talk to her. She told me about you and your marriage."

Wes picked up the glass of whisky and dashed the contents on the old man. Connie put her hand on Wes' arm. He needed to calm down.

"Wes, who is this guy?"

The old man wiped his face and blinked away the fumes.

"Andrew Cross," said the man with the shotgun.

"He's the ex-police Sergeant," said Wes. "He worked on Jane and Kate's case. Worked on covering his own tracks."

"You're Andy's Dad." Connie thought of the Sergeant locked in the coolroom. They had the same chin.

"She's pretty. It's going to be a shame to shoot her," said Andrew. "Where are the-" The old man's voice broke. He frowned, his attention shifting inward to his body. He cleared his throat and rubbed the tips of his fingers together, testing his sense of touch. His eyes fell on the bottle of whisky, and he pushed his glass aside. "Where are the skulls?"

"They were stolen," said Wes.

"I know Kipper stole them." said the old man. "I convinced Kipper to steal the bones. The night of the storm, I made a few calls, tracked him down to this place and got him on the phone.”

Connie had taken that call the night of the storm. She could remember the rasp of his voice.

“Kipper has a pending case against him as a peeping Tom. I told him I had a picture of him looking through windows. I said I’d keep it to myself if he got me the skulls.”

The old man’s words slurred.

“But, Kipper’s dead. It came through the two-way. Andy radioed it in. He said you, Wes saw Kipper fall from a cliff. So, I figure you’d have the bones. I called the farmhouse, no one answered, so I came here. All in a days’ work for an ex-cop” The silver-haired man slid the shotgun along the table, aiming the muzzle at Connie – staring at Wes. “You’ve got three seconds to tell me where they are, or I’ll fill her with lead.”

Connie’s heart leapt into her mouth. She wanted to duck and run.

“One.”

Connie glanced at Wes. The old man held the hard stare of the Ex-Sergeant.

“Two.”

“They’re in the coolroom,” said Wes.

“With the Sergeant, your son,” said Connie, furious.

The old man turned his steely blue eyes on her.

“Think you’re a smart bitch? Did you lock them in there?”

“No. I did,” said Wes.

There was a long silence, the old man eyeing them off, looking for the lie. A lifetime of policing must have told him they were telling the truth, and he reached for the bottle of whisky, pouring himself a drink.

“Then it’s all over,” he said, taking a swig, the gun still

aimed at Wes.

"I saw you at the creek yesterday." Andrew slurred, pointing at Connie. "You were with him." He faced Jakes, lying on the barroom floor. "And I know for a fact, he's not your husband. Who is he? Your lover?"

"That's none of your business," said Connie lifting her chin, defiant.

The rebuttal didn't seem to bother the Ex-Sergeant, who faced Wes, his head sluggish on the turn.

"She's a cheater. I can pick em. I was one," he grinned drunk at Wes. "Jane told me about your proble-" his voice broke again and he cleared his throat with another dram. "You had problems in the bedroom." The old man's grin was lopsided. "You were trying for kids. It wasn't working, was it?"

"We were fine."

The Ex-Sergeant shook his head, his shoulders slumping lower than they already were.

"No it wasn't, and you never kne-" his voice broke again, and he frowned, rubbing his fingers, touching his face and lips looking at the plate of bread, puzzled.

"Put what together?" said Connie, drawing Andrew back into the conversation.

The ex-Sergeant looked up, a horrible grin smearing his face.

"You can't have kids."

"What are you talking about? We had Kate," said Wes.

Andrew laughed a broken laugh.

"Kate wasn't your daughter. She was mine."

Connie felt a wave of shock hit her body.

She looked at Wes, the old man's face was drained of colour.

"You're lying," said Wes in disbelief.

"I was sure you would find out after her birth."

Connie looked at the Ex-Sergeant, and her mouth fell open.

"You shot your own daughter."

"She was a bastard, chi-." His voice caught again, and Andrew glanced at the plate of bread, then at Jakes. He picked up the piece of bread and put it to his nose.

"What is this?" he looked at Connie with fury and tossed the bread. "You fucking bitch. It's poison."

Andrew Cross, his hands searching drunk, fumbled for the shotgun.

Wes was frozen in disbelief.

If she didn't do something, they were going to get shot.

Connie took a breath and held it in. Bringing her feet beneath her, she pushed herself up, out of her seat, reaching across the table, for the bottle of whisky, taking it by the neck and pulled back.

"Go to hell," she said, swinging.

In a wide arc, the bottle collided with the silver head of the Ex-Sergeant, shattering and spraying Whisky and glass.

His head jerked sideways. Then the air filled with a deafening boom.

The blast from the shotgun punched Connie in the side. Hot iron seared her skin. Beside her, Wes slammed back in his seat, the window beside him shattering. The air all around her filled with tiny dots of shimmering red among constellations of shattered crystal.

Connie was falling. The hotel rolled like a ship capsizing. Across the table, the Ex-Sergeant, eyes rolled white, slid from his chair, and hit the floor, the shotgun bouncing away. Connie hit the ground beside him, her side exploding with pain, a scream streaming from her mouth into her ringing ears.

Glass from the shattered window showered her body,

tumbling across the timber floor and stopping at the prostrate body of Jakes. His eyes were half open, face slack, watching, distant.

Connie put a hand on her side, warm and wet, the pain terrible. Lifting her head, she saw blood, her clothes shredded. Wes was slumped in his chair, his chest a bloody mess of bone and flesh, his head slumped forward, eyes open, staring at nothing.

Dead.

In the distance, sirens wailed. Warm tears ran across her face, warm blood ran across her back, and a coldness crept into her arms. The room grew dark. Jakes watched. She reached for him, but he was too far away to hold. The sirens faded, her body became weightless, and the hotel went dark.

CHAPTER 44

Connie pushed herself into an upright position, wincing, and swung her legs out of bed onto the floor, her side awash with pain. The house was dead quiet. She took two pills with water and waited for the edge to come off. Morning light blazed in from behind the curtains. In the bed behind her was a large divot where John once lay. Guilt weighted on her. It had been three weeks since John had died. She'd been home from the hospital for four days and four nights. Too soon to replace the mattress.

Her bedroom door into the hall was open. She'd left it open to listen for Karla. Only when Karla became hysterical, hyperventilating, and crying would Connie go into her room. She would hold her or sit with her until she passed into exhaustion, curled into a ball and fell asleep. It happened up to five times a day, and after each episode,

Connie would try to justify why she'd killed John. The guilt was crushing.

Nobody knew what had happened up at the escarpment, although the police had questioned her closely and Connie had formed an affirmation, repeating the words in her head; this is for Karla, Karla can't know, No one can know.

Connie pushed off the bed, the pain in her side doubling then dying back and the pills kicked in. Halfway down the hall, she stopped at Karla's bedroom door. There was no sound. No crying.

A small blessing.

In the kitchen, the cupboard doors were still missing. She hadn't made the time to call the cabinet maker for repairs or a quote, yet. The damage was so bad she'd probably have to replace everything. That would cost several thousand, and she wasn't sure how much money was in the business. The bank accounts were under the company name, and John didn't have a will. Their lawyer had come to see her in hospital. He was dealing with the changeover, but the government and the banks were taking their time.

Connie reached for a mug and caught a strong jab of pain in the side. Her legs buckled, and she caught herself on the countertop. Another jab of pain shot through her hands as if stabbed in the palm with a needle and she dropped to the counter on her forearms. Maybe she deserved this.

She recovered and looked closely at the palm of her hand. Embedded in the skin was a tiny fragment of glass, a remnant of the night John wrecked her kitchen.

Connie flicked the shard of glass into the sink and washed it down the drain. These little things were like signs, telling her she'd done the right thing. And there were times when she believed it. Times when she knew she'd done what she had to do. And now she had to keep her nose clean, to protect herself and Karla.

The kettle boiled. She fingered the chip on the lip of her mug. In time, these little memories of John would fade.

The telephone rang, and Connie jumped. When her pulse settled, she answered. It was the voice of Andy Cross. She'd been fielding questions from the Sergeant from her hospital bed and knew his tone intimately.

"Sorry to call so early. Are you home today? We'd like to talk to Karla."

Paranoia edged into her thoughts, and she repeated her affirmation, that no-one could know.

"We're heading out, into town."

"We can come up now. What time are you leaving?"

Questions from the police were expected, and Connie had answered her fair share. Now they were going for a different angle. They were targeting Karla.

"Why do you want to talk to Karla?"

"She needs to give a statement. It's required for the investigation. I thought it'd be better to come to your place rather than have her come into the station. What do you think?"

Connie would prefer if they didn't talk to Karla at all. But she couldn't stop Karla from talking to the police. It was better to get it over. Connie agreed to the visit, ending the call.

The timeline for the day moved up. She had to get ready.

Taking her coffee with her into the bedroom, she placed the hot mug on the bedside table beside John's Nokia. The bandage on her side encircled the lower part of her torso. She unwrapped herself, peeling back the gauze, exposing a scattered pattern of stitches in dashes and dots like Morse code across the side of her abdomen.

She'd been lucky. She hadn't lost an organ, and unlike Wes, she hadn't lost her life, the pellets fired from the shotgun leaving only scars.

Connie reapplied a fresh bandage and dressed, putting on a pair of earrings while eyeing off the Nokia. It had been here for weeks, unanswered. She pressed a button, and the screen lit up. There were several unread messages. She checked them. Two of the texts were reminders for appointments. She opened them and saw a list of reminders for several meetings with a Doctor McNaughton.

The name wasn't familiar to her. In a small community, everyone knew everybody, but Connie didn't know a Doctor McNaughton. The name was fake, or the Doctor was from out of town, doing the rounds; a regular cycle of visitations to see patients in the different places across the cape. That wasn't uncommon.

But if John had been seeing a doctor, he would have said something. He'd been to the Doctors plenty of times over the years and told her about his complaints.

Connie rechecked the message. Each of the reminders and times coincided with John's trips into town. So there was a pattern. John was seeing someone for something. In the call history was a record of the landline John had called the Friday before he died. Curiosity got the better of her, and Connie took the mobile with her into the kitchen, picked up the phone and dialled.

A woman answered.

"Cooktown Medical Centre."

"Oh, is this the hospital?"

"No, if this is an emergency you need to call triple zero."

"It's not an emergency," said Connie, her brow

tightening.

"Are you calling to make an appointment?"

"Who is this?"

"Jan. May I ask your name?"

"Constance Harvey-Fairchild."

The woman, on the other end, drew a sharp breath.

"Connie, it's Jan Tucker. I heard about John. Are you alright? How is Karla doing, the poor thing?" The sympathy in Jan Tucker's voice was thick as jam. Connie didn't deserve it.

"Yes. We're alright. Was John a patient there?"

"Oh, Connie, I'm sorry. I can't discuss patients. You know how it is," said Jan.

"Is there a Doctor McNaughton that works there?"

"Yes."

"Can I talk to him?"

"Her. I can leave a message?"

"Is she there? I just want to talk to her."

"Sorry, Connie. She's not in, and I should tell you, she doesn't take consultations over the phone, unless you're a patient. Would you like to make an appointment?"

Connie considered her options. Is there anything available later today?"

Jan set an appointment for Connie with Doctor McNaughton and after several platitudes, hung up, leaving Connie holding the receiver, confused. John was seeing a doctor. A female doctor.

There was a loud knock at the door. Connie's stomach dropped, and her heart rate lifted, sure it was the police.

She was right. Opening the front door, Connie was met by Sergeant Andy Cross in full uniform, accompanied by a taller, uniformed officer. What she hadn't expected was the woman in the blue dress. She was standing behind the two men, looking inconspicuous, which was hard to do for a woman as attractive as she was. She had long, straight hair, sharp features and the clean, business attire of a professional.

Connie felt the pressure in her body rise.

"You didn't say you were bringing a friend," said Connie, ignoring the woman.

"Can we come in?" said Andy.

Connie stood aside. The three of them crossed the threshold, the smell of lavender wafting in with the woman in blue.

"You know Sticks." Andy waved at the tall, uniformed officer then at the woman. "And this is Doctor McNaughton."

CHAPTER 45

When it came to playing host, Connie was a professional. She brought them into the kitchen, offered them drinks and engaged in conversation. All the while, she watched the Doctor with interest. The Doctor was attentive to the conversation, but when she thought Connie wasn't watching, the Doctor's eyes drifted over the broken cabinets, peered into the quiet hall and threw furtive glances through the open door of the office. Connie saw a diamond ring. The Doctor was married.

"What kind of doctor are you?" asked Connie.

Doctor McNaughton gave a practiced smile.

"A psychologist."

John was seeing a psychologist. She didn't think he was capable of discussing feelings.

"Forgive me for being up front about this, but why are

you here?"

Andy shifted in his chair and cleared his throat drawing the attention of the room.

"We need your permission to talk to Karla, on her own."

"Without me?"

"If you agree, Doctor McNaughton will be present for the interview."

The Doctor threaded together the fingers of both hands, resting them on her lap and tilted head in a relaxed, natural composure. She seemed genuine, but impressions could be deceiving.

"Jesus Andy, you couldn't tell me on the phone?"

"Sorry. The guys taking over this case are rushing us with this. Whether you're there or the Doctor is with her it doesn't matter. Either way, we've got to get Karla's statement, and it'd be better to do it without you to avoid any suggestion of coercion down the track."

"I'm not coercing Karla."

"We know, but lawyers can see it different. We've had it before."

Connie crossed her arms, unhappy with Andy's approach. He must know that there was a connection between the Doctor and her husband.

The Doctor smiled.

"With your approval, I can talk to Karla. Maybe I can give her some tools to handle any feelings she's dealing with right now."

The floorboards in the hall creaked, and Karla appeared in the doorway, her eyes red and underscored with grief.

"What's going on?"

Connie scanned the faces in her kitchen for any indication of fuckery. They appeared to be genuine. She smiled.

"Karla, this is Doctor McNaughton."

*****

Connie left Karla with the police and the doctor and headed into the hotel, unsure if it was the right thing to do. In the bar, the window by the table where Wes used to sit had been boarded up with a sheet of ply and the smell of old meat was unsettling. She opened the doors and windows to let in a warm breeze.

The hotel had been cleaned by professionals, but some things wouldn't wash out. On the fibre cement sheet a dark, rusty stain marked walls. Tomorrow, the walls were getting new lining. On Monday the hotel was holding a memorial service, and from Tuesday onward, they were open to the public. This was the Lion's Den hotel, her hotel, with debts to pay.

Connie lowered herself into a seat at a table in the restaurant, wincing and thought of Jakes. The last time she saw him alive he was lying on the floor of the bar. It was tragic, and she wondered if Jakes would be with her now if she'd done something different. She could use someone to talk to, and Jakes knew everything. He'd seen her shoot John and Kipper. There would be no need to keep secrets from Jakes.

Forty minutes later, Andy, Sticks and the Doctor came in through the front of the hotel and took a seat at her table. Andy had his back to the place where his Dad died, leaving the Doctor to face the dreadful stain.

"How's Karla?" said Connie.

"She's making breakfast," said Andy.

"Have you found Fred Abe, yet?"

"There's been reports from people who've seen him as far south as Atherton. I don't think he's coming back."

"What about his mates?"

"They've been charged with assault."

"And that's it?"

"It's a serious charge, but yes. We know they were friends with Fred Abe and Kipper, but they weren't involved in stalking or trespassing, and they've never attempted any kind of assault on any woman." A waft of old meat blew across the table. Andy shifted in his seat, uncomfortable and glanced over his shoulder, looking for ghosts.

"Andy, why are you here? Shouldn't someone else be working on this case?" said Connie.

Andy brought his attention back to the table.

"We're short-staffed," said the Sergeant placing a thick manila folder on the table and sliding it over to Sticks.

"Do you mind if we talk?" said Sticks.

Connie waved a hand, a gesture of apathetic permission.

"The Sergeant is here only as a witness," began Sticks. "He won't be asking any questions. We've been instructed to hand over the files to an investigation team to keep things at arms distance. They're putting that team together today, and they'll be arriving Monday. We'll introduce them, and I'll stay involved in the investigation."

A team of detectives meant more questions. Worry gnawed at Connie's guts.

"We have a few follow up questions to the statement you gave in hospital. You don't have to talk to us without a lawyer, but we'd appreciate it if you could help us round out our files before we hand them over. Do you require a lawyer?"

This was sounding very formal, and Connie's worry threatened to rise in a flush of panic. She forced it down with a few measured breaths. None of these people knew she'd shot John. It had to stay that way.

"Do what you need to do." said Connie.

Sticks opened the manila folder.

"We need you to take us through the moments in the kitchen at the Wesselman farm after Reggie Morris attacked him."

"Who is Reggie Morris?" said Connie.

"Kipper. That's his legal name. After Kipper attacked Wes, what did you see?"

"Blood. A lot of it. Kipper had tied him up. There was tape around his wrists and ankles."

"Did you notice anything else at the time? Any other damage?" asked Sticks.

"There was a hole in the ceiling. From the gunshot."

"Did Wes have his glasses with him?"

"They were on the floor," she said.

"What condition were they in at that time?"

"They were broken. The lenses were cracked."

Sticks made a note.

"Was this the first time you noticed that his glasses were broken?"

"Yes, he put them on, and that's when I saw they were cracked." Connie had already covered some of this in her statement.

Sticks took a sheet of paper from the manila folder and placed it on the table between them. It was a photograph of Wes' spectacles. Both lenses had a spider-web crack.

"Are these the glasses that belonged to Wes?"

"Yes."

"When you saw them at the house, were they broken like this?"

"I think so," said Connie. "Yes."

Sticks took back the photo and put it in the file.

"Thanks, that's helpful. Just a few more questions. Did

Karla drive Wes back to the hotel?"

"Yes, but if you're going to charge Karla for driving without a-"

"We're not going to charge Karla," said Andy.

Sticks flashed Andy a look of warning, and the Sergeant lent back in his chair, crossing his arms. Sticks returned his attention to Connie.

"Why did Karla drive Wes to the hotel?"

"Wes was injured. He had a head injury."

"Did he say anything at the time about why he couldn't drive?"

"No."

"But he wasn't fit to drive?"

"Not at the time, but then he drove himself back to the farm, so he must have recovered."

Sticks nodded at his file. Connie waited.

"Andy reached out and pointed at something on the paper in front of Sticks, and the officer grunted, looking up at Connie.

"Do you know how far Wes could see without his glasses?"

"Without his glasses?" Connie looked around for an example. Wes often took his glasses off when he was having a drink. "About from the bar to the centre of the hotel," she said. "But not as far as the toilets."

"How long would you say that was, Sticks?" said Andy turning in his chair back and forth trying to estimate the distance.

"I would say ten metres," said Sticks

Andy waved a finger at the writing pad, and Sticks made a note.

All these questions and note-taking were starting to put Connie on edge.

"Are we done? I should be going," said Connie.

"Almost." Sticks put his pen down and sat back. "What we need you to help us with is how Kipper fell."

Connie felt a wave of panic. She felt the eyes of the psychologist on her.

"I told you, this already."

"Right. We've been up to the tin mine and found bullet marks on the rocks directly above where Kipper fell. Your statement is consistent with the evidence." Sticks tapped the manila folder. "You also said in your statement that you and Wes were behind a boulder when Wes shot John. Are you sure that's correct?"

Another wave of panic washed over her chest, rising to her neck. She'd already signed a statement saying all this. She couldn't contradict herself.

"Yes."

"And was Wes wearing his glasses when he shot John?"

Connie knew she was in trouble. With and without the glasses, Wes couldn't see. He'd have trouble shooting the side of a bus let alone hitting John in the chest.

"No, I don't think he was wearing them," she said.

Sticks shifted in his chair.

"You don't think, or you know?"

"I'm not sure. I saw Wes wearing glasses at some point, but I don't think he had them on when he..." shot John. She didn't want to say it.

Doctor McNaughton raised her chin slightly, watching, silent.

"O.K. Thanks for that. As I said, we've been up to the escarpment and taken some measures. I'd like to run something past you if that's alright?"

"Go on."

"We measured the distance from the boulder to John's body. It was fifteen metres." This was a trap. She'd said

Wes could see ten metres and he'd shot John at fifteen. Sticks stared at her, waiting for a reaction.

"O.K. If you say so."

"If you picture yourself behind the boulder again, looking up at the cliff, was Wes standing on your left or right?"

In her mind, Connie changed positions with Wes putting him behind the gun.

"He was on my left," she said.

Andy opened his mouth to speak then put his hand to his lips, his eyes narrowing.

Sticks wasn't watching, his head down, making notes.

"When you were at the escarpment, how many shots were fired in total?"

"Three."

"Three? Are you sure?"

Connie recalled pulling the trigger three times. Once for John, twice for Kipper. Kipper. She'd forgotten. Wes had shot Kipper.

"Four."

"Why did you say three just now? Which gunshot did you forget?"

Connie wasn't sure if she should say something. She needed a lawyer. She'd been thinking about it and put it off, worried that getting a lawyer involved would be a sign of guilt. But this was getting serious, now.

"I forgot about the last shot. The one that killed Kipper," she said.

"That was the gunshot to the head?"

"Yes."

"Before that, how many times did Wes fire at Kipper?"

"Twice."

"And where was Kipper when Wes fired at him?"

Connie's patience was running out. She really did need

to leave. They had an appointment to keep in town.

"Where was Kipper? He was climbing the cliff."

"Thanks. We measured those distances. Kipper was ten meters up in the air when he fell. What we can't figure out is how Wes, being short-sighted with broken glasses, shoots John square in the chest at fifteen metres but can't hit Kipper, a sitting duck at ten."

They were coming for her. No doubt about it, they thought she'd done something. They just didn't know what.

"I don't think Wes was trying to hit Kipper. He was trying to stop him from getting away with the skulls."

"Why wouldn't he shoot Kipper? He shot Scratch and those boys."

A drop of sweat ran down her side.

"Wes didn't shoot the boys because they stole the bones. He shot them because they killed his dog. And maybe he didn't want to kill Scratch." Connie had said enough. Maybe too much. It was getting harder to stick to a story where only half of the facts were true.

Connie made an obvious move to look at her wristwatch.

"I'm sorry, I really have to go. Can we do this later?" Connie stood and waited for them to stand then showed the two policemen and the doctor to the front door, locking it behind them.

The next time the police wanted to question her, she would bring a lawyer.

Back at the house, Connie found Karla at the kitchen table with a half-eaten bowl of breakfast and her cheeks stained with tears. Connie put her arms around Karla. There was nothing that could be said to take away her pain.

After a short cry, Karla straightened, and Connie stood

back.

"Did the police treat you O.K.?

Karla nodded.

"The lady was nice. We talked for a bit." Karla's voice had a strength that Connie hadn't heard for weeks. Maybe it was the talk with Doctor McNaughton.

"Would you like to see her again?"

Karla shrugged. It wasn't a no.

"We better get going. Are you ready?"

CHAPTER 46

As they took a seat in the doctor's waiting room, some locals offered their sympathies while others seated further away, stared and whispered. A doctor appeared, waving Connie and Karla out of their chairs, down a long hall into a small room, closing the door. Connie was glad to be away from prying eyes.

He invited Connie and Karla to take a seat and moved behind his desk, flashing a convivial smile.

"What can I do for you?"

"We'd like to get a pregnancy test done," said Connie.

"For you?" The doctor was looking at Connie.

"God, no. For Karla?"

Karla shrank into her chair.

He told Karla he would need to take her blood. Karla

agreed to the procedure, and the doctor got to work.

"How are the stitches?" he asked Connie.

"I changed the dressing this morning. They're fine."

"And the pain?"

"The pills help."

The doctor smiled.

"Good. While you're here, I'd like to check your bloods too. We ran some tests while you were in the hospital. Some of your levels were out of balance. It could be the transfusion, but I'd like to check."

Connie shrugged. She'd been stuck with needles so many times it didn't matter.

"Sure."

When Karla was done, Connie rolled up her sleeve and looked away. She didn't even feel the needle.

"The tests won't take long," he said and left the room with the two vials of fresh blood.

The room went quiet. Karla settled into a trance, staring at the desk. Connie put her hand over Karla's and they sat in silence.

The doctor returned and took his seat, placing two pieces of paper on the desk.

"Karla, your results have come back positive."

Connie's stomach sank. Karla looked confused.

"What does that mean?" she said.

"You're pregnant."

Karla burst into tears and fell forward in her chair, covering her face. Connie put an arm around her.

The doctor handed out tissues, talked about Karla's options and gave her a fist full of pamphlets on family planning. He typed some notes into his computer, then picked up the phone.

"Can you come in?" He hung up the phone.

"Karla, while you're here I'd like to do a check-up with

Mum. Would that be O.K?"

Karla, nodded and blew her nose. There was a knock. The doctor got up from his desk and opened the door. Standing in the hall was the woman they'd seen at the reception desk.

"Sarah will stay with you while you wait. We won't be long," said the doctor gesturing with open hands.

Karla got up with the box of tissues in one hand, the pamphlets in the other and followed Sarah into the hall.

The doctor closed the door, went to his desk and picked up her blood test. His mouth twitched and his face straightened. Connie got the feeling that something was wrong.

*****

She left the office, her head spinning and found Karla in a mess. They got into the car and Connie drove in no particular direction. She needed to talk to someone; not Karla, not the police, someone who could listen and tell her she was going to be OK. Somehow, the Pajero ended up in the carpark of the Cut Price Supermarket. She told Karla to wait in the car. Standing in the dairy aisle, staring at blocks of cheddar, Connie gathered her thoughts. She bought two cartons of flavoured milk and went back to the car. A stomach full of milk was as much comfort as she was going to get, but it wasn't enough to stop her head from spinning. She really needed to talk.

Turning down Helen Street, Connie stopped outside a dull-looking triple story building. The sign at the front read 'Cooktown Medical Centre.'

"What are we doing here?" sniffed Karla.

"Doctor McNaughton, works here. She's the lady who came to our house this morning. I made an appointment to see her." Connie got out of the Pajero, taking Karla with her into a small reception area.

The waiting room was empty. Connie saw Jan Tucker behind the desk, and keeping the conversation to a whisper Jan told Connie to wait. She didn't have to wait long. Doctor McNaughton appeared wearing that same blue dress and a smile.

"Connie. It's good to see you again." They shook hands. "Come through."

Connie stood up, but she didn't follow and turned to Karla.

"Do you want to go with Doctor McNaughton?" she asked.

Karla looked puzzled, but she stood up and the Doctor led Karla through a door into a large office with bright colours, couches and chairs. A single candle had been lit and placed by the window and the room smelled of wax and lavender.

Connie had stopped in the door way. John had been here.

"I'll leave you two to talk," she said, closing the door and walking out.

It was a short drive back to the Cut Price Supermarket where she chose a bouquet of frangipanis. Another short drive and she was at the Cooktown General Hospital. She'd been here for four weeks recovering from her gunshot wound and had become immune to the eye-watering smell of industrial-grade disinfectant. Navigating down the wide halls through double doors, bypassing reception Connie followed the signs to the nurse's station in the Intensive Care ward. She checked in, disinfected and walked through a glass, automatic door. The beep of biometric monitors filled the room. There were six beds and only two patients. In one of the beds, Scratch lay unconscious, a nurse at his feet reading a chart. The nurse returned the file to the foot of Scratch's bed, smiled at her and headed for the exit. In the bed beside Scratch was Jakes. Seated beside Jakes in a grey vinyl chair was his friend, Quicks.

Quicks looked up at Connie with a tired smile.

"How is he? she asked, approaching the bedside, searching his face for signs of consciousness. But his eyes were closed and a thick tube taped to his mouth and connected to a mechanical pump was helping him breathe.

"He still hasn't woken up," said Quicks.

"And Scratch?" she asked.

"His stomach lining is still torn to shreds. It'll take him a lot longer to recover."

"How are you?"

Connie shook her head. Unable to answer, the pressure of tears building up. She bit her lip.

The machines chirped.

Connie waved a hand at Jakes.

"Can you give us a minute?"

"Sure." Quicks stood up, slow. "Can I get you a coffee?"

Connie shook her head and waited for Quicks to leave. She moved to the side of the bed, replacing the flowers on his bedside table with the frangipanis.

Jakes' tan had faded, his jaw and neck was covered in stubble. She took his hand. It was cold, and she warmed it with her own.

"Jakes-" his name caught in her throat, the pressure built in her chest, and she let it go. A horrible noise escaped her mouth, tears burst from her eyes and she cried hard. When the emotion was all but out, she wiped away the tears and took a breath.

"Jakes, it's Connie. Can you hear me? Jakes, I'm

pregnant."

The machines skipped a beep. Jakes' heart rate changed pace, and his face twitched, his eyelids lifting.

THE END

Thank you for reading Road to Rumour.

If you have purchased this book online, please take a moment to return a review. Your comments will help others to find my book - and I love reading your feedback.

For bonus material and more books, please visit my author page at
https://sites.google.com/view/danwatters-author/home
and while you' re there, sign up to my mailing list for freebies.

You can also email me directly at
d_watters@hotmail.com

Acknowledgements

Thank you to the volunteers at the Cooktown Historical Society for taking the time to send articles from the local newspaper-your contribution has help to give context to the people and events in Road to Rumour. Thank you also to the community of Cooktown for fielding odd questions on Facebook. Thank you Belle Newman at the Lion's Den Hotel for the initial cover photograph, even if it didn't make the later editions. Thank you too to Heather Dusting-my Mum, Sabina Green, James Kay and Lesley Mosley who read early versions of my drafts, provided honest and supportive feedback and generously gave their time to editing and proofreading my manuscript. To my writing group, The New North Writers – your support and enthusiasm has propelled me to the finish line. Anyone who has ambitions to be a writer should join a writer's group. It makes a big difference. My last and lasting thanks goes to my loving wife, who continues to support me and my writing in so many ways.

About the Book

To get to the Lion's Den Hotel in Far North Queensland, you have to drive through Black Mountain. It's an unusual place. Geologists haven't been able to determine exactly how the mountain of boulders took form. When I visited with family in 2012, I was inspired to use the setting for a story. On that trip, we visited the Lion's Den Hotel and went to an exhibition at the Historical Society in Cooktown, showcasing the local history. There, I found a piece about the original owner of the Lion's Den Hotel, John Hatley Rose and his wife, Annie Watkins. While reported to be married, they did not share a surname which seemed odd for that time. It was reported that Annie's husband died from Malaria at a young age, leaving Annie to run the hotel. She remarried and her lover died of the same disease. I thought that was curious.

Road to Rumour seeks to understand how a loving relationship can transition into resentment and hate and explores the ugly descent into domestic violence, showcasing the worst aspect of the average male contrasted against the strength and power of a lioness.

WRITTER

In 1995 I was sitting in a blank room with one small window, the door closed, talking to my career councillor. I'm in my final years of high school with one job in mind. I've written it on an A4 sheet of paper that I hand over to a teacher that I don't really know. I've never taken his classes. I think he teaches clay modelling or photography or something.

He reads the single word.

'Writter. Well, you're not going to be a writer if you can't spell.'

We weren't there to talk about my spelling.

After that, I kept my aspirations to myself for a few decades, tapping away at the keyboard from time to time, trying out different starts to different stories and going nowhere. When you kick around a dream like a tin can, you eventually realise the frustration of falling short of your own expectations.

In 2012, I committed to completing my first novel — whatever it takes, whatever that means. The biggest sacrifice is time…eight years of it. Along the way, I've had to change my priorities, learn discipline, listen and learn and talk about a lot of stuff to do with writing and editing and publishing. It turns out that to be a writter, you have to act like one.